JUMPER

JUMPER

A Novel

Richard Barth

THOMAS DUNNE BOOKS • ST. MARTIN'S MINOTAUR • NEW YORK

THOMAS DUNNE BOOKS.
An imprint of St. Martin's Press.

Grateful acknowledgment is made for permission to reprint the following: "The Cow," from *Verses from 1929 On* by Ogden Nash. Copyright © 1931 by Ogden Nash. By permission of Little, Brown and Company (Inc.).

www.minotaurbooks.com

Design by Nancy Resnick

Library of Congress Cataloging-in-Publication Data

Barth, Richard, 1943–
    Jumper / Richard Barth. — 1st ed.
        p. cm. .
    ISBN 0-312-26608-1
      1. Coney Island (New York, N.Y.)—Fiction.   2. Government investigators—Fiction.   3. Accident investigation—Fiction.   4. Roller coasters—Fiction.   5. Serial murders—Fiction.   I. Title.

PS3552.A755 J86 2000
813'.54—dc21

                                                                00-031743

First Edition: September 2000

10   9   8   7   6   5   4   3   2   1

For Daisy, my April Flower who brings spring year-round

ONE

The man had been plagued by his son for over a year... ever since the boy hit fifty-four inches and could meet the height requirements for the Cyclone. But Astroland in Brooklyn was over an hour away on the subway and there was always something depressing about Coney Island. Its sense of despair was as heavy as the cloying smell of funnel cakes and undercooked hot dogs. Time had passed the place by, but it struggled bravely on. The rusty steel framework of the defunct Parachute Jump stood guard over a park that included carousel horses too tired to do anything but dream of their past glory years. Coney Island... once a fabled name to amusement seekers, now just a place where big kids went to buy drugs and little kids went to make their bones on the Cyclone, the one thing left on the strip that mattered.

You had to be fifty-four inches to ride the Cyclone because a kid that tall is supposed to have a strong enough grip to withstand the forces the Cyclone imposed. Since 1927 it had been tossing celebrities, politicians, criminals, and innocents around like so many sacks of flour. Charles Lindbergh once said that the thrill of the Cyclone even beat the thrill of flying. Its initial climb was almost nine stories high and then the track dropped at sixty degrees, pushing the cars at an incredible sixty miles an hour. For one minute and fifty seconds your heart stopped as your body slammed over three thousand feet of track, through six fan turns and nine shuddering drops. And then it was over and you could go back to school and tell your friends you had done the Cyclone. It hadn't changed in over seventy years, and now the kid desperately wanted it.

1

The man had promised in a moment of weakness, when his son was maybe forty-eight inches, and now it came back to haunt him. Haunt him, because even at fifty-four inches he wasn't going to let his firstborn climb into that thundering train by himself. And a gut wrenching was not his idea of adult entertainment either. But a promise was a promise, and so on that fine morning the man and his son found themselves on line for an experience for which his son had been waiting years.

It was the kind of day that inspires family outings. Maybe seventy people were in line, all jabbering with excited anticipation. The boy too, looking up above him at the miles of wooden framing that creaked and groaned as the Cyclone's cars rushed by, made silly comments to relieve his nervousness. The man was thinking only about how long it would take and telling himself never again to be so foolish with his promises.

The line moved fairly quickly, and it soon came to be their turn. But for the last seat in the train. This had been hotly discussed by the boy on the subway out.

"Not the last seat," he had insisted, "everyone's ahead of you. The best seat is the first one. If we could get that . . ."

And now it was a possibility. To be in the first seat is to be on your own magic carpet, swooping by yourself, dangling dangerously alone over every drop.

"We'll wait," the man said to the attendant.

The gatekeeper nodded and asked the people behind them in line but they were a family of four and wanted to stay together. So he just closed the gate, locked the safety bars, and released the brake.

The train slowly rolled down the slight incline and then caught on the lift chain that pulled the car up the eighty-five-foot incline. The man and his son watched it slowly rise, waiting for the next train to pull up for them. They could hear the metallic clanking of the chain dogs as they scraped over the safety ratchets, the sound of the connecting joints between the cars as the alignments shifted, the anticipatory screams of the people about to be Cycloned. Their train now pulled up and the man and boy excitedly slid into the first seat. The boy's eyes said it all: heaven. They watched as the train ahead of them continued to rise. And then they heard a noise unlike any other, a tearing sound, and then a loud bang. It was too loud for a shot, more like a steel beam collapsing.

Other people had heard the sound too and were looking in the direction from which it had come. Up the track, where the car ahead of them was now approaching the crest of the hill. Except now it wasn't moving forward; it was doing a crazy little dance maybe six feet from the top. For a second or two it would slowly slide backward, down toward the waiting car with the man and boy until something underneath caught and started bringing it back up. And then after a few feet the metallic tearing noise would screech again and another loud report would ring out and the car would slide backward again. The screams from the cars were now for real because there was no mistaking what was happening. Something horribly wrong was taking place underneath the train. The cable was still operating, but it was not finding much to hook onto.

The man recognized in an instant the danger they were in and pushed his son toward the platform. At that moment the train above them started rolling backward and kept going. Slowly at first, then faster as the angle increased, it made its way in reverse. The man pushed, then shoved, and finally just lifted and threw his son out of the car. He dived after him as the other people behind him tried to get out also.

When the damaged train was halfway down something did grab underneath for less than a second, only long enough to be sheared off in another frightful ripping sound. But for an instant it slowed the falling train to a near standstill. In that brief moment when the safety ratchet had held, a man from one of the cars jumped, flailing frantically at the wooden guardrail alongside the slanting track. But he couldn't hold his grip and tumbled down the wooden structure, keeping pace with the now plummeting train.

The attendant at the gate acted quickly. He released the brake and once again, the waiting train at the station slid slowly toward the lift cable. There were still three or four struggling people in it, but his thought was to have the crash away from the platform with its milling throngs. The two trains headed toward each other, one going slowly for the bottom of the cable and the other doing maybe fifty miles an hour in reverse. When they hit, the noise was deafening. The man took one look and just threw his arms around his son, hugging him tight. The compartment they had been sitting in no longer existed. It was pushed like a tight accordion into the three behind it in a space no bigger than a room divider. They would find out later that two people had died and several had been hospitalized, but for the moment, in their numbness, all they could do was hold each other.

TWO

Dr. Samuel Garvey was at his desk in the research facility at the Angelus Corporation's Park in Freemont, Texas. He was in the middle of a G-force calculation for the Jumper's blue section fifth drop when the call came in. The first four drops were within the acceptable range of under six Gs but drop number five had such a tight radius that Garvey knew it would be a problem. He was just about to plug in the weight factor when Jason Roper appeared over his screen and pointed to the phone.

"Sounds official. You better take it."

Garvey raised an eyebrow. "Official?"

"Someone in Washington. National Transportation Safety Board."

"Get a number. I'll call him back."

Jason Roper didn't move. He was Garvey's younger assistant. Hip, attractive, smart. The best ever, but with an attitude. The young man played for a moment with the little earring poking out from under his curly hair.

"She sounds cute. I can do the calculation."

"Yeah, I think you'd enjoy running the G force up to ten."

"Hell, why stop there? Blackout's at around ten nine. Besides, I thought you trusted me, Sam."

"I don't trust anybody with the Jumper." He leaned over to his right, reached over the crutch that was leaning against the desk, and lifted the phone. "Garvey here."

"Dr. Garvey, this is Rachael White. NTSB. Have you got a minute?"

Garvey sighed heavily and put his computer into pause mode. He ran a hand through his shock of prematurely white hair.

"Sure. Do I know you?"

"No, but I know you. At least I've been to some of your lectures. When you were up in Boston. Back here there are not many people with your reputation."

"What can I do for you, Ms. White? I'm pretty busy."

"I'd like you to come to New York. We'll arrange it. We have a situation here. We need some expert advice."

"I'm afraid that's out of the question. I have a deadline on the project I'm working on—"

"Two people are dead. We need you, Dr. Garvey. Whatever your project is, I think it can wait for twenty-four hours."

Garvey grimaced and looked down at his computer. Impulsively he flicked the switch and watched it go blank.

"I have a young daughter. I don't know if I can arrange for a sitter for overnight."

"I can send someone from our staff."

"Thanks, but it's better if I get someone Sarah knows." He looked over at Jason "Where will I meet you, Ms. White?"

"Coney Island. I'll send a plane for you."

THREE

Jason looked amused.

"She likes what at bedtime?"

"Ogden Nash. You know, 'The cow is of the bovine ilk: one end is moo, the other milk.' "

"I thought she was only five."

"You'd prefer she'd be like all the other preadolescents being nursed on TV spin-off characters?" Garvey scowled. "Personally I've always thought Miss Piggy should get mugged by the Grinch. No, it's Nash or nothing if you want to get her to sleep before nine." Garvey put a hand on the younger man's shoulder. "I really do appreciate this, Jason. They seem to think it's important up in Washington."

"Hey, Sarah and I get along just fine. Remember the time we all went to the car races?"

"Sarah does. She still calls it the 'sock-cars.' For one night you'll be okay. At eight in the morning, Rosita comes in to get her ready for school and then clean up the dishes. If you pick her up at school at three, I'll be back soon after."

Jason smiled awkwardly. "Um, you want to brief me about what I say about Fran? I mean, if she asks."

Garvey hobbled to the door, the crutch attached to his right forearm neatly missing all the children's toys strewn across the floor. "If she asks about anything it will be about heaven. And you've got carte blanche to make it as extravagant as you want. Think Spielberg doing a remake of *Stairway to Heaven*. All special effects; radiant lights, gauzy clouds . . . you'll be great."

"I think I can handle it, Sam. I'm strong on fable."

"Yeah, well, save your best stuff for the revised Jumper timetable. We'll have to hand one in next week. And if Dominici asks where I went, tell him research. It's a word CEOs respect."

FOUR

Mario Dominici was a man who had precious little respect for anything or anyone, especially if it didn't contribute to his bottom line. He was a man of great calculation and precision, a man who sought relaxation from his corporate wheeling and dealing in the painstaking restoration of classic cars. His oversized garage at home already had, in mint condition, a cherry-red 1935 Mercedes Benz 500K Special Roadster and a canary yellow 1937 Cord 812 Sportsman—all in working order. He brought to his corporate career the same determination that enabled him to find and install the original parts to some very obscure engines.

He always followed a policy of taking no prisoners, a policy that had gotten him to the boardroom of the Angelus Corporation, the multimillion-dollar entertainment company. Single-mindedness rather than subtlety was his strong suit. After revamping Bally's housecleaning computer system in Atlantic City so that the hotel could fire eighteen permanent employees, he looked at inventory control and came up with the wonderful idea of consignment. After that suppliers billed the hotel not on shipment, but on use, thus saving the hotel thousands of dollars on finance charges.

It is not clear whether it was single-mindedness that steered Mario into marrying Luisa D'Onofrio, the daughter of Tony De-O, owner of Las Vegas's biggest food service business. What is clear is that it was a career-enhancing move akin to Lana Turner's thirst-quenching dip into Schwab's. Within a year Dominici was living in Nevada and running the Grecian Forum, a thousand-room hotel and casino. When that was bought out by the Angelus Corporation in 1980, Dominici went along for the ride. It was a ride that would wind up with Dominici in the saddle and everyone else playing stable boy. And then he gazed on Texas.

The land outside Freemont was mostly flat with only an occasional hill to break the monotony. One hundred and fifty years earlier it had been a stretch of the old Chisolm Trail, one the steer runners liked because there were few dangers for the cattle. Over the years titles to the property changed, but the land remained the same; flat, unwatered, dusty, and cheap. Which was why, in 1989, under Dominici, the Angelus Corporation purchased a tract of Freemont land big enough to accommodate what would become one of the Southwest's largest amusement parks: Angel City.

Mario had seen all the figures. Demographics showed that there was a dead pocket of destination amusement centers precisely in that part of the Southwest. No more than four hours from both eastern New Mexico and central Texas, the potential of a large market existed for the kind of family entertainment that Astroworld was providing in the Houston area.

And so, Angel City opened in 1992 with sixty-five rides, eight restaurants, a fifty-acre parking lot, two aerial tramways, and a swimming pool complex called Tsunami Bay. The first year it was in operation it made twenty-seven million pretax dollars and sent the common stock of Angelus

Corporation soaring from 4 to 22 on the NASDAQ exchange. Angel City rose over the plateau like some alien encampment, visible from nearly fifteen miles away. It was all odd angles and tutti-frutti colors. It was a city unto itself with a medical building, its own security force, a day-care center for employee children, a six-story office building for Angelus's new headquarters, and, since it was committed to a program of one major new ride each year, a full engineering research facility. Since the opening, five new rides had been built, none of them nearly as exciting as what the engineers were working on now . . . a forty-million-dollar project called the Jumper.

Forty million was a huge number to dump into one project. But projections showed that revenues were slowing down and would turn flat in two years. Seventy-five-channel satellite television, the Internet, and cheap foreign travel were only a few of the things thinning out the flow of bodies to Angel City. Dominici decided that they needed something spectacular to reverse the trend. He envisioned a ride so incredible that it would become the benchmark for amusement parks everywhere. So in April of 1998 he green-lighted the project and called Dr. Samuel Garvey. Two months later the Jumper was on paper. When word got out about the plan, it was received with much skepticism. Getting it to work would be as complex as a shuttle launch, with layers of interconnecting, interdependent systems. But if it worked it would be just what Dominici wanted . . . a sensation.

And Samuel Garvey was the one man in America who could put it all together. The expert amongst roller coaster experts, he had read every journal, looked at almost every old blueprint, visited every working coaster, and had built seven of the largest running coasters in the country. As a child, while other boys were out playing baseball in back lots, he was drawing plans, first for a single, then a double-loop roller coaster for his erector set. His fascination only increased as he grew older, and when he was in graduate school and tacked on the Ph.D. to his name, it was for a study of vibration-stress metal fatigue in pre–World War I cast iron, material he analyzed on the cast butt plates of the Leap-the-Dips roller coaster in Altoona, Pennsylvania, built in 1902. And like some other obsessed people, he had given not only his soul, but a piece of his body to his muse. In 1988 he had been testing a coaster when it skipped the track and clipped his leg. Now there was more metal than bone inside and he was forced to move about awkwardly with his aluminum crutch. Other men of fifty-four dreamed of a perfect golf stroke, or perhaps of cruising the Aegean: Garvey dreamed of making a coaster fly. The Jumper would give him his chance.

FIVE

The ride from Texas up to New York on the government jet was a treat for Garvey. For a man who designed futuristic roller coaster cars, there was something compelling about the sleek body of the Lear 482B Stratocruiser. He had run his hand along the subtle transition from the window cowling to the door transom with admiration, had idly calculated the angles of the swept-back wings and tail elevator, had even, in his mind's eye, sectioned the plane where he finally came to sit to determine if its body at that point was totally round or slightly oval. Garvey was a man who saw his environment in geometric forms and air flow, and the Learjet was simply an unexpected treat. If only there was a way, he thought as the plane shot out of the small local airport and climbed toward the clouds, to put this thing on wheels and a track.

The countryside passed unseen below him. The flight was

going to take three hours, which would give him plenty of time to digest Rachael's report, faxed to him while the plane was still en route but before any meaningful inspection had been done. Still, it set the scene, gave an accurate timetable, and even had some preliminary pictures. Enough to get Garvey thinking along the lines of his own questions.

JFK International Airport was only a few miles from the scene of the accident. It took him barely fifteen minutes to make the trip from the tarmac where the government jet deposited him to the cordoned-off area where the two smashed trains of the Cyclone had come to rest. Even with the dozen or so police around, there was an eerie quiet over the scene. The lift cable had been shut off, as had the main bus carrying the electricity to the Cyclone in the fear that some rogue short circuit would occur. A bank of bright worklights illuminated the twisted metal. Rachael was waiting, as he had been told, under the track on a hastily rigged scaffolding. In her hand was an electronic camera, and she was so busy poking and prodding that she didn't even notice when he painfully pulled himself up the ten-foot ladder to her.

Cute was not exactly how Garvey would describe her, not at the moment anyway. Disheveled would have been too unkind, but in the ballpark. She was wearing a pair of blue jeans stained with grease from the track bed. The stains on her dark windbreaker with the four-inch NTSB initials were muted, but not the nasty rip over the shoulder where she had caught it on one of the sharper pieces of metal. To save her hair from the oil and dirt she had borrowed a dusty baseball cap and turned it backward, but her face had a streak or two of black grease. Garvey figured maybe thirty-two, thirty-three, but then he got a closer look at her eyes. They'd have to have seen a lot of twisted metal, he realized immediately, and shattered glass and charred bodies, to get that particular hardened look. They were the eyes of a beat cop after years in the worst New York City neighborhoods. That they happened to

11

be in a face that, washed up, could have stopped traffic in Milan was somewhat unnerving.

She extended a hand. "I'm Rachael White," she said. "Thank you for coming."

"Not at all," he lied. "It's my pleasure. But ladders," he added, "are somewhat of a problem."

She looked at the crutch still dangling from his arm.

"I didn't know . . ."

He held up a hand. "Hey, I needed the exercise." He looked around and immediately noticed the popped chain dogs on the lift cable. But that was a given. From what he had learned from reading the interviews with the passengers, the car had rolled backward a good thirty feet before being momentarily snagged by the safety ratchets. That kind of force would shear a dozen half-inch bolts easily. But before that drop, something had happened to disconnect the cable and he suspected it was under the car itself.

"Ms. White—"

"Call me Rachael."

"Get to the car yet?"

She looked behind her. "Briefly. Before I started mucking around under there I called in the local print guys . . . just in case."

Garvey frowned. "Isn't that a big stretch, Rachael? The last time I inspected the Cyclone was twenty years ago and it looked exhausted then. I recommended a complete refurbish, which I understand was only partially accomplished. Don't you think we can rule out anything deliberate?"

"We can't rule out anything yet." She reached into a pocket of her jacket. "Besides, this was found at the ticket booth." She handed him a note. "Don't worry, it's been dusted."

It was on simple blue-lined notebook paper, the kind kids in school use to write plodding term papers and leaden love notes. But this was no love note. All it said in pencil was: "Grapple with this problem." It was signed "Periclymenus."

"How's your Greek mythology?" Rachael asked.

"Dusty. Let's see . . . wasn't he the eldest son of Neleus?" Garvey handed the note back and removed a pocketknife from a side pocket. He started poking at the underside of the cable for a moment with the tip of his crutch. "Poseidon gave him boundless strength and the ability to change into any shape he desired. . . . Something like a Greek shape-shifter."

"If that's dusty, I'd like to see shiny."

Garvey smiled at her. "In high school everyone's heroes were football players, not exactly my type role models. Now Achilles and Heracles . . ." He moved to the edge of the scaffolding. "Look, this is interesting. These Pittsburgh Foundry crimp blocks held up real well." He twisted one to the side, a tunnel-shaped casting with locknuts on the four corners, and took a jeweler's loupe from his pocket. He inspected the metal not two inches from his face.

"The bolts went before the casting. If it's going to happen, normally it's the other way around. In any case, it came under a lot of strain."

"Anything else?" Rachael asked.

"No. I think it's the car that's important."

She helped him climb down the scaffold ladder and then the two of them walked to where the coaster's cars lay askew across the tracks.

"You have to help me a little here," she said. "I'm more familiar with the workings of planes and trains."

"That's because roller coasters are an endangered species, Rachael. You know how many there still are in North America?"

"I'd take a rough guess at maybe—two hundred and fourteen."

Garvey eyed her and a little grin appeared on his face. "And I'd take a rough guess and say that you've done some homework anyway."

"Not enough. The crimp blocks are connected to the cable and hook into the cars via the grappler arm?"

"And the chain dogs. But also there's a little spring pad

that cushions them. This one here." He got down on his hands and his good knee and touched a little piece of metal. "If the spring pads are broken, the jolt of the connection with the cable is severe on the riders and, in some cases, can actually break off one of the dogs or the whole grappler arm. From the interviews, it sounds like that's what happened." He turned over on his back and wriggled under one of the other cars.

"Be careful. I'm not sure how steady they are."

"That's not my only worry," he said. "These track beds are a nightmare of strange and sharp articles. Besides the open knives and box cutters that are tossed from riders' pockets, I can't tell you how many glass eyes, false teeth, and even prosthetic limbs I've crawled over in my inspections. Anything not nailed down comes flying out." Garvey played his flashlight under the car for a moment, his white hair flashing brightly as the beam crossed his face. "Just as I thought," he said after a minute. "Hey damnit, come here and look at this." In a moment she was by his side on the ground under the car.

"Grappler arm busted . . . backup safety grappler also busted . . . I'm going to have to remove the main grappler and bring it back to my lab to test it for metal fatigue. But that's not the real kicker. Look over here, no spring pad."

"It broke?" she asked.

"If it broke the ends would still be attached, one of them anyway. This one was removed."

"So, you're saying . . ."

"Periclymenus is real. And," he added, "he knows what he's doing."

SIX

Ever since Coney Island's glory days after World War I, Nathan's has been one of its required stops. Their hot dogs and knishes and creamy mustard are as much a part of a day's outing as a visit to Steeplechase Park. Over the years, Garvey had eaten at the original location dozens of times. Now he found himself once again sitting in a booth at Nathan's with a cream soda and a laden frankfurter, watching as Rachael fussed with her own dog. When she was finished, she came over and sat down.

"Salt and pepper," Garvey noted. "That's it?"

"Try it sometime. You can actually taste the meat."

"Meat? That's what that is? No one orders hot dogs for the meat. It's all about what's on top, the mustard and sauerkraut and onions. You must have grown up in the West somewhere."

"Miami," she said with a grin. "Only place I saw a cow was on a milk carton." She reached over and pulled a napkin from the dispenser. "So, you think we got a problem here?"

"There's always a problem when people die. For you. But for roller coaster people there's a secret trade-off. That element of real danger adds to the cachet of the sport." He bit into his hot dog and tried to keep the two inches of mulch balanced evenly on top. "I know of two other deaths on this Cyclone within the last thirteen years and still they come . . . more now than ever. In 'eighty-five a twenty-nine-year-old man was killed when he stood up and got creamed by a crossbar, and three years later another jerk decided to stand up and he got tossed out like a sack of potatoes. They never learn."

"No one stood up here," she said evenly. "And tomorrow I'm going to check their maintenance records. The government requires a safety inspection every six months and the condition of the spring pads should be one of the things noted. And you're going to let me know about the metal?"

Garvey nodded. He finished chewing and leaned back.

"Can I ask you something? I don't want to seem out of order or anything, but how'd you get involved in this?"

"Very simple, my boss picked up the phone and told me to fly to New York."

"No, I mean, this whole safety thing. Your job."

Rachael smiled. "Gee, Dr. Garvey, you ask all the guys you work with the same thing?" Her blue eyes pierced into him.

Garvey nodded. "Actually, I do, even though it sounds like a dinosaur question. I like to know who I'm working with."

Rachael thought that over for a moment. "Okay, fair enough . . . this time." She leaned back. "I started out my life in college as a sociology major. But summers I worked in my dad's garage fixing transmissions. In Miami it was either that or lifeguarding and I couldn't think of anything more boring. Three years into Northwestern I realized I was more interested in what made engines misfire than in what made families dysfunctional. But then my dad was a far better teacher than any professor I had at school."

"No doubt you were his best pupil."

"Except he wasn't so happy when I told him I was quitting school. We went back and forth on that one. Then he got sick and the smart SOB made me promise to stay in school. Appealed to my filial weakness, pulled every heartstring he could."

"Your mom?"

"Took a powder long ago. God knows where. So he told me running a garage was not what God had intended for anyone with brains, and as I was the smartest person he had known, he was selling the place. Luke Williams had always wanted a piece of it, so he got the whole thing." She took a bite of her naked hot dog. "And I transferred into engineering. The rest was just luck."

"He die?"

"Nope. Retired to Phoenix. His sickness turned out to be remarkably short-lived. I see him once a year when we vet the airport. Played me like a little toy doll, he did. But hey, I like what I do. I should thank him."

Her face was now cleaned up and she had taken off the baseball cap. Her hair was a reddish brown, the color of fine cherry veneer. But now, sitting across the small table from her, Garvey raised his estimate to the late thirties, maybe even forty.

"Any kids?" Garvey asked. "In all this."

"Hard to have kids without a husband or something like one," she said evenly. "Besides, they're too complicated. Too inconsistent."

Garvey laughed. "They will surprise you," he said. "But that's their special joy."

"So, do I pass your test?" she said with a little more edge.

"It wasn't a test. I'm always interested in where people come from and why they get into this business. I think I came to it from a different temperament than you . . . not engineering, but art. I see coasters as forms in space, ribbons of light, that kind of conceit."

"And that's not the only way we're different. You construct, I deconstruct. I figure out what happens when things go wrong. For me, it's kind of like a puzzle."

"You always need an answer?" Garvey said.

"I do." She nodded. "And it's always there, somewhere."

Garvey smiled. "Sometimes you just can't find the black box. Then what?"

"There's always a black box, even if it's not called one. Some clue, some thread, some solution to every accident."

"Sounds like it's a game to you." Garvey said innocently.

She was bringing the hot dog to her mouth when she stopped and glared at him.

17

"No, I see the bodies. More than I care to think about. I do it so there won't be more bodies. There's no 'sport' to flayed skin hanging on tree branches."

She sat back in the small booth.

"You asked me how many roller coasters there are in this country. Now it's my turn. You know how many individual parts there are on a Boeing seven-forty-seven that keep it flying?"

"Not a clue," he said.

"Over thirty thousand. From little set screws deep inside those enormous engines to huge turbine blades. And any one of them can malfunction and lead to a disaster. Speedometer's misread, thrust reversers deploy because of faulty valves, wire systems degenerate . . . and ninety tons of exquisite engineering tumbles out of the sky. On average ten planes a year, from little to big, and that's not including the times things go wrong and by some miracle, or sheer pilot effort, the plane gets down safely. And every time we get a disaster I get this feeling out of nowhere . . . did I screw up? Could I have noticed something on a different plane that I should have called attention to? We can't predict pilot error, or microbursts of quirky weather, but when it comes to equipment, all of us are parents to a million daily fliers. It's not a game, Dr. Garvey, least of all an amusement ride."

"I'm sorry. That came out wrong."

She looked at him closely.

"Dr. Garvey, apology accepted."

"Call me Sam," he said. "And we'll leave it at that."

SEVEN

Jason was being an elephant. Or maybe it was a horse, but he was down on all fours with Sarah on his back, jerking from side to side as he rambled across the lawn. He didn't notice Garvey until Sarah screamed out, "Daddy!"

She slid off and ran the ten yards to jump into his arms.

"Forsaken for a biped," Jason said, getting up slowly. "How'd it go?"

"Triped," Garvey corrected. "I've got some metal samples I want to run this evening. But by the looks of it there could be a situation up there. Some nut may have sabotaged one of the trains." He gave Sarah a big kiss and set her down. "How'd it go with you?"

Jason shrugged. "I thought I was good with females of all ages. Sarah taught me a few things about modesty."

Garvey raised an eyebrow.

"An hour after I picked her up from school yesterday she told me she thought I was very good with children. Took the wind right out of my sails."

"Daddy, Jason and I had a lot of fun," Sarah added. "We built a domino house, then cooked supper for Mrs. Mouse and her family. Can you go away again?"

"Maybe," he said, laughing. "But not right away. Did you go to bed okay?"

"Just like you said," Jason supplied. "Ogden Nash."

"And questions . . . about *la mère?*"

The younger man shook his head.

"A good sign. Rosita is inside?"

"Yeah. But Sam, something's come up with the Jumper."

19

"What else is new. I'll ride in with you." Garvey bent down and took his daughter's hand.

"I've got to go to work, darling, but I came back to see your domino house. Can you show it to me?"

"Sure," she bubbled. "Jason is real good at building things. Just like you."

EIGHT

The idea was a simple one. Two identical track layouts facing each other, two trains running the loops, rolls, drops, and switchbacks simultaneously, except that after a third of the ride, the trains jump courses over a sixty-foot gap between seventy-five and ninety-five feet in the air . . . then, a minute and a half later, jump back. The first time one train jumps over the other, the second time it is reversed. It was to be a little ballet of sixty tons of hurtling steel with eighty passengers on board, to take place as elegantly as a Pavlova and Baryshnikov pas de deux. Wheels would leave pipe tracks and find them again by infrared guidance systems, wind effects would be neutralized by perpendicular and horizontal thrusters, distances measured by lasers, speeds adjusted by instant-time computer-controlled braking systems. Everything was taken into consideration, including the sound effects . . . all so that thousands of scared-shitless passengers couldn't wait to tell their friends they had done it . . . had ridden the Jumper.

That's what Garvey was building, and three hours later Garvey was scrutinizing the readout on the laser deviations for the second drop of the Jumper's track. There were problems. The positioning system was one of the keys to the Jumper's success and in turn, the key to the system's success

20

were lasers that stayed within a precise frequency range. Jason had realized that in the middle of the Jumper's drops when G forces turned negative, the wavelengths altered enough to create, at the speed the train would be traveling, a deviance of close to eight millimeters. That was too big to ignore. Garvey was working on a response when Jason slid into the chair beside him.

"So?" Garvey asked.

"Given a heat massage." Jason said simply.

"Annealed?"

"And not from a New York heat wave. That baby was torched. Under the grease you could still see the color bands. Had to be acetylene. Whoever did it, he or she waited until it cooled down, rubbed some grease over it, and left. Routine maintenance wouldn't have spotted it. But that metal was almost as soft as brass, so it was just a matter of time before it gave out."

"Especially if the spring pad was removed," Garvey said. "I'll have to call Rachael White and tell her this." He turned back toward the figures in front of him.

"Jason, give me a hand with these laser divergences before Dominici gets wind of it." He heard the heavy door to the engineering office slam shut and turned.

"Damn, too late. Here he comes now."

Mario Dominici was steaming down the aisle toward them like a man on a mission. For a little man he brought along a lot of atmosphere, but then he traveled in his own ecological system, one of fear and intimidation. He walked right past Jason and pointed a finger to the middle of Garvey's chest.

"I hear you got a problem. You gonna tell me about it or just wait until September the goddamn third to drop the news? Or maybe you thought I wasn't interested," he added.

"Mario, you're the last person I'd ever accuse of that," Garvey said. "Come on in. Jason, bring in the printout for Mr. Dominici."

"I don't need to see the numbers. All I want to know is can it be fixed? It's the positioning system, right?"

Garvey looked at Jason for a moment. Jason, pencil in mouth and papers strewn on his desk, was waiting for something.

"Yes, it can be fixed. We just have to spike the effects of the negative G velocity. It'll take some math, that's all. What I want to know is how you get your information so fast. Jason just told me."

"There are a lot of loyal people who work for Angelus Corporation, Sam, and my name is on every paycheck. You guys are just the temps." His face relaxed. "Don't let it get to you. I need to know everything that goes on around here . . . especially with the Jumper."

"Mario, I promised you the Jumper. You'll get it and on time," Garvey said. "What I don't need is people looking over my shoulder."

"Everyone's telling me it's a long shot, Sam. I got a hell of a lot riding on this."

"You'll get it."

Dominici looked at him closely, then turned suddenly and strode away. Jason listened for the door behind him to close, then threw his pencil hard onto his desk.

"It's that asshole Hotchkiss, I bet. I asked him to get me some tables on laser deviations. He must have figured out we were getting into some bugs."

"Hell, sometimes I wish Dominici would just stick to playing around with his classic cars," Garvey said. "But he *is* the guy paying the bills. I think bad news should come from me, that's all." He looked at his assistant closely. "So just be careful what you show Hotchkiss." Garvey looked back down at his calculations.

"Now, what was I going to do before Dominici butted in?"

"Rachael White," Jason said. "The grappler arm."

"Oh yeah, another easy one. Christ, Jason, how come there are no more challenges left in life?"

NINE

Garvey wouldn't admit it to anyone, but another challenge was the last thing he wanted. He'd just come through the biggest ones of his life and he was not sure he had recovered from them yet. First there was the disappointment in Boston with the Demon Dipper, the only critical failure in his whole career. People came, rode, and shook their heads. And they said, "Garvey designed this?" But he got over that. It took him a lot longer to get over Fran.

Now, by all outward signs he was operating on all cylinders. He had managed to make the decision to come to Angel City, to take the two-bedroom rental house Dominici's assistant had found for him, and most important, to think again about his work. That was progress. For eleven months he had thought of almost nothing but her.

The acute osteomyelitis had come on suddenly from some rogue infection. Carried in the blood to the bones in her spine, they were told the blood would also carry the antibiotics to cure it. But after massive doses and bed rest for several weeks, it became obvious that an operation was necessary.

Fran held up well. After the operation, the pain went away for a while, and she was able to get back on her feet. But it was only a temporary respite. After a few months Sam began noticing her wincing when she moved too quickly. It took her longer to find a comfortable position to get to sleep, and waking up and getting out of bed was an effort. The pain came back and stayed with her, but now there was only one fallback position. The painkilling drugs had always been an option, but one they both felt was a dangerous, addiction-

23

ridden choice. The doctors hoped the pain might pass even as they kept draining the fluids from her spine. Her chief specialist, Dr. Paul Ivey, suggested Vicodin, insisted it would only be temporary, and gave her a prescription for a mild dosage. Garvey watched every day as she took her pills, waiting, as she was, for the need to subside.

But it didn't subside. It got worse, and Garvey found himself arguing with her to stay with the original dosage . . . to give it a chance. In the back of his mind he held the horrible image of a fuzzed-out Fran losing all concern except for her daily pain fix. He felt helpless against her pain, just hanging on for something, anything to change the course of events.

Then something did, the pain-management clinic she found at Boston General, and things seemed to get better. She found the breathing exercises and yoga and meditation all seemed to help, and she stayed, with much support from him, with her two daily tabs of Vicodin ES. She put a good face on it all, and he thought they had turned the corner, right up until the moment he got the phone call at work that she had overdosed.

By the time he arrived at the hospital she was in a coma. Then three days later she was gone, and he had to deal with both his unbearable sadness and his guilt at his role in keeping her in such pain. She had succumbed in one massive drug fest. They found her with enough of the drug in her blood to sedate a horse. On top of that was the pain of comforting his four-year-old daughter.

Somehow he seemed to forge a way through the tragedy, but it had taken time and a lot of tears, and a lot of chocolate milk shakes with Sarah. All through it Angel City had been an option he had been rejecting until one morning he simply said, "Why not?"

For her part, Sarah seemed like a happy child. She had a dad who could cook strange meals with mysterious ingredients, who could balance beach balls on the end of his crutch like a seal, who made trains do acrobatics on steel tracks. But the best, absolute best, was that she had a dad who came home, gave her a big hug, and told her stories. And her favorite story, the one he always told her at least once a week, was about her mommy who was up in heaven sitting on the fluffiest, whitest cloud, looking down at her. In her dreams, riding the trains her dad built, she would loop around this mysterious woman in the sky, blowing kisses, and feel as though she were floating on a cloud too. Now her dad told her he was actually going to make a train fly. She could hardly wait.

TEN

Rachael's office in Washington gave the appearance of being smaller than it was. On every flat surface lay pieces of twisted or fractured metal tagged with ID numbers. The walls were covered with black-and-white photos showing crash aerials, and one wall had a bookcase with numerous volumes of aircraft and railway specifications sheets. A small space had been cleared away on her desk for a computer and a phone, and on the corner balanced against the wall, a photograph of an older man with a wry smile and a wrench in his hand. The floor was linoleum tile, which made it easy to clean up the occasional oil leak from one of the many broken pieces resting on it. A narrow pathway through this garden of damaged parts led from the desk to the office door, the pathway that Rachael now used to grab the ringing phone.

Out of breath, she said, "Rachael White."

"Don DiGardino, Ms. White. DiGardino Maintenance. You get those faxes I sent yesterday?"

Rachael looked down at a stack of papers in front of the computer.

"I looked at them this morning," she said. "They check out with the Cyclone records. Everything appears normal. The spring pads were tested and I even see where two were replaced."

"Cars number five and twelve."

"The car that we're looking at is number nine. Your report on nine is clean."

There was a pause on the line.

"Ms. White, we've been doing the maintenance on the Cyclone for over twenty years and this has never happened. I want to be frank with you, they're our biggest client and we're very careful, know what I mean? Can't afford to lose them. Normally it's a one-man job inspecting the grapplers, chain dogs, and pads, but I send out two . . . just to be on the safe side. So soon as I heard, I wanted to know what the hell happened. I pulled the job sheet and last night went out and talked to both of my guys. Been with me a total of twenty-two years . . . they know their stuff and they both said that there was no way that pad was missing or damaged or the grappler broken when they inspected. No way. I don't understand it."

"Mr. DiGardino, no one's pointing any fingers yet. We're just getting started. I appreciate your concern and as soon as we establish anything positive, I'll let you know."

"Meanwhile I'm having sleepless nights and looking at a ton of lawsuits. You can't give me anything at all?"

Rachael debated with herself for a moment and finally answered.

"There's been some tests made on the metal. A report came through indicating there had been some tampering. That's all I can say."

"Tampering?"

"Thank you, Mr. DiGardino. I'll call when I have something more." She hung up the phone and leaned back.

Garvey had said positively the steel had been annealed. So that led in only one direction. She picked up the phone again, hesitated, then slowly dialed a number. As she waited she tapped a pencil nervously on the keyboard of her computer.

"Federal Bureau of Investigation, where can I direct your call?"

"David Pouncy," she said. After a moment a man's voice came on.

"Pouncy."

"Mr. Pouncy, it's Rachael White. NTSB. I think I've got something for you."

"Yes, Rachael, what is it?"

"The Coney Island crash. Can I come over?"

"It's beyond the local jurisdiction?"

"I'd say so."

"Yes, I'll look at it. Can you make it by six?"

"I'm on my way."

ELEVEN

David Pouncy's office was the opposite of Rachael's. There was a fine-weave wall-to-wall carpet on the floor, immaculate chrome-and-glass credenzas, and a desktop made out of sleek gray-and-red Tennessee marble. The FBI treated their senior officials well, and Pouncy, third in command to the director, was no exception. A career FBI man, Pouncy was pushing retirement age although he still oversaw several important areas. Transportation security was one of them and in that role, he had considerable contact with the NTSB and their different investigators. The crash of the Sunset Limited in Arizona landed squarely in his lap. Rachael had worked with him on that as well as an earlier hijacking that went bad. She liked his intelligence and directness, although there was something in his demeanor that prompted her to call him Mr. Pouncy. It wasn't just that he was her senior by close to thirty years; there was a paternalism which at times could get infuriating.

"Come in, Rachael," he said when she poked the door open a few inches. His clear eyes followed her as she entered and sat down. "I'm having a scotch. At my age it's medicinal. At your age it's just good taste. Care to join me?"

"No thank you. I'm still working."

"So am I, dear. So am I." He got up and poured himself a small glass from a side bar, then brought it back. "Now, what's this about Coney Island?"

She laid out for him exactly what she had. The report from Dr. Garvey, the note, the inconclusive fingerprint smudges from the NYPD, the maintenance reports from DiGardino and the Cyclone. When she finished she sat back.

Pouncy smiled. "I think you showed your customary good judgment in coming. We may have a very serious problem indeed, one that certainly should be addressed by this organization. It's too large for the locals. I'll start the ball rolling right away."

"We can start with the disgruntled employees of the Cyclone," Rachael said, "then riders who might have been hurt and never received compensation . . . then suppliers who have not been paid, insurance beneficiaries—"

Pouncy held up a hand. "Rachael, one bridles when another presumes to tell him his job." He stood up. "Be assured we have done these sorts of investigations before. I think we know the routine. These people always leave a trail. In some subconscious way, they want to be identified with their successes. You'll see, we'll have this wrapped up in no time."

"I hope you're right, Mr. Pouncy. There are two hundred and thirteen other roller coasters after the Cyclone."

"Is that so?" He said impassively. "Never having ridden one, I suppose after this I'll have to see what all the fuss is about. Thank you, Rachael. I'll be in touch."

28

TWELVE

Samuel Garvey turned the doorknob slowly and entered the one-twentieth scale indoor kinetic laboratory. The research facility at Angel City also had a large, two-acre flat field for larger-scale mock-ups. Not every proposed ride transited from one scale to the next, but Garvey was taking no chances with something as important as the Jumper. Even though the laser system was not built yet, the one-twentieth scale lab could give readings on inertia, trajectories, friction coefficients, and other motion data that would be necessary for the final calculations. Preliminary scale models of the car and of the track layout had been painstakingly crafted in the Angel City machine shop and now stood poised in the middle of the large, white-walled space. Work on the quarter-scale models had begun and would continue up to the point when final specs on weight and electronics were needed. But ringing the track right now was a jumble of wires, cameras, sensors, and banks of lights to record every second of every rolling test. On a bench along one wall were three computers taking in all the information. If this little one-twentieth scale model was the patient, then this room was the ICU. Even the temperature was controlled.

It was a Saturday morning, and Sarah crept in silently behind her father. The only other person in the room was Jason, rubbing the track down with a moist rag. Sarah's eyes took in the science fiction–like set and opened to the size of nickels.

"Wow."

"Don't touch anything, Sarah," Garvey said. "Everything is perfectly balanced." He said hello to Jason, then limped over to one of the foot-long models and rolled it along the track to the top of an arc at about his eye level. He let it go and watched as it rolled down the incline and around a vertical loop bow tie, then a fan turn, and finally came to a pause on the top of another hill. He glanced over toward one of the computers.

"Three Gs, thirty-three miles an hour. Nothing to write home about. We need another four to six feet on this hill, Jason."

"Daddy, what's this?" Sarah asked, pointing to a part of the track that dipped into then under a hologram simulating a pond. "People gonna get wet?"

"They'll think they will. A special picture of water, something like a movie, is shone on the top of the tunnel the train goes into, so it looks like it's going into a pond." He bent down to his daughter. "Do you think that would be fun?"

"Scary."

"Let's hope so." He moved over to the area where the actual jumps would take place and studied the spacing carefully. Two flare-shaped metal attachments rode on the front of each car to catch the ends of the open pipe rails at the end of the jump. An extended floor and two angled walls channeled the leaping car into the correct position to align the funnel with the rails. Even without the laser positioning system with its compressed air jets, chances were high that the car would successfully negotiate the jump. The high-tech stuff was for 100 percent accuracy.

Garvey looked at Jason, who was standing with the hose in his hand. "You doing another rain test?" he asked.

"I don't think we calculated the reduction in friction enough."

"Okay, Sarah, watch." Garvey pulled another car to the top of the hill preceding the jump, watched one of the computers as he ran the speed up, then let it slide away. As it gathered more speed and headed for the open space, the screen on the computer started dancing with numbers. The little model hit the end of the track and then flew into the air over the three-foot gap. Sarah let out a squeal. The car had been designed with gyroscopic stabilizers and aerodynamic fins so that as it traveled through the air it remained perfectly aligned. But space is a matter of three dimensions, and as the car made it across to the other side, it was a half inch too high. The car hit the track with a glancing blow and then skidded, unattached, until the next turn, when it fell over the side. Garvey cursed.

"I thought we'd allowed enough for moisture," he said.

"It's an easy fix," Jason answered. "Just a matter of slowing her down by brake."

"I don't like it," Garvey said. "I don't like relying for primary alignment on the computers. They should be backup for fine-tuning."

"You want to close the ride down when it rains? I don't think Dominici will go for that. Short of a thunderstorm, I mean, when the Jumper would become the best lightning rod for miles."

"We've got to find another way." Garvey shook his head. "Some way to dry the track pipes. Rain is usually only an issue on brakes; no one's ever tried to jump a car before."

"Heat or maybe air . . ." Jason offered.

Garvey was deep in thought. Finally he looked up. "Spin 'em, like they do for ship's bridge windows in the navy."

"Daddy . . ." Sarah was tugging on her father's pants. "I have to go pee."

"Can't spin the whole track," Garvey said thoughtfully as he bent down slowly to pick Sarah up. "But maybe the last fifty feet and use air to dry the wheels . . . I'll be right back," Garvey said. "Then we can run it again."

"Sam, take a break, it's Saturday. I can run it."

"I brought a coloring book and crayons just in case. That'll give me a half hour minimum. After that it gets dicey,"

31

Garvey said and limped out of the room with his daughter balanced on the arm on his good side. Jason watched the door close slowly after them, then turned back to the track.

Five minutes later father and daughter were back. Sarah sat down with her crayons and Garvey came over to the track.

"You know, I never understood why you insisted on taking out the clothoid loops in front of the jumps," Jason said. "I thought an inversion tear drop three-sixty going right into the flight would have been incredible. But now I think I understand. There would have been no time to incorporate anything corrective like a spinner that way. That was good planning, Sam."

"That's not why I took them out." Garvey smiled and gestured at the entire layout of the Jumper. "Listen, Jason, if you ever want to master this craft, you have to approach each coaster not as an engineer, but first as an artist, then as something of a psychologist. You have to know your customers and what they want. And let me tell you, they don't just want to be scared. The most terrorizing rides are not the best ones. They also want beauty, which is why we build in some purely gestural, swooping curves; they want speed, which is why we build some rabbit-hop sections close to the ground where the visual references are going by much quicker. We even add landscape trees close to the track to enhance that feeling. And they also want anticipation, which is why every coaster benefits from that slow, agonizing climb up hill number one. I took the clothoids out because it removed the anticipation of the jump. They have to see that coming, have to focus on their moment of truth several moments before it happens or else it's just one more trick in a ride full of them. And lord knows, we all have grab bags full of tricks to throw at any ride. Alternating track heights to bounce people back and forth, fan turns to slam them into their seats, camelback waves to build up negative Gs, *fin de capo* duck-unders to make them think about decapitation. I see that, but also

32

something different. This jump will be a personal baptismal, and I wanted nothing taking away from that."

"If we ever get it past this one-twentieth-scale limbo."

"We will, Jason," Garvey said. "We will."

THIRTEEN

David Pouncy looked angry. Two younger men stood before him, shifting uncomfortably. He had lost the air of studied graciousness shown to Rachael and was now turning on the screws. His posture was ramrod straight in the chair and any trace of a smile had left his face.

"What do you mean *nothing*, Jacobson? This is the FBI damnit, not some backwater two-man sheriff's office. Up the ante . . . tell them we'll pull one of their licenses, threaten them with an INS investigation. I'm sure they employ some illegals."

"It's not that they were uncooperative, Mr. Pouncy," the one called Jacobson said. "They had nothing. We spent two days in their files, checked on the few complaints they logged, on the two employees they had fired in the past year, interviewed all of their suppliers . . ." He looked at his partner for support. "The Cyclone Corporation had no leads. We have to look somewhere else."

The partner spoke up. His name was Delaney and had green eyes and hair the color of flax.

"No one had a clue who the hell Periclymenus was. We gave the note to our lab and it shows up pure vanilla. Standard paper, standard pencil," checking his notes, "Eberhard number two, obviously no prints, no oils, no unusual atmospheric contamination." He looked up. "Nothing."

Pouncy permitted himself to lean back a few inches in his high-backed chair.

"What are the locals doing?" he asked.

"NYPD, are you kidding," Delaney said. "They're delighted we're taking it on. Get the New York press off their backs."

"So we're the ones that come up empty." Pouncy added. "Well, damnit, I don't like that role. I told Rachael White of the NTSB we'd handle it, and if this is all we can come up with, it might as well have been the locals. There's nothing left?"

"There's always something," Jacobson said. "But it's going to take time."

"Enlighten me," the older man said, not trying to hide his annoyance.

"There's kind of a community of roller-coaster freaks. You know, have to ride on every coaster, conventions each year at different amusement parks. That sort of stuff. We can try to tap into that . . . see if they have anything of interest. Maybe one of them's gone off the deep end, spouting Greek or something."

Pouncy scowled. "Pretty damn thin, but okay, do it. Let me know if you get anything." He nodded them out, then ruefully looked down at the phone. Reluctantly he lifted it up and placed a call to the NTSB.

FOURTEEN

Tapping into the coaster network proved easy for Jacobson and Delaney. They had a computer, they had a phone line, and they had a dictionary to confirm that roller had two /s. In less than an hour they had the names and telephone numbers of five locals who could be found every day chatting on a website called Coasterworld.com.

"Is this Lanny Mason?" Jacobson asked on the phone.

"Yeah. You the guy on the Net said he was gonna call?"

"Name's Jacobson. FBI. I need to talk to you and not on a public website chatline."

"Coney Island, right?"

"How'd you guess?"

"Everyone's talking about it. Sure, come on over." He gave him the address. "It's not a residence."

"What am I looking for?"

"Don't worry, you'll know it when you see it."

Washington had many auto body repair shops, but Mason's was the only one with a four-car coaster train on the roof. Mason wasn't waiting for them. They found him under a 1989 Ford Bronco checking out a crushed fender panel.

"Found me, huh," he offered as he slid out. The two FBI agents needed no identification to show him. The last two pair of wingtips observed on his gritty, diamond-plate floor had been on a team of Jehovah's Witnesses. "Spotted the train on the roof?"

"A block away."

"What got me started . . . five years ago. An auction when they took down Ronelle Park. I saw those banged-up cars and said to myself, Hey, I could really make them into something. I think they were going for thirty bucks each . . . just above the scrap metal price." He wiped his hands on his jeans and lit a cigarette. "Really sumpthin' about the Cyclone, ain't it? Now, what is it you boys want to know?"

"Anything you can help us with," Delaney said. "Any rumors, any theories, any personalities of interest, you know . . . some background."

Mason smiled. "Going fishing, hey? You got the wrong guy, pal. I let my wife do the gossiping."

Jacobson moved in a step closer. He lowered his voice. "Lanny, we're not fishing. We already hooked onto something." He nodded at the spray booth. "Looks like you got a direct vent outside. As I recall, EPA regs call for an inline air scrubber for paint booths. And that's without even asking to see if your certificates of compliance for the welding tanks are up to date." He let that sink in. "Now, usually we throw back the undersize stuff. But sometimes on slow days we just throw it in with the rest of the catch." He winked at Mason. "You get my drift?"

Mason glanced over at the paint booth and sighed heavily.

"Christ, I'm just a little guy with a body repair shop."

"Yeah, and we got a bunch more like you to talk to," Delaney said. "And we don't have all day. So, like my partner said, all we want is background. Anything you think might help us."

"Well, there are a few ideas kicking around. All mostly bullshit as far as I'm concerned."

"Yeah?" Jacobson said.

Mason shrugged. "Let's go in my office. I got some chairs, we can sit down."

FIFTEEN

There are five roller coasters operating in Michigan, but the Screamer on Boblo Island was the one that seemed to attract most people. Boblo's original name was Etiowiteedannenti, not an easy bit of locution for a family seeking a nice place to picnic. Originally named by the Huron Indians who had no idea that one day there would be a major amusement park on their tribal land, the name was finally changed by the

French. They renamed the island Bois Blanc for the trees that were there. By 1929 the name was formally changed to Boblo because that's what everyone was calling it anyway. Boblo it has remained to this day, giving Detroit's amusement-starved weekenders a place to which to escape.

The Screamer, built in 1985 by Vekoma, was a steel-pipe track that featured two 360-degree loops called a classic double corkscrew. By the middle of the track the cars reached speeds in excess of forty miles per hour which, while not particularly fast on a thruway, are jarring on a tight coil. Passengers usually left the Screamer reeling, but with grins on their faces. There were always long lines of people who couldn't wait to subject their bodies to such pleasure, especially on a warm early spring day.

March 27 saw the clouds roll back long enough to treat Detroit to its first bonafide let's-do-something-outdoors Sunday since September. Boblo Island was overrun with sun and thrill seekers and by one P.M. the line for the Screamer had reached back eighty feet. Every ninety seconds another six-car train would enter the double corkscrew to the loud screams of its passengers, bank out, go around a few more switchbacks, and finally come to a crashing pneumatic halt to let its riders out. At that moment, another car would be filling with more riders some fifty feet down the track. When one train was empty, the other would be full, and both would advance. In this manner the Screamer could accommodate two trains on the layout at one time and keep the line to a manageable length.

At 1:06 another train left with a full load and started up the first incline. It raced down the hill, hit the bottom, and twisted left and upward. At that moment, the people on the line who were following its progress saw something fly out from underneath, hit the ground hard enough to chip some concrete, and come to rest miraculously within three feet of some picnickers forty yards away. It was a flat piece of metal, rounded on one side about the size of a shovel blade. It looked curiously like a shark's fin, but the short, flat section seemed to have sprouted a steel hangnail.

Nothing extraordinary happened. The train kept rolling along the track, negotiated the double corkscrew without incident, banked, and headed for home. The smiles on the faces of the people in the back seats were still in place as they careened into the exit area and continued onward without the slightest hesitation. Only the people in the front seats were treated to a last-moment premonition of their fate. It took less than one second to traverse the fifty feet of track to where the forward train was embarking riders. The noise of the collision was sickening.

SIXTEEN

It had been a simple act and once again it had gotten him into trouble. Garvey wanted to change into a heavier sweater and went rummaging in his closet. He had originally placed them there neatly folded on a shelf, but after several months of use they had become a confused interwoven mass of wool, cotton, and synthetic fiber. As he fumbled through, looking for a favorite blue-striped number, his eye came to rest on a little plastic-wrapped bundle. His hand stopped for a moment, then slowly reached out to touch it. Hesitatingly he removed it from under the weight of fabric and brought it out.

He hadn't really forgotten about it. It was instantaneously recognized; and just as quickly it produced in him a gripping melancholy. The bundle was the size of an airplane pillow, wrapped in a large Ziploc bag. He opened it and withdrew a neatly folded cotton woman's blouse. He laid it on the bed quietly and stared at it.

Fran's blouse. The one she had worn the first time they had met. Years . . . ages ago. The young journalist covering the Agawam, Massachusetts, city council hearings on the zoning variance for the proposed new roller coaster. The Black Widow . . . Garvey remembered now, 1976. She had spoken to him after his testimony about noise levels, questioning him closely about how he could know the levels before the ride was built. And the whole time Garvey had been trying to answer, keeping his eyes off her honey-colored hair and incredibly tight body poured inside this red-and-blue checked blouse. Of all her personal items he had gone through and reluctantly parted with, this was the only thing to survive. He knew when he had packed it away that he was flirting with the obsessional . . . that keeping one of Fran's garments was ultimately not healthy, and yet he felt incapable of disposing of it. There was something just too irrevocable about such an act. A final good-bye. This blouse summoned up random waves of alternating sweet and melancholy memories but he dared not part with it. Today's unexpected session produced nothing but pain.

He stared at it for several moments without moving, this piece of cloth that had framed her body so often, and then the phone rang. Like an adolescent about to be caught with a skin magazine, he hurriedly folded the blouse back into its bag and replaced it on the shelf. Then he lifted the receiver.

"Sam, is that you?"

"Yes. Who . . . ?"

"It's Rachael. Rachael White. NTSB. Remember, Coney Island, the Cyclone, three weeks ago."

"Of course, Rachael, I'm sorry. I was busy with something."

"Can you give me some time?"

"I'm sorry?"

"There's been another accident. I need to talk to you."

He hesitated for a moment. "It's too late to get anyone for my daughter."

39

"No, I'll come. It's just one piece of metal. I need a quick read."

"Where are you?"

"Detroit. I'll be at your office in three hours."

"Rachael, was there a note?"

"Yes."

SEVENTEEN

The San Miguel County Bank of Western Colorado had their head office and only branch in the little town of Ironwood, Colorado. As banks went, it was only a single picket in a fence of regional independent lending institutions stretching throughout the South and West of the United States. It performed its small role well, lending money to ranchers to get them to their next market dates, providing mortgage money and home equity loans, and offering a conservative 3.5 percent to people who had, in such a depressed community, any savings to harbor.

The chairman and chief lending officer of this organization was Patrick Moore, a thin Episcopalian with a pale complexion. In appearance, Moore was as proper as a small-town banker should be. He was close-cropped, wore a conservative suit and tie, and had a fascination for expensive cowboy boots. Not that Moore rode horses. For transportation he used his Chevy Blazer which, in Ironwood, was as ubiquitous as cow pies on the open range. At sixty-three he was considered one of the town's respected elders.

But beneath the facade of this buttoned-down financial bureaucrat, Moore had a deeper passion, one that few people in Ironwood suspected. While some men in privacy cross-dressed or read Anthony Trollope, their Wharton-trained banker was one of a small group of roller coaster freaks who visited a website called Coasterworld.com. Behind the closed doors of his office when things got slow in the bank, Moore would log on, chat, and e-mail his far-flung buddies to see what was happening on the tracks.

But even in this group, Moore was special. Because of his experience in working with numbers and crunching statistics on coasters, he was one of the few men who could accurately price a coaster ride. He was the guru of roller coaster supply and demand elasticity curves, and as such, he was frequently consulted by management before they set their prices. Before coming up with a figure, he had to consider what the other rides in the park were, how long the ride took, how different it was, what the riders were like, and how long the line was. Patrick Moore had carved out his little hobby niche purely out of curiosity, and it had carried him throughout the United States. Everyone knew how to get hold of him.

The problem was, Patrick Moore also spoke Greek and used the screen name Socrates on America Online. Lanny Mason knew it, and it wasn't long before David Pouncy found out from Jacobson and Delaney.

And the little town of Ironwood got to see their first FBI agents in years.

EIGHTEEN

The little piece of metal on Garvey's desk looked innocent enough. It was three-eighths of an inch thick and seven by nine inches with one of the long sides slightly curved. One of the short sides had a six-inch sawed rough cut that stopped an inch from the end. The last inch had been torn and ended in a jagged, curving claw of metal. Garvey picked it up, turned it over once, then put it back down.

"A Philadelphia Toboggan Coaster air brake fin. Seen a thousand of them." He looked up at Rachael. "They ride under the car and enter between two steel rails. The fin triggers the air pressure and is in turn stopped by the closing rails. The system is rated to stop a six-thousand-pound car going thirty-five miles per hour in under fifteen feet."

"But they don't work if the fin is hanging by a shaving as this one was," Rachael said.

"Hardly. Did you inspect the cut?"

"The lab report indicated that it was done with a regular-power Sawzall. Took maybe seven minutes."

"The accident happened when?"

"Yesterday."

"And the car was in service the day before?" Garvey asked.

She nodded. "And there were no problems with it."

"So it happened the night before, the night of March twenty-sixth."

"I know where you're going, Sam. I spent all this morning checking out the nighttime procedures at the Screamer. There's a watchman, but his rounds include two other rides, the farthest being about sixty yards away. It takes him about twenty minutes to make a circuit. And that's if he is diligent and not stopping for a smoke."

"Plenty of time for someone to get in, weaken the brake fin, and disappear."

"And the security at Boblo Island isn't too terrific either. There are a hundred places someone could have hidden until after closing hours . . . maintenance shacks, rest rooms, bushes. They do a cursory check, but nothing serious."

"No one heard anything? A Sawzall, as I recall, makes a hell of a racket."

"This guy is really good, Sam. Know why he chose the Screamer? Because fifty yards away on Boblo someone was breaking up some pavement with a jackhammer. They were laying some new fiber-optic cable. It covered any noise he was making."

"Who knew that schedule?"

"I'm working on that. At least a dozen people at the moment, from the workers actually breaking up the pavement to the secretaries at the maintenance firm. Also the introduction of fiber-optics at Boblo had been mentioned in some of the trade journals. And they'd been working for two nights so if you include the people who saw the equipment staged right there, that number goes up to several thousand park goers."

Garvey thought for a minute. "I'd follow up on those people who knew earlier. This guy isn't local. First New York, now Detroit. He must have known ahead of time." He frowned. "How bad was it?"

"One dead. Five serious injuries. Sam, what the hell's going on? The note said, 'Give me a break. Periclymenus.' Whoever it is wanted us to know it's the same person."

"And to let us know he has a really bad sense of humor."

"What for? What's it prove? This is really sick."

"But very deliberate and experienced." Garvey glanced over at his desk and the piece of metal. "You must have seen this sickness before?"

She shook her head. "Usually there's an agenda. Something political, something for money, maybe from insurance. The people who died were just unlucky enough to be in the car when the metal finally ripped."

"Oh, but there *is* an agenda," Garvey said. "We just don't know what it is yet." He winked at her. "That little black box is still hidden." He slowly got up, locked the crutch to his arm, and hobbled to his window. He looked out over the quarter-scale court for a moment before turning back to her.

43

"Why did you came back to see me, Rachael? Anyone could have told you what that piece of metal was." He smiled at her softly.

She returned it without coloring. "I guess you could call it intuition." She hesitated. "God knows I hate to trot out that old sexist word, but there's something about you I think I can trust."

"Thank you. And what is that?"

"You ever see *My Cousin Vinny?*" she asked.

"The movie?" He shook his head no.

"There's a woman in it who is an absolute ditzoid. Judy Holliday of the nineties. All tight skirts, big suburban mall hair, and an in-your-face Brooklyn accent. Except in the end she emerges as this kind of automotive guru . . . more experienced than a room full of Mr. Goodwrenches. Seems she came from a family of mechanics and knew tire tread patterns and transmission ratios for every car produced from the fifties onward. Well, I kind of identified with her . . . accent and all. That's the way I wanted to be, one part femininity, one part testosterotech. Now," she said, turning up the wattage on her own smile, "you understand that's not an easy mix. Not many men would buy it. My dad did. Vinny did. And, Mr. Garvey, in my brief glimpse, I think you would also. I guess that's why I'm here. You're right. I didn't need to come about the brake fin. I needed to come to ask you to help me . . . not patronize me, which is the feeling I'm getting from my normal channels. Can you understand that?"

"Yes, but to be frank, I'm not sure I can give you the time. We're on an incredibly tight schedule here. I can't go running around at will." He lifted his crutch and smiled. "I use that word advisedly."

"I'm not asking for your body, Sam, just an okay to phone you whenever I have questions. And don't tell me there are a lot of coaster people out there to help me—you're the best." She looked at him hopefully.

"Some people would argue that."

44

She nodded. "Yes, I heard about the problems with the Demon Dipper at Boston. I just figured it was budget constraints, not a bad design."

He smiled. "That's generous. The fact was I could have made it better within the limits the financial people set. When it was all said and done, it came out an average ride and got a bad rap because people expected more. I was not proud to put my name on it." He shook his head. "I just didn't push things far enough."

"Everyone has bad days. Maybe it came at a bad time in your life," she said. "So now you won't make the same decisions on the Jumper."

"Generous and curiously optimistic, I like that." He looked at his watch. "So, okay, if I can continue to help with this investigation, I'd be glad to. I'll make the time."

"Thank you." Rachael breathed out. She replaced the piece of metal in the container she had brought.

"You know a man by the name of David Pouncy?" she asked.

Garvey shook his head.

"FBI. He's working on this case."

"Mr. Patronizing?"

She nodded. "He's found someone. Sounds crazy to me but they're checking him out."

"You don't think it amounts to anything?"

"Just because he speaks Greek?" She shook her head. "Puerile."

"There must be some other connection, otherwise every coffee shop owner in New York would be under suspicion."

"He loves coasters. Other than that, he's a small-town banker. They're checking out his movements on the two days in question."

Garvey's eyes narrowed.

"Don't tell me it's Patrick Moore they've found?"

This time it was Rachael that started.

"You know him?"

45

"He's a friend and one of the all-time great guys in the world. I've known him for years. Your Mr. Pouncy is barking up the wrong tree. Greek is only one of four languages he speaks."

"Unfortunately it's also the one Periclymenus spoke." She stood up and walked to the window. "You'd vouch for him?"

"Absolutely."

"Well, I'll tell Pouncy. I better get back to Washington anyway with this . . ." She hefted the metal fin. "Think you could call me a cab?"

"I'd be glad to drive you, but I have to go to the shareholders' meeting. I'll get my assistant, Jason." He picked up the phone and in a minute, the younger man entered the office.

"This is Ms. White, Jason. She needs a lift. You need some fresh air. Work it out."

"Be delighted," Jason said and took the package from her.

"Thanks for coming, Rachael," Garvey said. "Call me when you need me."

As they pulled away from the parking lot in Jason's red Miata sports car, Rachael looked out the window at the immensity of Angel City, her eyes darting everywhere. All of the rides were running, there was motion everywhere.

"This place looks like it would be fun to work here."

Jason nodded. "Yes, I'd say it has its benefits. You meet a lot of interesting people." He looked at her closely and she felt strangely uncomfortable.

She asked quickly, "And Dr. Garvey, is he one of them?"

"I'd say so," Jason answered. "He's been good for me."

"So tell me," she said, "what's this Jumper all about?"

NINETEEN

The shareholders' meeting was being held in the auditorium of the Bronco Buster, a quasi-ride, multimedia historical journey meant to put the viewer in the midst of an old-fashioned horse roundup. The Frederick Remington–like series of film clips flashed on a 360-degree, three-story screen accompanied by a frighteningly chaotic sound track and seats that bucked and twisted pneumatically. For the shareholders' meeting, the bouncing was turned off and the screen showed not frightened horses and dusty cowboys, but financial graphs and charts of cash flow and stock movement. Dominici presided from a lectern fronting a long table where his backup team of trustees and financial whiz kids sat. This was the first shareholders' meeting held at Angel City. The idea had been to divert some of the harder questions about the corporation's flat performance with a more exciting environment. And if need be, if the meeting got too hot, Dominici had a fallback option . . . show stockholders what Angel City did so well by turning on the ride. They were expecting no more than two hundred attendees, but when Garvey got there, the three hundred seats in the gently sloping auditorium were almost all taken. He found a seat on the end of the director's table and levered himself in. In front of him were the shareholders of Angelus Corp., an incredibly mixed bag of people of all ages and in all manner of attire. Garvey suspected that both Giorgio Armani and Kathie Lee had supporters in the crowd.

"I am very positive about the coming year," Dominici began, "vis à vis our financial profile. We are currently retiring some older debt and with the restructuring and consolidation of our training facilities under one roof at Parkhurst, we are anticipating considerable savings. Also we are looking at a pretax write-off from the unit in Wilmington of about . . ." he looked behind him for confirmation ". . . Approximately three-point-four million, right, Gus?" The man so addressed nodded. "Which will considerably improve our operating picture. The gate at Angel City and the other amusement facilities, while not increasing, remains firm, while our market share has increased. The Jumper will substantially increase this, but not until the fourth quarter." He stopped for a sip of water. "All in all, two thousand is shaping up to be a year of continued strength and by all accounts, one of a buoyant stock price." He looked around, smiled, and added, "I'll take all your questions now."

A few hands shot up in the air. Garvey knew they were the plants, one or two loyal employees who had been given the softball questions that Dominici could field easily. When he got through with those he found himself facing the hard-core questions by analysts and disgruntled shareholders alike. But Dominici was an experienced performer who dodged and weaved with skill. He pointed quickly to another woman for a final question. She was middle-aged and dressed in what looked like a Wal-Mart January sale days warm-up suit.

"Mr. Dominici, we have heard much about the Jumper's role in the expected phoenix-like resurrection of attendance figures here at Angel City. For some time we have heard one refrain: . . . *Wait for the Jumper to come on line.* Well . . ." she gestured to all of the people around her ". . . I think many of us feel that the Jumper is something of a black hole. It will suck up more than forty million dollars of our equity and presents the single most dangerous commitment of funds that I know of in the amusement industry since Euro Disney . . . and we all know what happened with that stock. I'd like to know what the status of that project is, what the actual timetable looks like, and whether you have any contingent financial safeguarding plans if the Jumper proves unfeasible. Also you claim that the cash flow from continuing operations is sufficient to finance this project, but only, I believe, by retiring some of the senior debt you promised last year and not increasing that debt with the issue of new bonds. Would you please speak to these concerns." She folded her hands, and like the resolute Wal-Mart shopper that she was, remained standing, awaiting her itemized receipt. It would teach Dominici a lesson about judging a book by its cover.

"First of all," he responded, "we do not use the word *unfeasible*. The Jumper will be built. We have the best team in the country working on it, including Dr. Samuel Garvey." Here he looked back and motioned to Garvey, who obligingly nodded. "Dr. Garvey is renowned in this country. He is the only person I know who could engineer, build, and ensure that this fabulous ride will be up and running on time. It was only when he agreed to this project that the board of directors and I felt comfortable committing the funds." He turned back to Garvey. "I'll let him speak. Could you tell us, Sam, if you are anticipating any delays in construction?"

Garvey reluctantly rose to his feet and took the few steps to the mike. He hated being put on the spot like this, but he couldn't refuse. That's why there had been a seat reserved for him at the dais. He cleared his throat and leaned into the microphone.

"We are pretty much on schedule right now," he said. "We've had a few minor problems with some of the strategies for varying weather conditions, but at this time we are content that we have them solved. We are working hand in glove with our suppliers and Madondi and to date have experienced no delays in that regard. We should come in pretty close to the target date." He looked awkwardly around the room then turned simply and limped his way back to his chair.

Dominici continued. "Thank you, Sam. Let me add that we have the best facility here to engineer it, and along with

49

the subcontractor, Madondi, the most experience to build it. I believe at this point it is just a matter of working out all of the primary and backup safety systems so that we can confidently go before the state certification board for our license. Most of that has been already done."

Garvey had to smile. Men like Mario Dominici got places by riding the thin edge of partial truths until they either fell off or it widened out. At the very least, Garvey thought, you had to admire their balance. The safety test simulations for the cert board had not even been scheduled yet.

"And as far as a timetable is concerned, we are shooting for an opening on September third, but revenues won't show up fully until next year's first quarter. The first of two scale models has been built already and the second one, the quarter model, is about to be installed. Now, as far as financial safeguards, I am unaware of any insurance we could purchase to cover the remote possibility of our not bringing this project to completion. While our personnel is the very best, they can be replaced in case of emergency. This is not the movie industry, where one insures the actors' pretty faces." A smattering of chuckles filled the auditorium and he waited until it subsided.

"All I can say is that we are moving ahead prudently, spending only what is necessary to continue to the next phase of the project, and watching our expenditures critically. Our professional management team," and here he motioned behind him, "is the best and only safeguard I can offer. Finally, we are at this time absolutely not planning any further bond issues in regard to the Jumper or any other project. We are skillfully managing what debt we have, which is at a level with which we feel comfortable. More debt at this point would only add unnecessary pressure. I hope that answers your question, madam." He smiled thinly in her direction. "Thank you all for coming. I think refreshments have been set out in the Silver Dollar Saloon just next to the

Bronco Buster, where I'll be able to meet with you on a more informal basis." He turned and shook some hands behind him on his way to an exit. With this signal, people started to get up and move away. Garvey also made an exit.

So the one quarter model "is about to be installed"? That was news to him. He'd have to ask Dominici where he was hiding it.

TWENTY

Rachael made sure a general advisory was sent out the next day. The Detroit accident played as a local news item and none of the national news organizations had yet put it together with the Coney Island incident. But it wouldn't be long. Someone from the industry or one of the groupies that surfed the Net would make the right phone call . . . and Rachael's office would be deluged. Might as well cover all the bases early.

The advisory was sent to all the operators of the two hundred and fourteen coasters in the United States and extended to all operators of amusement parks with similar mechanical rides. It explained the nature of the two accidents, requested that heightened security be enforced, and gave a number to call in case more information was needed or could be supplied. The advisory ended with an admonition that while there was no need to cause alarm in the coaster-riding public, it made sense to check equipment thoroughly on a daily basis. This would raise some eyebrows, she thought, and some hackles, but it was safer than sticking your head in the sand.

The next thing she did was call David Pouncy to relay

Garvey's information about Pat Moore. But Pouncy surprised her. He told her Garvey had already called at nine A.M.

"I thanked him for his call," Pouncy told Rachael, "and told him nothing. I asked him how he knew about Moore and found out about your . . ." he drew the word out ". . . association. You could have told me."

"I thought I did," Rachael said simply. "He's the best guy on coasters there is. So what about Moore?"

There was a pause on the line. "Moore was questioned in Ironwood. His story and movements on the dates in question are being investigated now. That's all."

"It's a long shot, Mr. Pouncy. Garvey says it's impossible he's the guy."

"So I heard. But we have our protocols, Rachael. No matter how important someone's friends are. Or how squeaky clean they may seem."

"Moore's like that?"

"Like rubber on linoleum. And as annoyed as a smoked hornet. But if he's not our man, he'll get over it. Now what have you got?"

Rachael told him about Garvey's analysis on the brake fin. And about the advisory.

"Good," Pouncy said. "I'll let you know about Moore when Jacobson and Delaney finish checking on his story." He rang off and left Rachael holding the dead receiver. She looked over at the brake fin lying on top of some twisted wires on her floor. Now what? The secretaries at the maintenance firm and all those people who knew beforehand about the jackhammers at Boblo. She opened a folder on her desk and picked up the phone again. It was going to be a long day.

TWENTY-ONE

Patrick Moore was still fuming about his treatment at the hands of the two FBI agents when the call came through. He was at his desk at the bank trying to work. But every time he reviewed a mortgage application file or checked on some portfolios he'd see those two smug faces and replay their insinuating questions and his eyes would lose their focus.

"A Dr. Garvey on the line," his secretary said.

Moore picked up the phone quickly.

"Sam, don't tell me the goddamn FBI's been visiting you too."

"I heard, Patrick. It's this mess up at the Cyclone and now at Boblo. They're just fishing."

"Well, I wish they'd a stayed out of my little pond. Ernestine, my secretary, has got a mouth as big as a feedbag. Christ, by now the story's probably around the whole county. People around here don't like their money and their gossip under the same roof."

"I called the guy at the bureau who's handling the investigation," Garvey said. "Pouncy. I told him he was crazy to think you'd be involved."

"Thanks, Sam. I appreciate that, but I'll get through it. I haven't been out of the state in four months. It's just damn annoying."

"Good. So . . . ," Garvey hesitated. "Any ideas?"

"I haven't heard anything if that's what you mean. People have been chatting on the boards, but there's nothing."

"I was thinking maybe not on the boards. Somewhere else."

"Like where?"

"Financial."

Moore chewed that over for a moment. Finally he said, "I don't know what you mean."

"I'm not sure I know either. It was just a thought. The investigation is looking for people. Maybe it should be looking for money."

"And the angle? So far, to keep two roller coasters from running for a few days. Hardly. Insurance? You know what this will do to their rates?"

"I guess you're right. I was reaching. Anyway I called to lend some moral support."

"Much appreciated. Say, you coming up here any time soon? I've got a client runs a few ponies around his ranch and I just know Sarah'd love the ride. You can't be more than a day's drive away."

"Thanks, Pat. Maybe when the Jumper is finished. I'll let you know." They said their good-byes and Garvey hung up the phone slowly, staring at it for a moment. Then he looked up and saw Jason watching him through the open door of his office. He had a curious expression on his face.

"What's up?" Garvey asked.

"The quarter-scale track just arrived." Jason said. "Madondi's crew is coming tomorrow to begin setting it up." He frowned. "I didn't think we were quite ready yet. I'd done the calculations and drawings on the last section of spinning track, but we hadn't tested it on the smaller model yet."

Garvey frowned. "They were supposed to wait for delivery until we called with the final specs. Did you . . . ?" Jason shook his head.

"I didn't either. The spinning sections are included?"

"Madondi says they are. How could they have gotten the drawings?"

Garvey got up angrily, holding onto the desk. He didn't even bother with his crutch. "I'm the only person authorized to send the requisitions in . . . by way of Dominici. God-damnit, how did he get the information?" He limped along his desk. "I've a good mind to send it all back."

"It would save us a couple of weeks if we started in on it tomorrow, Sam. We'll just do the preliminary tests on the larger scale."

Garvey looked at him. "Jason, I don't like cutting corners. Even if the CEO wants it. We're dealing with a basic safety feature here. We were going to build a minimodel of the spinners."

"Doing it at the quarter-scale level would be more accurate, Sam."

There was silence in the room as Garvey mulled this over.

"Who else knew that you finished the drawings?" he said finally.

"You, me . . . maybe Hotchkiss if he entered the Jumper files on his computer. They're networked."

"Shit. Okay, get him in here. I want to have this out right now." His expression was dark. "And Jason, don't give him a chance to call Dominici. I don't want any interruptions in our little conversation."

Martin Hotchkiss was a man of about forty with thin shoulders and a pinched face. As he entered he looked nervously around him. Eye contact was not something he favored. He sat down lightly and smiled at a spot about a foot to the left of Garvey's face.

"You wanted to speak to me?"

Garvey sat silently for a moment, watching Hotchkiss's eyes slowly, reluctantly drift closer to his.

"Martin, I used to think there were only two things in life I couldn't stand, intolerance and stupidity. You've shown me there's a third . . . betrayal."

Hotchkiss produced a dry laugh that barely made it out of his narrow throat.

"What do you mean. Surely you don't think I've done anything—"

"Dominici ordered the quarter-scale track and models brought in. How did he get the drawings of the spinners to send to Madondi? What the hell are you doing looking into the Jumper files? Your responsibility is solely for development of EV stuff. Electric visuals and decoration. When we need your help on that stuff, we'll ask for it." Garvey was getting heated. "We're not playing with little neon lights here, sir. If something goes wrong with one of those cars or the track, we're not going to have some short circuit or blown fuse. There'll be real blood and shattered bones and it will be my ass, not yours, on the line."

"And Dominici's," Hotchkiss offered smugly.

"Screw Dominici," Garvey said. "He's only looking at the bottom line anyway. He buys enough accident insurance and he's covered. I'm the designer and it's my reputation. You can't cover that with a Met Life policy."

Hotchkiss looked behind him at Jason, who was still standing by the door, unmoving.

"Come on, guys," said Hotchkiss. "Dominici just wanted to know how close you were to moving on to the quarter scale. All I did was tell him where to look for Jason's latest report and drawings. I had no idea he'd go ahead and get the spinners built and jump-start things. Besides, you guys know you're behind schedule as it is."

"There's no such thing as 'behind schedule' when you're talking about safety," Garvey said grimly. He got up and this time grabbed his crutch. He moved to stand over the slighter man. "And if you ever do something like that again the first thing I will do is walk, kiss the Angelus Corporation and the Jumper good-bye. And you know what? Maybe without a project your own job won't be so secure. Mull that over. Now, you get on your special direct line and tell that to Dominici." He motioned toward his door.

Hotchkiss levered himself slowly out of the chair like a

parochial school kid with too much attitude, suddenly released by his principal. He shuffled past Jason, mumbling something inaudible.

"What do you think?" Garvey asked as Jason stepped closer to the desk.

"I still don't trust him."

"Me either. In any case, we better program in a password right now to all the Jumper files. I can't believe we forgot to do it when they did the Y2K fix."

"Okay." Jason sat down heavily. "What do you want?"

Garvey shrugged. "Pick something."

Jason thought for a moment. "Okay, what did you get on your high school combined SAT score?"

"Excuse me?"

"Your SAT score. Everyone says they forget, but no one does. Not that number. They only say they do if they get under twelve hundred. What was yours?"

Garvey smiled. "1483 . . . something like that."

Jason punched the right numbers. "One thousand four hundred and eighty-three it is. Now what about Madondi and the track. We go ahead with it?"

"Okay," Garvey said. "Let's see how those spinners you designed work."

TWENTY-TWO

Rachael found a cab at the Detroit airport and gave the driver the address. Marsden Maintenance, 1401 Appleton. No doubt another location under some freeway or along some migratory route for eighteen-wheelers. Maintenance firms always seemed to be housed in old cinder block buildings whose main architectural feature was chicken-wire safety glass. Marsden was no different: 1401 Appleton was along a stretch of concrete poured during the Depression and now lined with scrap yards, beverage wholesalers, and small foundries. Rachael reminded herself that her job description had not touched on aesthetics.

"You want me to wait, lady?" the cabby called.

"No thanks. I don't know how long I'll be."

She pushed open the front door and entered the small waiting room. She was right on time and there, waiting for her, was Maria Ricciardi, the small firm's office manager.

"Ms. White?" the heavy-set woman asked. Rachael nodded. "Follow me."

The two women went into a small office with two desks and several good old-fashioned filing cabinets. On one of the desks was a file marked *Boblo, April*.

"We're the subs for all the paving work for the amusement park. After you called I did some research. This work was placed in January."

"But when was the schedule set?" Rachael asked.

"Let's see." Maria opened the file and looked at some of the earlier papers. "February twentieth, a definite work schedule was set for the last week in March. The work order was written the next day and the crew selected."

"And notified."

"No. They're on staff. It just meant blocking out their time. I do that, along with our foreman, Mark Evans. We're a small shop here, so not many people get involved in the process."

"And who placed the order?"

Again Maria referred to the documents. "Like I thought. Jack Walker. He's Boblo's GM. He places most of the orders with us."

Rachael thought this over for a few moments. "So, up to a few days before the work actually began, how many people would have known it was about to happen?"

"I guess Jack, Jack's secretary, my boss Anthony Longo, me, Mark, and maybe Mark's assistant, who had to make sure the equipment was ready."

"Did your firm also lay the cable?"

"No, that was Sytech. We just prepared the trench for them."

"Didn't they give you specs. I mean on how wide and deep?"

"Yeah, right here."

"So they would know also when you were beginning. I suppose they were coming in right after you finished. You couldn't leave open trenches lying around."

Maria nodded. "I forgot them. Yes, they knew too. I called a week before to remind them."

Christ, Rachael thought. A ton of interviewing. Not even including those at Boblo who might have known, like their security and operations departments.

"Oh, and then we had the call from some guy at *AM*."

Rachael looked lost.

"*Amusement Monthly*, the trade magazine. They had run something about the new cable in February and he was wondering if we had finished yet."

"Was that usual to get a call like that?"

Maria thought for a moment. "No, now that you mention it, normally those would go to the Boblo office."

Occam's razor always worked for her. Rachael thought, Why not now? Occam, a fourteenth-century philosopher, changed the face of science by stating that the simplest theory that fits the facts usually is the correct one. The simplest theory here being that whoever wanted to find out when the jackhammers would be blasting simply called up.

"Do you remember the call?" Rachael asked.

Maria closed her eyes for some time, taking deep breaths. It was obvious that she was going on a random access tour of her memory so Rachael waited with her, not saying a word.

Finally the other woman opened her eyes. "Dan something, he said his name was. Said he wrote the story. All I can remember."

"Did he sound young, old . . . have an accent or bad grammar, a cough . . . anything distinguishing about his voice?"

Maria turned behind to the top of one of the cabinets. There she rummaged for a moment and came down with a slim, dusty magazine with the heading *Amusement Monthly*. "Call him up," she offered.

Maria took the magazine, found their office number inside, and called. While she was waiting for an answer, she was looking at the masthead.

"Dan please," she said when she got the operator.

"There's no one here by that name," the bored voice came back.

"A writer," Rachael continued, "Dan something?" She looked back at Maria for confirmation.

"You mean Frank Danville?" the voice asked.

"Yes, Mr. Danville."

"I'm transferring you."

Maria waited, frowning. Finally a man's voice said, "Yeah."

"Mr. Danville, I'm Rachael White from the NTSB and we're looking into something up here at Boblo. I wonder if you can help me. I believe you wrote a story in February about their installing some new fiber-optic cable?"

"That's right. They're one of the first planning on using it to connect individual ride terminals."

"Did you ever subsequently call Marsden Maintenance to check on whether they had begun laying the cable?" Rachael looked over at Maria.

"No. As I recall it was a small item, buried in a section called 'What's New.' I wouldn't have followed up."

"You're sure?"

He sounded impatient. "Yes, Ms. White, I'm sure. We have a small operation here, only six people. This is not a daily newspaper. We have enough to do getting this thing out each month as it is. Follow up . . . ?" He laughed.

Rachael was silent for a few moments, considering. "Mr. Danville," she finally asked, "how can one get your magazine?"

"Subscription. It's not sold on newsstands if that's what you're asking." Rachael felt a smile beginning.

"And your list of subscribers, is it large?"

There was a hesitation on the line. "National Transportation Safety Board, right?"

"Uh huh."

"And I can call you if I need some information on these accidents."

"These accidents?" Rachael asked.

"Brooklyn, now Detroit. The advisory you guys sent out." Rachael felt her voice go cold.

"How many on your list, Mr. Danville."

"Ten thousand, but if you want it, you'll have to speak to the owner, and he's not in now."

"Damn, ten thousand?" Rachael said involuntarily.

"We do a good job here, Ms. White. I knew you'd be impressed."

"*AM*? Yeah I get it," Garvey said later that night into the phone. "So do all the people involved in the management of theme and amusement parks across the country. What of it?"

"Our saboteur read a piece about Boblo there," Rachael said. "Then he pretended he was the reporter and called up to confirm the maintenance schedule. So I guess I've narrowed the search down to their subscription list of only ten thousand."

"Probably more," Garvey answered. "Those magazines are left lying around. No telling how many people read each issue."

"Oh, and it's a man."

"Great."

Rachael sighed. "I know. Precious nothing to go on. So how's the weather in Texas?"

"Hot. You back in Washington?"

"Yeah, cherry blossom time. You ought to see it."

Garvey was silent on the phone for a long time. Too long.

"It's funny," he said finally. "Every year my wife would say how much she'd love to see the cherry blossoms. We never got around to it. You postpone and postpone until it's too late."

"But they're as beautiful as ever," Rachael said. "Your daughter would like them. Think of your wife seeing them through her eyes."

"*Très poétique.*"

"I do my best."

"Which is not bad at all," Garvey said. "I'll think about it for next year."

"There's no time like the present," she said lightly.

"The present," he said, "is all booked up. We just set up the quarter track for the Jumper. There's a lot to do."

"Well, good luck. I'll call if I need you on anything else. I'll send you a picture of the mall in full bloom."

"Rachael . . . thanks."

"What for?"

"I don't know. For making me see how inappropriately maudlin I can be sometimes. You're right, life goes on."

"Unless you happen to be riding the wrong roller coaster."

TWENTY-THREE

There were some benefits to being an online addict. You stayed warm and dry in the worst weather, saved on movie and gasoline money, and never ran the risk of tearing an ACL or pulling a hamstring. Also it made one adept at electronic snoopery. Patrick Moore, with an infinite number of resources at his command, had raised this skill to an art form. He spun from data bank to bulletin board to newspaper morgue to chat forums to home pages to financial services with the speed, grace, and precision of a Chinese acrobat. His hands moved without a single wasted motion.

He was seated at his desk at the bank three nights after his conversation with Garvey, fingers tapping steadily at the keys of his computer. All the personnel had gone home, the doors had been locked, and only the desk lamp illuminated his work area. It was the time he liked best. Everything was quiet and he was alone with his thoughts playing out visually in front of him on the color monitor. Tonight, as in the past two, his thoughts had taken him on a nationwide tour of amusement parks. But he was not only visiting their home pages to read their publicity blurbs. He was touring their finances, digging for some magic truffle that would reward his patient efforts. Some number out of the ordinary, some movement of money that looked irrational, something that would confirm Garvey's suspicions. "The investigation is looking for people, maybe it should be looking for money," was what his friend had said. So Moore was looking.

So far, besides visiting various home pages, he had been back and forth to the Dow Jones information service, the

Bond Reporter morgue, Crain's business service, Lipper, the AOL financial chart utility, and a dozen other agencies that kept the most arcane financial records. He had turned up a lot of information, enough to put a roomful of analysts to sleep, but nothing he could call suggestive.

He looked at the clock in the top right-hand corner of the screen and realized he had been at it for over three hours without a break. Moore flexed his fingers and was about to click on the close-all-windows prompt when he noticed something. He was looking at the balance sheet of a ten-million-dollar company in Boulder City, Nevada, called Virtuland. It appeared to be a thirty-thousand-square foot indoor arcade site with the most recent virtual environment games plus a few slot machines and a small outdoor roller coaster. Still, a cap of ten million dollars was way out of synch with similar sites. Twenty to thirty entertainments in that space was pushing it, at a hundred thousand each . . . would be two to three million max. Another three-quarter million for the small coaster. Building, offices, infrastructure . . . maybe another one and a half. Someone had pumped a lot of money into this venture, money that was not showing up in the inventory or fixtures. Moore leaned closer and clicked on the second page of the balance sheet. Company wasn't even listed on the main NASDAQ . . . simply a small cap stock listing. Fun and games with that accounting, he thought. He scrolled through the lines slowly until he found what he was looking for. Real estate was listed at six million. Huh? For maybe three acres in Boulder City if you included the parking? He clicked back on the Virtuland home page but there was nothing indicating what other land the company owned. This was where Moore had to get creative.

He went back to Dun and Bradstreet (fortunately his bank was a subscriber) and opened on Virtuland. No real estate investments listed, but he noticed a fifty thousand share holding in something called The D. Kang Fund, Inc. Okay, what was that? D and B had nothing, so he went to his databases to find them. Standard and Poors and Moody's on bonds, Morningstar and Lipper on mutuals, even a Merrill Lynch research index. Still nothing. Not even on the Canadian Penny Stock Reporter. He figured it was probably a private hedge fund and started a state-by-state search through individual Secretary of States and Department of Law's offices. Some had accessible databases, some had 900 numbers to call, which he listed for calling the following morning. But that wasn't necessary. An hour later he found D. Kang in the corporate lists on the New York database, which came off the NY form M-11. When he opened on it, he got a filing address and a list of directors. Fortunately, New York had no secrecy laws and even required a current corporate address and list of directors every two years. He printed out the information, stuffed the paper into his pocket without inspecting it, then finally turned off his computer. It was well past ten o'clock. Besides his eyes bothering him, he still hadn't had dinner. He could just get to Milly's before it closed and if Milly was still in a civil mood after more than fourteen hours behind a griddle, he'd try to talk her into fixing one of her chicken-fried steaks . . . the best ones in Ironwood.

Milly's restaurant was down a dirt road about fifty yards from the state highway. It was a peculiar location for an establishment that catered to the public, but everyone in Ironwood knew where it was. If you didn't, she figured, you weren't worth feeding. It had originally been the Lougher farmhouse, but after her husband had died eight years earlier, Millicent Lougher sold off all her land and farming equipment, enlarged her kitchen, converted the two downstairs front rooms of her house into one large sunny space, and put up notices all over Ironwood. Her cooking had gone public much earlier in dozens of church suppers and July fourth picnics, so when she opened her doors, she had no lack of customers. And Patrick Moore was one of her most loyal.

He found a seat at one of the back tables and poured

himself a coffee. One thing about Milly, she kept a coffeepot going nearly eighteen hours a day . . . and not that tinned stuff either. Fresh ground, sent all the way from Denver in little bags. And fresh-baked doughnuts too, if you wanted to send your HDL skyrocketing.

Milly heard the bell over the door and came out of the kitchen for a look. She was a little black woman, more gristle than fat, with no pretensions to political correctness. On her head she wore a bandanna that could have jumped right off an old pancake mix box. She never made excuses, neither for her food nor for the way she looked.

Her face brightened and she greeted him warmly.

"Well, if it isn't the FBI poster boy himself. You want supper or sympathy?"

"You heard?"

"Who hasn't? Honey, that news went around town faster than Sue Ellen's abortion and you know there were at least half a dozen relieved gents spreading that one. What can I get you?"

"The usual if you're up to it."

"Why not, then you can tell me what this is all about."

She left Moore sipping his coffee and looking vacantly at the room's decorations. Milly had a fancy for paintings of cowboys around chuck wagons, and all of them had the same down-home realism. You could almost smell the biscuits and stew lifting off the canvas. The one over the woodstove on the side wall was Moore's favorite. A black cowboy was raising a tin mug of coffee to his lips while a scruffy white dog was watching him carefully, waiting for any and all donations from his plate. Moore always wondered if Milly hung this for the allegory or whether she just liked the scene. He studied it for a few minutes and then remembered the paper in his pocket. He pulled it out, put on his glasses, and slowly read down the list of directors of D. Kang, Inc.

"You want fries or hash browns?" Millie called from the kitchen. But Moore's eyes were narrowed and his forehead furrowed in thought. She had to ask him again, this time from the doorway before he looked up.

"What?"

"Fries or hash browns. Don't be going to sleep on me now."

"Fries. And Millie, put the light up a little. I got to read something."

"Oh, you paying my power bill now?" But she leaned over to her left and hit a switch and the ceiling lights came on brighter. She went back into the kitchen as Moore raised the paper closer to his face.

Six minutes later when she brought his plate out he hadn't moved. But his eyes were looking through the paper and concentrating on something far away. When she put the plate down he didn't budge.

"Hello . . ." she said. "You have a mind to eat or burn holes through that paper?"

"Sorry," he said. "I was thinking of something."

"Man, all you bankers float away like that? No wonder we had an S and L crisis. More coffee?"

"Thanks. Why don't you sit down?"

She refilled his cup and sank heavily into the seat across from him. She watched as he began eating.

"So what'd they want? I mean the FBI."

"I guess they thought I killed six or seven people." He smiled for the first time that evening. "But don't worry, Milly, 'cause if I did it must have been when I was concentrating so hard on something else that I don't have a single memory of it at all."

She laughed. "Patrick, you sure are a hard customer. Six or seven? Man, what'd they do, miss a mortgage payment?" This time she even slapped her knee. "Or maybe tried a Christmas club withdrawal in October?"

"Milly, you are too smart. Damn if you didn't see me out. It was the Christmas club."

"Figures," she said. "You guys hate to see cheap money fly

67

back out of the teller's window." She got up and poured herself some coffee and came back. "Seriously, now . . . you in any trouble?"

Moore shook his head. "No, Milly. No need to worry." He looked back down at the paper by his plate. "At least, not yet anyway."

TWENTY-FOUR

If impatience was a disease, Patrick Moore would have been, at that moment, at death's door. Instead, he was sitting uncomfortably behind his desk at the bank the next morning, listening with half-glazed eyes to the problems Abel Yorkum was having with the new irrigator. Well, not exactly new, as Abel explained, but "new fer me." It seemed that Abel felt it should put more than two-inch holes into the ground and no matter what he did, that's the maximum depth he could get.

"What good is two inches gonna do me or my corn?" he asked, not in the least rhetorically. "About as much good as it would do a mare in heat."

Patrick shifted his legs over each other and took a glance at the clock. Twelve-thirty, half an hour into his lunch time, and Abel was still going strong. He had to think of something. He knew where this was all leading, he just had to find some graceful transition.

"It's not under warranty?" Moore asked.

"Expired after six month. One of the problems with second-hand goods." He snorted. "I'll have to send it up to Junction. Might take a week or so to fix it." He lowered his head, but raised his eyes so he could keep the banker in his sights. "So the corn will be late a coupla week. And it ain't gonna be a good spring, Patrick. Almanac says so and it's never wrong.

Predicted damn near every major storm to hit this county since 'seventy-nine. Nope, gonna be a bad spring . . . means I guess I might be a little late on the seed loan I got from you guys."

"That all that's bothering you, Abel?" Patrick Moore said and stood up. "I think I can work out a coupla weeks postponement on that loan. On account of the irrigator, that is."

" 'Course, it's the damn irrigator's fault," Yorkum affirmed.

"S'long as you keep up the house mortgage payments on time."

"No problem there," Abel Yorkum said with a grin spreading across his face. "That's very kind of you."

Moore bent down to shake his hand and in the process usher him out of his chair. "Now don't you worry about a thing," he said. "I'll tell Edna. She'll flag the loan so she won't put it in the late pile." He smiled broadly as he led the older man to the door and closed it quietly behind him. Now, he thought to himself, where was I? He returned to his desk and pulled out a scrap of paper.

"D. Kang," he said aloud. "About time I see what you're all about."

From the New York operator, he got a telephone number for the listing of D. Kang at the address he had scribbled down. A woman answered on the third ring with a curiously slow, friendly-sounding voice.

"Good afternoon, D. Kang. How can I help you?"

"I'd like to speak to Mr. Frank Tartaglia, please."

"Sorry honey, Mr. Tartaglia isn't in. Maybe someone else can help you. Mr. Massio is here."

"Thank you."

A moment later a man's voice answered. "Robert Massio."

"Mr. Massio, this is Patrick Moore from the San Miguel County Bank of Western Colorado calling. I'm chief officer here and of course one of my responsibilities besides loaning

69

money to individuals is finding safe, interestin' investments for our stockholders. Now recently your fund was mentioned to me by an associate and I was hoping I could get some information on what it is you all do."

"I'm afraid, Mr. Moore, this is not a hedge fund that is open to the general public. Can I ask who recommended us?"

Moore thought fast. "Someone down in Nevada. Boulder City, I think, but it could have been Vegas. Another banker or CFO I met on one of our regional meetings." He hesitated.

"Well, I don't know who it could be, but this is strictly a fund run for some select individuals around the country. Was it George Manfredi by any chance, the man who gave you our name?"

"Manfredi . . ." Moore turned it around slowly on the phone. "Nope, doesn't sound familiar. Well, I'm sorry to trouble you. I like to follow up on any lead I get. Usually do pretty well with them. Thanks anyway."

"No trouble," Massio said and hung up.

"Manfredi," Moore said and leaned forward to the intercom on his desk. This was pitching the ball back in his field and he felt a lot more comfortable.

"Edna," he said after pushing the button. "Who do we use in Las Vegas on credit investigations?" A moment later she came up with a name. "Get him for me, would you?"

TWENTY-FIVE

The quarter-scale track for the jumper took a week to set up in the open test lot behind the engineering building. Even though the highest point of the structure reached over twenty-seven feet, the tubular steel pieces fit together like some precision surgical instrument. Madondi was by far the best construction firm in the United States for coaster cars and tubular steel-track coasters . . . quick, accurate, and careful. The Madondi engineers had had some questions on the original design, but Garvey worked them through the strut redundancy and convinced them that everything was quite within the parameters of tubular steel specs.

Looking at the gleaming structure the Thursday morning when everything was in place, Garvey felt once again like he had just been presented with a Christmas bicycle, one not quite big enough to ride in, but big enough to give the illusion of the real thing. Quarter-scale models always made him feel like a kid again. After the crew had put the final touches on the paint job, he just stood there for a quarter of an hour looking at it. It reminded him of something surreal, like some exploded helical-genetic structure. But this one was special. Besides its innovative shape, the Jumper incorporated three untried safety features now installed on the quarter-scale model. One was the spinners to dry the track, another was the laser positioning system using compressed gas to compensate for windage, the last was called the TOA, or trajectory override adjustment. The TOA was crucial due to the variance in weight of each carload of passengers. It worked by sub-track weighing sensors at the loading station, feeding information to a separate computer which then fed settings to hydraulic pistons under the final track section before the jumps. The pistons moved no more than a few centimeters either way, enough to increase or decrease the arc of the flight several feet, depending on the car weight. This was one of the features that had not been tested yet on the one-tenth scale model but awaited them now.

Garvey was admiring its repeated-mirrored shape when Jason walked over and put a hand on his shoulder.

"You won't like this," he said. "The test cars' sheathing is over twenty percent too heavy."

Garvey swiveled around as quickly as his bum leg would allow. "Can't be. We worked it all out."

"I know what we did," Jason said defensively. "I went over the numbers half a dozen times to make sure. I thought we agreed at eighteen gauge. But Madondi used sixteen-gauge sheet steel. It's going to fly short."

"They didn't catch the mistake?" Garvey asked incredulously.

"No, they reported the manufactured gauge. I couldn't believe what I was looking at. That's why I double-checked it. I just spoke to Don Madison over there. The specs as delivered on the quarter scale call for sixteen gauge."

"They misread them?" Garvey was furious.

"You're not hearing me, Sam. They were *delivered* at sixteen. Came from us that way. That's what they're saying."

"No way!" Garvey was adamant.

"That's what I thought until I looked at our own records here on the computer. Says sixteen, plain as day. So why did I remember eighteen? Something's fishy." Jason shook his head. "You'd better speak to him. He's your buddy. You might even have to travel out there. But for now, we can't work with these two cars. They have to be resheathed and that's going to take at least a couple of weeks. Maybe you could convince them it was their mistake and they have to prioritize it."

"Came from us that way," Garvey repeated. "How . . . could we really have made that mistake?"

"I don't know." Jason shrugged. "Someone has to check Madondi's original prints. But you know," he said, and gave Garvey a meaningful glance, "the specs on the cars were delivered two months ago . . . and at that time we had no password on our files."

"Hell!" Garvey turned quickly and walked into the engineering building. Jason followed closely behind.

"Just how I like to spend my Fridays," Garvey said. "In beautiful Cincinnati. I'll have to tell Rosita to stay late with Sarah."

"Call me if you need me to cover," Jason said.

"Beautiful track, the spinners even came out looking okay, the TOA ready to go except now there's no goddamn cars to run," Garvey said almost to himself as he reached for his phone. "What a joke."

"Who's laughing?" Jason said.

TWENTY-SIX

The Madondi plant was set on the outskirts of Cincinatti in a building that had previously been a steel distribution warehouse. When Riblet Steel went bankrupt in 1991, Madondi, one of its more successful customers, saw an opportunity to move closer to their own clientele and in the bargain pick up some distressed real estate. They got five acres, a fifty-thousand-square-foot cinder block building with a hundred fifty-foot traveling two-story crane, a detached forty-ton truck scale, three loading bays, and plenty of parking and outside storage. The two-story office was in the northeast corner of the building behind some soundproof glass windows and gave a good perspective on the operations below. Garvey met with Don Madison at two o'clock later that day after a frantic rush to the airport to make connections.

Madison was a big man, the kind that only looks good in open-neck shirts and hard hats. His glasses had, years earlier, left two imprints into the sides of his face where the steel ear pieces had pressed mercilessly into the flesh. Behind the glasses were eyes that were equally incisive. Right now they were searching the column of specification notes for the item on the sheathing gauge.

"Here it is," he finally said. "If that's not a sixteen, I'll eat my hat."

Garvey leaned closer and looked where he was pointing. Sure enough, the number was a six, not an eight.

"You didn't double-check?" Garvey asked lamely.

"I would have double-checked if it had been eighteen. Sixteen is pretty standard for these cars."

"Except when you're trying to save weight to fly them," Garvey said disgustedly. "Let me see the signature."

"Here it is, next page."

Garvey saw his signature but that didn't help any. Three pages of specs, signed only on the last page. He'd never had a problem before, but now he could see the opening.

"I should have signed each page," he said. "Jason and I looked over everything, checking each other. I can't believe we both missed it."

Madison looked skeptical. "You think someone substituted this page in?"

Garvey didn't answer.

"Well, it didn't happen here. This is just what I got," Madison said. "The original never left my desk."

"Damnit, Don, I'm not accusing you. It's just that we've got a hell of a problem now. This will set us back long enough that we won't make the target date. All hell will break loose. I've got to have these cars back by next week."

"Oh, a stand-up comic?"

"I wasn't trying to be funny."

"Yeah, well then come with me." Madison motioned and Garvey followed him out the door and onto the production floor. They waited for two fork-lift trucks carrying bundles of twelve-foot steel tubes to pass them. Then they turned down an aisle to the right. A moment later they stopped in front of a seven-foot-high steel brake, a machine used for bending sheet metal. The sheet is fed onto the brake's table, a bar clamps down, then the front of the table swings up hydraulically with a whoosh and presto, the metal becomes three dimensional . . . all automatically. At the moment there was a stack of gleaming sheets three feet high waiting to be processed.

"This is a job for the Laser, Dorney Park. Twenty-four new cars to be delivered next week. That's joke number one." Madison waited through one cycle and watched as the bent sheet was pushed out of the machine, then walked farther. Past a guillotine shear spitting out little triangular reinforcing stubs, he came to stop next to an automatic forty-ton press. A man was locking in place flats of stainless sheet over a die bed, then pushing a sequence of several buttons. Slowly, the positive die head came down and pushed the steel into the shape below it. With a metal clang the ejector rod popped the now hollow part up and into a waiting bin.

"The Python, Busch Gardens," Madison said. "Seventy replacement wheel caps and attachments. Due tomorrow. Joke number two." He smiled. "Wanna have more laughs?"

"I get your drift."

"All good customers," he continued. "What am I going to do? Rushing your cars out I postponed all of them. Now you want me to stick it to them again?" He shook his head. "I can't, Sam."

"Yes you can, Don. This is the Jumper we're talking about. Those others are just regular coasters."

"You used that one on me before. Won't work twice."

Garvey banged his crutch against the hydraulic press in frustration. "It's just the goddamn sheathing on two cars . . . two quarter-scale cars. You could do that in three days. You delayed them already, you said so yourself, so what's another few days? They're still going to operate. But the Jumper may not ever get off the ground if we keep up these delays."

"But, Sam, it wasn't our fault." Madison looked defensive.

"Didn't say it was, and you can point the finger squarely at me. I'll take the heat. But I need those cars. Come on, Don, I'm laying twenty years of working together at your feet . . . that has to mean something."

Madison thought for a moment. In his silence, noises swirled around them in a symphony of predigital clicks, clangs, thumps whirrs and screeches. The music of industry; Garvey took it all in and waited.

"If you get the cars here by Monday, maybe I'll have them by Friday. I can put a crew on over the weekend, but it's going to cost you."

Garvey smiled. "Thanks, Don. Whatever it is, we'll take it."

"Wouldn't do this for anybody else . . ."

"Nor should you. Get me to a phone and I'll have Jason send them back out right away." He looked at his watch. "And then I'll get a cab. The last flight back's in forty minutes."

Madison laughed. "Cut it pretty close, didn't you?"

"Nah, Don. You always had a sensitive side."

TWENTY-SEVEN

Rachael White was having her coffee break two days later when the mail was dropped on her desk. It settled in between the heaps of metal and plastic parts like fall leaves on broken shale. Some advertisements, some standard directives, junk mail, even a reminder from Ford about a recalled part on her car. She almost missed the small envelope wedged between a torn fuel strainer and the broken fan blade from a DC-10. She snaked it out with her two fingers and turned it over.

It had the look of evil even before she opened it. It was a cheap dimestore white envelope with her name and address glued on from magazine cut-outs, the kind of thing you'd see in movies. The postmark was from Denver. She was careful opening it, as if Kaczynski weren't already in prison for the rest of his life. Inside was more of the same magazine wording on some generic blue-lined school paper. She dug out her tweezers from the desk and held up the paper to read.

YOUR INVESTIGATION IS ON TRACK, BUT WHEN THE WIND UP IS OVER YOU'LL SEE WHAT I SAW. WOULD YOU BOW TO THE KING? I THINK IT BEST. PERICLYMENUS.

Shit, what was this? She sat back and stared at the paper for several minutes. Authentic . . . yes. They'd not given out the name Periclymenus to anybody. Only the people involved with the investigation knew. But nothing new had happened, no accidents, no reported tamperings. And how had he gotten her name. But that's not what bothered her. She had a feeling that what she was looking at was not a boast, although there was that too. It was a warning . . . no, a challenge. It said: You think you're so smart? Figure this out. And the feeling in her gut told her that if she didn't, a bunch more people would die.

A wordsmith, but not a good one. "Grapple with this," "Give me a break." The two previous notes were sophomoric in their ex post facto punning. This one too? She looked at her watch. It was 10:30. Too early to call Garvey in Texas. Pouncy? What help would he be? She swallowed the remainder of her coffee in one gulp and looked back down at the note. Okay, she thought, I'm on.

There were seven adult roller coasters at Paramount's King's Dominion in Doswell, Virginia; plus seven adult coasters at Paramount's Kings Island in Kings Island, Ohio, including the King Cobra, America's first "stand-up" steel looping roller coaster. Those were the only places in America that had "King" in their title. Fourteen coasters. The first thing she did was call up the parks, over four hundred miles apart from each other, and speak to their head operations managers. She asked, then pleaded with each to send out crews right away to check on their coasters. Each told her no problems had been reported, that they checked their rides nightly, especially after the advisory, that there were huge lines even now to get on, and that to stop the rides under the circumstances would be financially disastrous.

"How financially disastrous will it be if someone gets killed," she countered and wrenched from them the assurance that they would try to send someone out to each ride.

"Close them down," she begged.

"Not without a court order," they answered. They had a point, she thought. She was asking them to forego hundreds of thousands of dollars of revenue on her hunch. Now what? She went back to the letter.

YOUR INVESTIGATION IS ON TRACK, BUT WHEN THE WIND UP IS OVER YOU'LL SEE WHAT I SAW. WOULD YOU BOW TO THE KING? I THINK IT BEST. PERICLYMENUS.

"Sophomoric," she repeated, "double entendres and puns," and then she started working with the words. She hated crosswords, hated codes and acrostics, hated all forms of confusion in communications. That's what got pilots and air controllers in trouble. She liked words to mean what they said, and here she was trying to peel away some silly word game to save lives. *On track, wind up, what I saw, would you bow, think it best*. Where was the connection? The similarities? She looked at her watch again. Eleven o'clock. Screw the Ford catalytic converter recall. She'd hop in her car and work on it on the way down to Doswell. Couldn't be more than an hour and a half away. Maybe she could get Garvey on the phone on the way out. She copied the note on a clean piece of paper, put the original in an envelope for safety, and headed out of the cluttered office.

TWENTY-EIGHT

Rosita was saying something into the phone that Garvey didn't understand, something about Sarah's teacher calling. But then Garvey seldom understood Rosita's heavy Spanish accent before the second run-through, and then only after a lot of hand signals. Talking to Rosita on the phone was very difficult.

"You peek up," she said. "Sarah seek."

"Sarah?"

"Seek. Mus go get."

"At school?" Garvey asked.

"*Sí. Venga. Ahora.*"

"With what? She was okay this morning."

"You call," Rosita said now on firm ground. "I no car." She hung up and left Garvey staring at the phone. Of course Rosita had no car. She had no driver's license either, a little fact which seemed to elude her. The only way she came and left work was by the good graces of her twenty-year-old son on his way to and from his auto-painting job. He sighed, dialed the school number, and in under a minute he had the director on the line.

"Sarah's sick?" he asked. "I just dropped her off an hour ago. She seemed okay."

"Dr. Garvey," the woman said patiently, "Sarah's been acting strangely lately. I thought perhaps it was time to bring it to your attention. She seems fine for the first ten minutes, then slowly she disengages. In half an hour she is sitting by herself in a corner not talking or playing with anybody. This is so new for her we were concerned. She is usually such a pleasant little child. Her teacher, Mrs. Johnson, and I thought perhaps something happened at home . . ."

Garvey was stunned. "I'll be right there," he said and hung up the phone. He left his computer on with the simulation he was about to run and reached for his crutch. A short time later the phone on his desk rang but there was no one there to pick it up.

"What's the problem, sugar?" Garvey asked, picking up his daughter and hugging her. "Mrs. Johnson says you're not joining in any of the games or having any fun." After a moment he put her back down and sat next to her in a tiny chair in a corner of her kindergarten classroom. "Something bothering you?"

"Ralph."

"Who's Ralph?"

"Him," Sarah said and pointed nervously to one of the little boys playing with blocks nearby. "Ralph says I can't run as fast as him. And 'cause I can't run as fast as him, I can't play with the blocks."

"Well, of course that's ridiculous, Sarah. Of course you can play with the blocks. Didn't you tell Mrs. Johnson that?" Sarah grabbed her dad around the neck and started to cry. Through her tears she managed to blurt out, "Ralph said if I told Mrs. Johnson, he would hit me with a block. And he told me I couldn't play with clay either."

Garvey took out a handkerchief and wiped his child's tears away. He kissed her lightly and said, "You wait here, honey. I'm going to have a little talk with the principal and then you and I are going out for a soda, and when we come back, I'll bet Ralph will let you play with him." He got up slowly and motioned to Mrs. Johnson. "Come with me," he said, and the two of them walked into the principal's office.

"Okay," he began. "Here's the deal. Between nine A.M. and three P.M. on school days it is your job to take care of Sarah. That includes finding out if someone has threatened to assault her and if so, to remove that child from the class. I'm taking Sarah out of here for half an hour. When I get back, if you haven't spoken to Ralph about his threat to assault my daughter and correct the situation, I am going to call the police." He got up. "And if you think I'm angry, you're right. Mrs. Johnson, I can't believe this goes on behind your back in your classroom. Maybe Sarah is not the only child threatened with a heavy block. And for you, Principal Walker, to suggest that there was some problem at home rather than on your own premises goes beyond effrontery. 'One of her moods,' as you called it was a result of your school's negligence. And I want you to call Ralph's parents. This is a public school, Mrs. Walker. The only kindergarten in this part of the county. Everyone has to learn how to be civil with each other." He turned out the door and walked back to his daughter's classroom.

"Now," he asked her, "what's it going to be, a milk shake or an egg cream?"

TWENTY-NINE

I've been trying to get you all morning," Rachael said frantically into the phone. "Where have you been? They couldn't find you anywhere."

"A parent thing," Garvey answered. "I'm not sure you'd understand. I just got back. What's up?" She told him quickly about the note.

There was silence on the line for a long time. Finally Garvey spoke. "It's not Doswell, it's Cincinnati."

"How do you know?" she asked. The cell phone was to her ear as she sped past cars on I-95. "From the words?"

"No. It's just a hunch, but look at the other attacks. New York, Boblo, now Ohio. He's moving west, not south."

"But I'm headed toward King's Dominion. I'm only a few minutes away."

"Turn back," Garvey said. "Get yourself to Kings Island. Can you do that?"

"Pulling some strings, yes."

"Call me when you're in the air. I'll work on the note."

"I think I got part of it," Rachael said as she turned off the southbound interstate and swung north on the cloverleaf. "I think it's a woodie. 'Would you bow . . .' "

"Good," Garvey said. "But which one?"

"What if you're wrong about Cincinnati?" she said.

"Just about even odds," he said. "Funny, I was just there Friday."

"Funny," she said. "You should have stayed."

The helicopter landed two hours later in a corner of the least-occupied parking lot. Peter Taber, head of Kings Island security, was waiting for her in one of their security Jeeps. He was a tall, lanky man who looked as if he spent a lot of time out in the sun. He introduced himself, then told her that they had checked out all of their woodies as she had asked in her second call.

"Everything is perfect. No cuts in any track support beams. Nothing's been sawed through even partially. Besides, in most of the structures there's so much redundancy it would take cuts in over half a dozen beams to accomplish anything. Would be easy to spot. Everything's secure."

"No," she said. "Something's been done." Her cell phone rang as they entered the park and she quickly answered.

"This is Garvey. Look, the names of the coasters at Kings Island are: Vortex, a steel; King Cobra, a steel; Top Gun, a steel; Outer Limits Flight of Fear, a steel; the Racer, a woodie; Adventure Express, a woodie mine-type ride; two kids rides, and finally, the Beast, a woodie. The note said he thinks it best; I think it Beast."

"Got you," she said. "Good memory."

"I looked it up."

Anything else?"

"Not yet. Keep your phone on."

She turned to Taber and said quickly, "Let's go to the Beast." He looked at her curiously, then spun the wheel.

"I was just there," he said. "Myself. It's working fine."

"Listen, Taber," Rachael said evenly. "Understand this. Planes work fine up to the moment they drop out of the sky. Trains glide smoothly down their tracks and then flip onto their backs. Things 'work fine' until some little thing goes wrong and tragedy strikes. That's why I'm here. Now," she sat back. "Tell me about this ride. Why do they call it the Beast?"

"Wait until you ride it."

"I don't intend to."

He laughed. "Okay. It took three years to build and is the longest ride in America at around seventy-four-hundred feet. Takes four minutes and thirty seconds to do one circuit, which is about the longest ride in time too. There are three tunnels, one of which dives into the earth, another encloses a five-hundred-and-forty-degree helix at the finish when the train is going approximately sixty-five miles per hour. Let's see, the biggest drop is a hundred and forty-one feet." He smiled and looked at her sideways. "That a good enough description? Those are only numbers though. Its reputation is as the granddaddy of all terrain coasters."

"Terrain coasters?" Rachael looked confused.

"It's built on thirty-five densely wooded rolling acres at the back of the park. It follows the contours of the ground. It's hard to spot from the rest of the park, but," he pointed off to the left and Rachael saw some wooden track shooting through the open space between two trees, "there it is."

"Wow," she said involuntarily as they approached closer. The wood structure was constructed of solid timbers and if anyone thought a "terrain coaster" meant low and slow, they had another think coming. The Beast used the land in spots, gracefully following the undulations of several rises and hills, but then it swooped upward at an impossible angle, jerked to the right, and dove down toward the earth like some crazed Midway divebomber. As she watched one of the trains, a two-car, twenty-four-seat jointed affair, slammed by at over sixty miles an hour, sounding like the A train on steroids. They were over forty feet away from the track and out in the open and she still felt the rush of air as the train carved its way through the afternoon heat. She didn't need to hear the screams from the delighted passengers to know that they were getting their money's worth.

"That's the Beast," Taber said after the noise receded.

"You couldn't have checked every timber," she said in disbelief as she saw the entire layout. "It's only been two hours since I called."

"Every one," he assured her. "We're good at what we do. Maintenance has a cherry picker, which we got right over. We also checked the ground under the track. Not a speck of sawdust." He smiled. "Maybe there's something else to look for?"

She pulled her scrap of paper out of her pocket and looked at the words again. There was a swirly wind coming from the large body of water surrounding the park that made the paper flutter in her hand. She was careful to hold on tight; the last thing she wanted was to have it fly away into the nearby woods.

"Always this windy?" she asked.

"No, somedays it's worse than others. If we get a north-wester coming in off the lake it can be annoying."

She looked up and saw the trees moving in the wind as another gust passed, then braced herself for another train to thunder by.

"Right on time," Taber said, looking at his watch. "Four minutes and thirty seconds apart."

Then she had it. Of course! She peered at the note again. "It's all here!"

"What?" Taber asked.

"Follow me," she shouted. "Can we follow the track in the car?"

"Most of the way. Some places it takes a detour."

"Can we get to one of those places where the track is low to the ground?"

The lanky man thought for a moment, going over in his head the length of the entire track as it dipped and rose and twisted along its almost mile-and-a-half length.

"Yeah, one spot. Road's about seventy feet away from the track. It's close to the end."

"Let's go," she said hurriedly and jumped into the car. She heard the cell phone ring and snapped it open.

"Yeah," she shouted.

"You think 'bow' could be 'b-o-u-g-h'?" Garvey said, spelling it out.

"Bet on it," she answered. "Especially on a windy day."

"Wind," Garvey said, mulling it over. "Of course!"

"And, Sam, it's goddamn windy out here!"

"You got a lot of trees to check?"

"Don't ask. Has to be over a thousand. But I'm on my way, playing a hunch."

"Want me to call someone?"

"No, stay on the phone. I may need some technical help." She put the phone on the seat between herself and Taber and held on as the other man jolted down the road next to the overhead structure. Up ahead she saw the road dart right as the track came down and dove into the tunnel starting the

540-degree turn. When it emerged it was uncovered, off to one side in some thick wood. She saw the road rejoin it about one hundred feet farther on.

"Over there," he said.

"I see it." She also heard behind her the sound of another train making it down toward them, maybe a minute away. Taber stopped where the road swung right, and Rachael jumped out.

"Can you get some help down here right away," she called over her shoulder. "The more eyes the better. Maybe some rope . . . or chain."

Taber nodded and pulled out his walkie-talkie. He spoke into it, dropped it on the seat next to Rachael's phone, and in another thirty seconds he was right behind her in the wooded area.

They both saw it at the same time. The ground had been recently raked by a litter-gathering maintenance crew, leaving the dark brown earth looking evenly colored, except in two places, where there were little white discolorations, as though it had snowed only briefly. The little piles of sawdust had been sheltered down at ground level, but up on high, the trees continued to bend back and forth in the wind with loud swishing noises. The track was barely ten feet above them and now rumbling as the train neared.

Taber looked up. The trees they were standing under were old oaks and had limbs the diameter of hubcaps. The branch above his head arched up and almost over the track, but twenty feet higher. He didn't need binoculars to see the wedge-shaped cut that had been made only a foot from the trunk. He saw where it stopped also, perhaps with only two inches of wood left to support the massive weight. As the train approached, its noise was so overpowering he didn't hear the microburst of wind as it bent the treetops above him. The oak bent back, then forward, then the limb snapped with a sound so loud it pierced the train's metallic

86

screeching. The splintering limb gave forth a percussive grinding and tearing noise that happened in the space of an instant. And an instant was all it took for the limb to come swinging down just as the train passed underneath. One of its smaller side branches just grazed the last car, missing a person's head by inches.

The heavy branch smashed against the coaster's track and balanced there for a moment, swaying up and down. Rachael and Taber were transfixed for a few dazed moments, watching the seesaw movement above them. The horrendous thing was straddling the track, but slowly the weight on its inner end pulled in ever deeper swings, up and down, until the entire branch, inch by inch, slid toward them. In one final arc the heavier part pulled the rest over.

"Watch out," Rachael called, but it was too late. The ton of wood came down like a sack of sand, gave the ground a thudding blow, then toppled over on its side. In between two of the wrist-size branches lay Taber, unconscious, a smear of blood staining his forehead. Rachael had been five feet farther away and miraculously had been touched by only a few twigs.

All was quiet except for the rustling of the wind in the trees.

Then Rachael screamed.

Garvey heard it over the cell phone in Texas, but they didn't hear it a quarter of a mile away through the thick woods at the control booth of the Beast. She screamed again, and again, and when no one answered, she got hold of herself and figured she had to go for help. Except the way out was blocked by the fallen branch and she had to slowly negotiate around it. It took her a few minutes to get out of the woods and back to Taber's car. She heard another train tearing down the track behind her, now harmlessly littered with splinters and pieces of bark. God, was that lucky, she told herself. She found Taber's walkie-talkie and turned it on, but she needed a channel. There were too many buttons to press, and shouting into it over and over she got no response. She threw it down and picked up the cell phone.

"Sam, you still there?"

"Still here. Jesus, what happened?"

"No time. Call the Beast, or management, or whoever here at Kings Island. I'm right where the big turn exits, in the woods. Taber is down, unconscious, hurt pretty bad. I'm going back to stay with him. I need help."

"Hang on," he said. "I'll call."

She found a first-aid kit in the Jeep, took the phone with her, and went back. Taber was still unconscious, the blood still flowing although less copiously. She opened the kit, unrolled some gauze, and pressed it to his wound. Another train went by overhead, rattling the earth beneath them. The branch over them swayed and for a moment she thought it might shift on top of them, but it settled harmlessly. She felt for a pulse, found one, then watched his breathing. Vital signs seemed okay, just a lot of blood loss. She took off her jacket and carefully raised his head with it, then pressed down on the gauze. Christ, where was someone? Why was it taking so long? Seconds felt like minutes. Then she remembered something and chill fear stabbed through her. There had been two scatterings of sawdust, against two different trees! She looked around her, trying to remember where the other one had been, and that's when she heard the voices off near the road.

"Over here," she called frantically. "We're over here."

The voices came closer, then she heard some cracking of lesser oak boughs as two men clambered over the fallen branch. One dropped down next to her and heaved a length of heavy rope to the side. The other took one look and got on his own walkie-talkie to call for an ambulance.

"What the Christ happened?" the first man said. "He called in for some rope."

Another train screamed by, another moment of praying for

88

the fallen branch not to move and the second sabotaged limb to stay upright.

"We have to hurry," she said. "Another one might go any second." The two men looked up and this time Rachael spotted it. An even bigger branch, higher up, this one ten feet closer to the road. "There," she said. "See the saw cut? Call the control booth. Tell them to hold up the next car."

"Can't," the man with the walkie-talkie said. "This only goes to maintenance. They'll have to relay it."

"Just do it," she shouted as a new gust of wind rumbled through the trees, and at that moment, the other branch gave way. The report was not as loud since this branch didn't separate; it splintered and just drooped enough to lose support and came swinging down to rest across the track.

"Holy mother of God," the man next to her said, looking up at the huge limb and how it lay across the track. "If a train comes tearing through here at over sixty miles an hour, you're going to have twenty-four decapitated heads raining down on us."

Rachael looked over to the man who was still talking on the walkie-talkie. Too late, she thought. If the other train had passed ten seconds ago and he was still talking, it was too late! The next train was already on its way, and sure enough, when she listened hard enough, she could hear the screams of the people in anticipation as they climbed the first drop hill. They had a little over four minutes before the disaster happened.

"Leave him," she shouted at the man next to Taber. "The rope, come on!"

She jumped up and ran to the base of the roller coaster. The man with the rope was right behind her.

"What . . . ?"

"Give me an end. Take the other and work it out to the truck."

"I don't know if it's long enough."

"Then you've got to bring the truck closer. It's the only

way." She grabbed the end, tied it around her waist, and started climbing. She was wearing the wrong shoes for this, the low soft leather pumps that happened to match her blue skirt. But then who knew this morning back in Washington that she'd be pretending to be a human fly with some twenty-four lives at stake? She reached up, got a hold of the crossbeam above her, and twisted her legs over her head. Also the wrong clothes too. She already felt her panty hose in shreds and that blue woolen skirt full of splinters. But she had under four minutes to get up to the track, put a wrap around the branch, and pray that the other end reached the maintenance truck.

Down on the ground, the two men were pulling on the rope to get it to the road. The shortest route lead through some heavy brush, and without a second's hesitation they crashed through, the wood tearing at their overalls. The line snagged in several places, but within a minute they had it pulled through. The road was another forty yards away past some thin spruce and pine trees, and they ran toward it without stopping.

Rachael was almost there. She was up to the last crossbeam, a few feet below the guardrail and track bed ... maybe twenty seconds away. She was tired from the exertion of climbing the fifteen feet, bloody from the scrapes to her now bare legs, and frightened she was going to be too late. She stood on the last crossbeam and was reaching for the guardrail when she felt the rope around her waist snap her backward. She screamed and clawed out with her hand and just managed to grab the steel guardrail before her feet were pulled out from under her. She slammed down and smashed her knee into the crossbeam and felt a shock of pain travel upward. She hung on with her single hand, reaching desperately with her other one. But the rope was still tightening around her waist, still pulling her grip away from the railing. She shouted out again, and this time she felt the rope release. With one last effort she lunged out and felt her hand make contact. She hung there for a second, balancing her weight and catching her breath.

"Slack, give me some slack," she yelled finally. Slowly, she climbed back up and, with great effort, swung herself onto the track bed. The broken limb was a few feet away and dangling at a forty-five-degree angle across the rails. As she started to untie the rope from her waist she looked around her. There were no extended platforms, no escape from the speeding train except over the side. She had to work fast . . . the rails were already starting to vibrate with the closing train. But what the hell to do?

"Slack," she called again. "More slack!" She pulled on the rope and gathered several coils in her hands. She was about to put a wrap around the branch when she stopped herself. Think, she told herself. What's that going to do? Pulling on the limb might tear it off the tree, but then it would still be lying across the track and most likely snagged. The rope led away to the truck in the same direction the smaller branches pointed. It would be like trying to drag a grapple with a hundred barbs the wrong way over a grating. It would never work. She heard the truck engine start up and the truck back toward the woods.

One of the men shouted at her. "Can you give me some rope!"

"Not yet," she called back and looked out to where the train was moving. It was darting up the second hill, halfway around the track toward her. As she followed the track's course her eye spotted something closer to her. There, some ten feet higher and only a few feet away, was another large tree limb. It was her only hope. She ran down the track until she was on the other side of it and picked out a spot to aim her throw. Between two secondary branches there was a space of about two feet and with only one practice swing, she underhanded the rope coil upward. It unraveled smoothly, bounced on the horizontal limb, then fell over on the other side.

"Hurry," she heard one of the men say. He was underneath her now, holding onto the rope as it lead toward the truck. "Maybe two minutes left."

She rushed to the dangling end of the rope and reached up. It was there, just out of her grasp. Maybe four inches. She could jump, but there was no telling if she'd land back on the separated beams of the track bed, or in the empty spaces between and break her leg. The only thing to do was jump looking down and hope she could grab the rope blind. She tried it once and got a fistful of air. The second time she grazed the rope but couldn't catch it. Twice more she tried, and twice more she timed her grab badly. She hadn't counted on the wind swaying the end of the rope. She was already exhausted and this was taking her last reserves of energy away. She had to do it the other way; look up and hope she landed right. She took a breath, looked at the rope carefully, and jumped. She got the end, held on tight and prayed that her feet came down on something solid.

"Hold on," the man beneath her called out as he saw one of her feet land half-over the wood beam. Rachael twisted backwards, about to fall over the edge, when the man yanked on his end and pulled the rope taut. Rachael held on long enough to catch her balance with her trailing foot and stood upright.

"Okay," he called out. "I can give you some more slack! Only hurry!"

Rachael didn't need any encouragement. She pulled the rope savagely behind her, snaked it around the middle of the dangling branch, and threw a quick bowline in it. Her hands were shaking as she pulled the knot tight.

"Okay," she screamed. "It's yours!" She leaned exhaustedly against the limb for a few seconds, then felt the track rumble beneath her feet and slowly pushed away. The train must have been very near now because the wood beams themselves began to tremble. She made it to the side, threw a leg over the guardrail, and hesitated. She didn't know if she had enough strength to hold on, especially with all the wind and vibration. But there was nothing else to do. She couldn't climb down . . . not yet anyway. She was so weak she could hardly hold herself steady, but it was suicide to stay where she was. She threw the other leg over the guardrail and waited, taking big gulps of air. Out of the corner of her eye she watched for some movement in the dangling limb.

The maintenance truck had been backed up as far as it could go. Its rear end was snug against a two-foot spruce tree with the motor idling, and the two men were looking in anguish at the end of the rope still four feet away. That meant they needed at least eight feet more to make the connection.

"What do we got in the truck?" one of them asked frantically.

"Nothing strong enough."

"What, what? We can double, triple it."

"Just the nylon rope we use for the crowd lines."

"Get it," the other man said. "We got to try something."

They got the yellow roll out, stripped out some fifty-five feet, ran it back and forth six times between the truck's axle and the small loop on the end of the rope, and tied it off.

"Go, go," the first man said. "Slow at first. Snug it up." The man now behind the wheel put the truck into gear and crept forward. The nylon webbing and rope tightened like a piano string, but the truck stayed in place.

"Nothing's happening," the man behind the wheel said. "I ain't moving."

"Give it more gas."

Rachael felt the pressure of the wind on her face before she saw the train. She was doing her best to hold on, but now the wood beneath her feet and the metal guardrail were shaking so hard it felt like an earthquake. She locked her hands together and looked to her left. The limb hadn't moved an inch even though the rope was now as taut as a bow string. The train approaching from her right was no more than fifteen seconds away. When she turned her head

93

back she could see the curve of the track smoothly bending toward her, could hear the joyful shrieks of the passengers innocent of the disaster awaiting them. She wondered how their shrieks would change as they saw death looming before them. Idle, crazy thought. She wanted to close her eyes against the carnage, but she couldn't will herself to blank this out so easily. She waited for the first glimpse of the train, knowing fatalistically that the entire horrible sequence would be imprinted on her memory for the rest of her life. Nothing she could do . . . helpless. She took one more look to the left and thought she saw, yes, did see, the heavy limb jiggle upward. Maybe it was just the train's vibration moving it. But then she saw it move, maybe a few inches, actually move, and she bit her lip. It moved up a foot, then another, but it would be too late. The train was only a hundred yards away and bearing down. And now the limb was nearly parallel to the track, and at the exact height to decapitate.

The truck's wheels were spinning wildly, carving little troughs in the dirt. Thin wisps of smoke were rising where one of the wheels was burning rubber against a submerged rock.

"Hold it," the man outside called, moving toward the truck wildly. "Let me do it! This ain't no drag race." He shoved his partner over to one side and slid in behind the wheel. Quickly he reversed the gear and, aided by the weight of the limb pulling on the rope, the truck rolled backward and out of the troughs. He slammed the gear into low range, flipped a lever to four-wheel drive, yanked the steering wheel to the left, and said, "Keep your fingers crossed." Slowly, gently the truck pulled forward, missed the ruts by a few inches, and kept pulling.

Unbelievably, she saw the heavy limb sag once again toward the track and she felt a cruel disappointment. But then, like a miracle, it started to rise again, and this time its movement was steady. Was there time? She looked at the train, now only a dozen feet away, and motioned frantically with one of her hands. "Get down," she was telling the riders, screaming it out at the same time. The train blurred past her, the airstream from its front nearly knocking her off her perch. Had they seen her? Had they ducked? Her eyes followed the back of the train, half expecting to see spouts of blood . . . but there was nothing. Just the rustling of some leaves from the lowest branch over the track, maybe six inches above the tops of the cars. And an empty cowboy hat, now spinning to a stop upside down on the wood crossbeam directly under the branch.

"Oh my God!" she heard herself say.

The truck was continuing to pull forward when the men inside heard the webbing part. It sounded like a snapping whip, loud, percussive, and the truck bolted forward. Five yards later the driver regained control, but not before crashing through a little sapling. The rope recoiled like a shot and the limb came crashing the six feet back down to the track. It came to rest on top of the upside down hat, flattening it like a supermarket flyer. Rachael looked at it, at the train now heading toward the station with heads bobbing merrily along, and she slumped over the rail to wait for help.

THIRTY

The hospital in Cincinnati where they took her was ten miles from the park. Now, six hours after the incident, she lay in her semiprivate room, looking up into the concerned face of Sam Garvey and the somewhat-perplexed face of the little girl by his side.

"It's nothing to worry about," Rachael said. "A few scratches and bruises. I don't know why they're keeping me here overnight."

"Observation," Garvey said. "Which covers a multitude of sins. Apparently you were pretty banged up and shaky." There was a genuine note of concern in his voice.

"I never did like heights," she said with a little schoolgirl grin. "Funny, huh, an NTSB agent with vertigo."

"Very funny." He pulled a chair over and sat down. "This is Sarah. She wanted to meet a real live heroine."

"Hello." Rachael smiled. "You look like your dad."

"Hello," Garvey's daughter said.

"The way I heard it from the people at Kings Island," Garvey went on, "you saved a lot of lives." He pulled Sarah onto his lap and smoothed her hair. "I thought that merited at least a job-well-done committee. To tell you the truth, Rachael, when your cell phone went dead, I simply hung up and called the airport. I had heard enough." He reached out a hand and squeezed her arm. She smiled and looked at Sarah.

"If it hadn't been for your dad, there would have been an accident. I was on my way to the wrong park. Wrong coaster. Didn't have a clue where—"

"Yeah, we make a great long-distance pair," Garvey said.

There was an awkward silence for a moment as Sarah hopped down off her dad's lap.

"What's this?" she asked looking at the IV drip bottle and the tube snaking into Rachael's arm.

"Dinner," Rachael said. "Want some?"

"Ugh!" Sarah shook her head.

Rachael shifted up in bed. "I'll be out tomorrow. First thing I want to do is have a big steak."

"On me," Garvey said.

"Why Dr. Garvey, I'd be honored. You're staying?"

"Till you're back on your feet. Besides, I always wanted to show Sarah Cincinnati."

"Yeah, sure."

"So what's happening out at Kings Island?" Garvey asked.

"I called Pouncy. His people should be there right now."

Garvey shook his head. "I don't know, Rachael, this one just seems kind of clumsy. The other two incidents were more—elegant. Annealing the main grappler arm, removing the spring pad, slicing the brake fin . . . all took an expert. Sawing through two branches was amateurish."

"It almost worked," Rachael said.

"I know. But we have so little to go on we have to work what we have to death. There were other things he could have done that would have succeeded, ways to sabotage that coaster you never would have found. The sawdust was too obvious. Plus, he actually told you where and what to look for. He's changing his MO—why?"

"He's getting a conscience?"

"I don't think so." Garvey shook his head. "I think he wants our attention."

"He's certainly got that."

"Then I think he wants us to find something."

"Like what?"

"I don't know."

THIRTY-ONE

Jacobson and Delaney were scouring the ground under the trees at Kings Island like two north woods trackers looking for week-old spoor. The footprints they found were a confusion of Rachael's and the other three men's. Beyond that there was only old leaves, pine needles, and squirrel shit. They were not pleased with the last two hours they had spent searching on their knees. They were less pleased with the two hours of interviews they'd done with employees who claimed not to have seen anyone in the woods during the past week.

Jacobson got up, brushed off his pant legs, and walked to one of the trees that had been sawed into. He lit a cigarette and casually looked at the bark next to him.

"Nothing," his partner, Delaney, said disgustedly. "Nothing anywhere."

"Yeah, so how did he do it?" Jacobson said. "How did the son of a bitch saw those branches? Got to be over twenty-five feet up. There's not a spike mark on this trunk. What'd he fly?"

"He used a pole saw." Delaney got up and walked to the larger of the two sawed branches. He pointed to the partially splintered cut end. "We take this end sample, maybe we can figure out how wide it was, tooth separation, curvature . . . give us a model number or something."

"A pole saw? You think he walked around carrying a twenty-foot pole and wasn't noticed? Come on, Delaney."

"Telescoping. I've seen them."

Jacobson shrugged. "Maybe. How we gonna get that sample? That end is over eight inches thick."

"Maintenance department. They probably have a chain saw we could borrow. Remember the two guys we spoke to?"

Jacobson took another drag and turned to walk out of the woods.

"Okay, let's go back."

The maintenance shed was a garagelike building with two wide truck doors and an interior space the size of a tennis court, filled with shelves that went floor to ceiling. A middle-aged man in green workclothes was sitting behind a wooden desk, looking at a maintenance report. In red thread over one of the pockets was stitched the name VINNY. He was one of the maintenance men who had helped Rachael the day before, the one who had moved the truck forward at the last moment. Jacobson walked over and planted himself by the desk.

"You still here?" the maintenance man said. "You find anything?"

"No, but we wanted to take back a cut end of one of the downed branches. Take measurements. You got a chain saw we could use?"

"Sure. Back here." He got up and walked to one of the shelving bays. "I could go with you."

Jacobson nodded. Delaney was right behind him, looking around at all the equipment. There were hand trucks, crowbars, paint sprayers, shovels, pickaxes, clamps, electrical conduit, and dozens of other things that were usually found in maintenance sheds around the world.

"You got any pole saws?" Delaney asked abruptly.

"One," Vinny said. "I think it's standing up by the ladders." He pointed and Delaney sauntered over to where he was pointing. Vinny turned back to reach for the little chain saw on one of the nearby shelves. As he was shaking it to hear how much gas was inside, Delaney called back.

"Now you got two. Jacobson, take a look." He emerged from one of the aisles holding a new pole saw on a telescoped base. The whole thing was maybe six feet tall. "This yours?" he asked.

Vinny shook his head. "Never saw it. Ours is an old one, strapped to a twelve-foot one-by-two." He walked closer and looked at it. "Nice-looking. Must have just got here. They're always buying us things they think we need."

"Who put it back here?"

Vinny shrugged. "Ask Hector. He's the other maintenance guy works in here." He looked at his watch. "He should be back any minute. He went out to get our coffees."

Delaney was holding it with a handkerchief, turning it around slowly to look at its business end. It was a quarter-inch-thick arc of steel eighteen inches long with teeth on the inside curve. It looked like the profile of the upper jaw of some prehistoric beak. "This sucker's sharp," he said.

"I think we're going to need to take that," Jacobson said.

Vinny's eyes opened. "You don't think that's the thing . . ."

The door opened and a younger man entered carrying a brown paper bag. Without preliminaries, Vinny shouted out, "Hector, where's this from?"

Hector looked at the pole saw Delaney was holding and shrugged.

"I found that leaning against the building about a week ago. I thought you'd picked it up. I just put it back with the other one. Why?"

"I never picked it up." Vinny said.

"You never picked it up," Hector repeated with a frown. "So where's it from?"

"Well, it's been used," Delaney interjected. "There's some residue of sawdust and some sap or moisture of some kind near the haft. You guys never used it around here?"

Both maintenance men shook their heads.

"Any one else might have used it?" Jacobson asked.

"In the last week?" Hector looked doubtful. "Only Vinny and me work the grounds. We got machinery guys, electricians, steel guys, but nobody would need that thing."

"Okay," Jacobson said. "Can we use that chain saw now? Then we'll be out of your hair. Wrap that saw up, Delaney, I don't want to smudge any prints. Maybe it's not been such a bad day after all," Jacobson added. "Makes sense. Guy carries the saw in to use, then ditches it near where it would fit in . . . unnoticed. Beats walking out of the park with it."

"Son of a bitch," Vinny said.

"Yeah," Delaney said. "A real saint."

THIRTY-TWO

Patrick Moore was looking at the credit report on his desk with genuine disbelief. This guy, George Manfredi, 43 Pinion Way, Las Vegas, had the kind of credit-manipulating skills that gave bankers sleepless nights. Besides playing twelve credit card companies back and forth like a symphonic conductor, he had stacked up several loans using collateral that was dubious at best. Yet his Empirica score and Beacon score were in the mid-seven hundreds, which indicated that he was a good payer and could keep on getting people to loan him even more money. It was just a matter of staying one step ahead of next month's interest charges. His current debt balance was over six hundred and seventy thousand dollars, which was pretty hefty for a guy who lived in a neighborhood that was described by one of Patrick Moore's friends as "marginal."

This is crazy, he thought. A wheeler-dealer debtor tying in with D. Kang, and then Virtuland . . . what am I doing? But he let his fingers do the walking.

"Is George Manfredi there?" he asked when a woman's voice answered the phone.

"Just a minute." More like three minutes later, a high-pitched man's voice came over the wires."

"This is George."

"Mr. Manfredi. This is Patrick Moore at the San Miguel County Bank of Western Colorado here in Ironwood. We've recently been purchasing some incidental home equity and assorted collateral loans from some of our affiliated organizations in your area and a few of your loans came into our portfolio."

"No one told me nothing."

"I'm telling you now. I'm also telling you that you appear to be somewhat overextended when we pulled up a credit report."

"Hey, I always pay on time."

"Yes, and I think I can see just how you do it. Now, Mr. Manfredi, if you want us to cooperate with you on maintaining your loan, then we would need some cooperation from you."

There was a pause on the line.

"Who'd you say you were?"

Moore repeated the information.

"I'll call you back there. I'll get the number from information."

"My pleasure," Moore said and pressed the disconnect button. A minute later Manfredi was back on the line.

"Where the hell is Ironwood?" Manfredi asked.

"The center of Colorado banking . . . least as far as you're concerned. Now you know who you're dealing with, Mr. Manfredi, here's what I need. We have an individual who has an interest in a particular hedge fund and he has proposed putting his shares in that fund up as collateral. We know nothing about the fund, we can't get any information other than a few names of some of the other investors. Lo and behold, your name was one of them. You see where I'm going. It would be a great help to us to have some independent corroboration of the kind of fund and some of its particulars. We have other equity for this proposed loan, but this would round it out to our committee's satisfaction."

"Who's the guy?" Manfredi asked.

"I'm afraid that's confidential information, Mr. Manfredi," Moore said. "He doesn't want anyone else to know that he has asked for a loan or the nature of the securities that he has pledged. You understand that."

There was another pause. Finally Manfredi came back. "You just want info?"

"That's right. Won't cost you anything. And your own loans will continue as usual."

"Well, what've I got to lose," Manfredi said airily. "What do you want to know?"

THIRTY-THREE

It wasn't explosive, but it was certainly interesting. Manfredi's information detailed a hedge fund that was unlike any other he had ever heard about. Most funds prided themselves on consistency and impressive yearly earnings or appreciation. D. Kang prided itself on confidentiality, a hedge fund specialty. The fact that their flat return rates were unusually uncompetitive didn't seem to bother any of their investors. Manfredi couldn't remember any of the details about what the fund was investing in, except that it was somewhere in the gaming industry.

"They do everything," he said. "Options, a lot of short sales, leveraged buyouts. You know, they're players. But I can't remember any specific names."

Moore attempted to jog his memory. "Ever hear of Virtuland?" he asked.

"Yeah, I think that was one of them. Place in Boulder City, Nevada, right. Near here."

Moore cracked a thin smile. "Thanks." A few minutes later he hung up. There were Ponzi schemes, questionable commodity straddles, and all sorts of crazy derivative manipulations that balanced on the thin margin of illegality. This went over the edge. It was something like an equity reverse. New with hedge funds, it worked like this: A small public company with excess cash invested money in a fund that then turned around and bought newly issued shares in the company with the same cash. A wash on paper, except that two things happened. First, the money got laundered—the original cash could have been skimmed from unreported gambling earnings, avoiding the corporate income tax; second, the price of the public company's stock would be artificially supported. Effectively, the company transfers dirty money into clean hedge fund shares, plus they get the money back by releasing their own in-house shares. The fund makes out okay because they set their exchange rate favorable to them. It was a cozy, illegal scheme that relied on confidentiality and mutual trust, which explained why D. Kang was not available to the general public.

Okay, Moore thought. So he uncovered some small-time financial shenanigans in Nevada. But what did that have to do with roller coaster sabotage? Just because Virtuland had a small coaster? He'd call Garvey with the information and see if he could make anything of it. But before he did that, out of habit he logged onto Coasterworld.com, just to see what the chat was. It wasn't long before the innocuous little posting jumped out at him:

What was Dr. Samuel Garvey doing in New York a week before the Cyclone accident? What was Dr. Garvey doing in Cincinnati on Friday, two days before the Kings Island near-disaster? Coincidence, Dr. Garvey?

THIRTY-FOUR

Someone's trying to frame you, Sam," she said, "and all you can do is smack your lips and ask me to pass the Worcester-shire sauce."

"Hey, I can't remember the last good steak I had. Let me enjoy this one for a while." He leaned down and cut into another juicy mouthful.

"You're not going to do anything about it?" Rachael asked incredulously. "You're just going to let the FBI start poking around in your private life, poisoning your professional life?"

Garvey laughed. "On a rumor. Come on. Besides, you're the one that works for them."

"Not for them, sometimes with them, sometimes reluctantly. But there's only so much I can do to deflect them. And I've just about run out of any capital I had."

"Patrick Moore thanks you. He told me so himself just last night."

"After he told you about that Internet posting?"

"Well, that and other things. Now, give me a moment here." He put the piece of steak into his mouth and closed his eyes, savoring the taste of the meat. "Mmm, that's what they say, the best meat comes from up North. Eat, eat," he said, motioning to Rachael's plate. "You were the one that wanted steak." He looked to his left at his daughter, who was crayoning on the table mat, a picture that looked like two disarranged copulating spiders. "How's your hamburger, honey?"

"Good," Sarah answered.

"You haven't eaten much of it."

"I'm taking an art break," she said.

"I think your stomach would rather you take a protein break."

She sighed, put her crayon down, and lifted the sandwich in front of her.

"Seriously," Rachael continued, "Pouncy can be pretty dogged."

"I'll deal with it," Garvey said.

"How about you practice with me first. Like, what were you doing in New York a week before we met at the Cyclone? I thought you told me the schedule on the Jumper was so incredibly tight."

Garvey flushed. "You *are* persistent."

"Wait till you see Pouncy."

Garvey sighed and put his fork down. "Well, it's personal."

She shook her head. "Not good enough, Sam. They'll get your Visa records, your phone records, they'll know more about where you touched down than you can remember. But they'll want to know what you did. If you're not straight with them, it gets worse."

Garvey leaned back and looked down at his hands. Then he stole a glance at his daughter.

"So, it was the anniversary of Fran's death. I went back to the cemetery just to," he shrugged, "pay my respects. She grew up in New York, her parents still lived there . . . the family plot was there."

"A long way to go just to pay your respects."

"Yeah, well, I guess it was maybe a little bit more. I didn't want Sarah to forget that she had a mom."

"Sarah came with you?"

He nodded and put an arm around his daughter. "We sent Mommy some flowers in heaven, didn't we, sweetie?"

"Red roses," Sarah said. "A big bunch. Want me to draw a rose, I know how to?"

"So you were only gone a day?"

"Two days. It's the way the airplane reservations worked out."

"Two days? Away from the Jumper?"

"Like now." He smiled. "I take time for things that are important. Besides, it was at a time when Jason could run some simulations. They were waiting for me when I returned." He leaned forward. "Hey, are you only playing devil's advocate here or is there something I'm not picking up on? You're acting uncharacteristically annoying."

Rachael looked at him for a moment in silence.

"I got a call this morning at the hospital just before you picked me up," she finally said. "From Pouncy. He had no idea you were here. He wanted to tell me about the Internet posting about Dr. Samuel Garvey. They tried tracing it and got nowhere. It was sent from a computer out of Basel, Switzerland. There are these off-shore websites that specialize in conferring anonymity as they pass along e-mail. Kind of electronic laundromats for obscene and threatening messages. Throws up a firewall against investigation."

"I was wondering about that," Garvey said.

"There's more," Rachael continued. "Pouncy also wanted to let me know the latest on their Kings Island investigation. They made some tests on the pole saw his agents recovered yesterday at the park. It definitely was the saw used to cut the two branches over the coaster. There were traces of the same type of wood in the saw grooves, the width of the blade matched precisely the width of the cut, and the pattern the teeth made on a fresh piece of wood also matched with the cut sample. He had no doubt they had the right saw."

"Good. So they can concentrate on tracing that."

"They are. But that's not all they found on the saw. They also found traces of mesquite and saguaro." She let that sink in for a moment. "Not two species usually found in or around Cincinnati . . . but, as I recall, they are in abundance around Angel City."

"Yes, I think you're right. As well as over half the goddamn Southwest. This is getting ridiculous, Rachael; someone points an anonymous finger on the Internet and a saw turns up that could have come from anywhere south of Dallas, and all of a sudden I'm the number one suspect? The FBI needs more than that."

"Of course. And maybe they'll get more or be presented with more." She let that sink in for a moment. "Don't you see what's happening, Sam? This is a warning. What it's saying is 'back off.' If you don't there'll be more incriminating stuff and then maybe it will be enough. The FBI has already got you on their radar. The problem is that you can only react. You won't know where Periclymenus's next shot's coming from."

"Unless we find him first."

"Yes." She sounded skeptical.

"So, I wonder . . ." he said, leaning into his steak again and cutting off another large piece. "Just who knew I was both in New York in March and in Cincinnati last week."

"Maybe you can find that out when you get back to Texas tonight."

"You kicking me out of Ohio?"

"I am. I myself am heading back to D.C."

"You must be feeling better," Garvey said. "You think it's the steak?"

"If you weren't so stubborn, I'd say it was the company."

"I'll drink to that," he said and raised his beer mug.

THIRTY-FIVE

The new cars came in the next day, a day earlier than Don Madison had promised. This time they had the right eighteen-gauge steel for the sheathing. Garvey had them installed right away on the track and he and Jason began their tests. In each car they positioned force monitors to check on both vertical and horizontal pressure on track shifts. The more airtime, or weightlessness, they could build in on the camelbacks the better. The more slamming, or side thrusts, on the straightaways helped make the ride more exciting. There was also a "trick track" section where one rail dipped lower than the other and then reversed to give the riders the sense they were being dumped overboard on alternate sides. The forces had to be just right, based on the curvature and placement of the track and with the quarter-scale model they could finalize their calculations. Clothoid loops and heartline spirals now produced accurate scaleable measurements on the instruments. The computers put everything together and gave recommendations for infinitely slight changes to the track alignment. This was done with one-inch metal shims and built-in expansion sections where Garvey knew they were going to need some adjustments. A four-man crew responded to Garvey's instructions, climbing over the track with their tools after each train run, tapping shims in, shortening or lengthening track. It was a painstaking day, but by five-thirty they mostly had it; everything but the jumps. They ended up working on blue drop number five, which required a lot of attention. G forces went up to 5.8, the most on the ride, and both Jason and Garvey wanted to make sure the release came quick enough. Both men were looking at the final printout after the adjustments when Garvey asked casually, "Can you boot up the initial simulations we ran on this drop?"

"The initials?" Jason walked over to a computer that was on a nearby table. In a moment, he had the graphics program up and running and a simulation of the drop was playing over and over.

"This has a date on it?"

"Is there a problem?" Jason asked.

"No, I just don't remember this simulation too clearly. I didn't make it, did I?"

Jason peered at the tag line on the screen and said, "It was done March eighteenth. I did it. As I recall, I think that's when you went to New York. You checked these when you got back."

Garvey nodded. "That's right. March eighteenth. My trip to New York." He straightened up and looked solidly at the younger man.

"Jason, this is important. You didn't by any chance tell anybody I was away that time. I mean, you remember I told you to keep it quiet. I didn't want anybody to know I was going back to put flowers on Fran's grave. I didn't want people to think I was still . . . emotional about things."

Jason looked back down at the computer. "Why, Sam? Something's come up?"

"Yeah. Something's come up. It's about the coaster accidents."

"What about them?" Jason asked.

"People have died, and more people will die if these things continue. Three days ago a note was posted on an Internet site that was meant to either scare me off or begin to implicate me. Whoever posted it knew both the FBI and I would hear about it."

"Yes?" Jason looked confused.

"The note asks what I was doing in New York a week

before the Cyclone accident. Now, not too many people knew I was there."

Jason's face drained. "You can't think that I—"

Garvey shook his head. "No, no Jason. Not you. I know you didn't go to New York, or Boblo, or Kings Island. But maybe one of the few people I told; you, Rosita, Sarah's teacher, one or two others, maybe someone inadvertantly mentioned it. It's too much of a coincidence to think I was spotted in New York by the same person doing all these horrible crashes."

Jason was silent for a moment. The gleaming track for the Jumper scale model swooped over both men and then arced back down to the ground where the scale train awaited another run. The four men in the crew were looking at Garvey and Jason, waiting for their next track adjustment.

"I might have mentioned it to Hotchkiss," he said awkwardly. "I think he came by looking for you and it might have just slipped out. I'm sorry, Sam, I guess I forgot. Yes, I remember now, it was Hotchkiss. Before we had our doubts about him. I'd told him you were coming back the next afternoon from New York. Damn, I'm sorry."

"Hotchkiss?"

Jason nodded. "Hotchkiss."

"Thanks."

"I am sorry, Sam."

"Just be a little more discreet next time, Jason."

"What about Hotchkiss?"

"I'll have to talk to him." Garvey moved away from the table with the computer and up to the small crew of workers.

"Okay, guys, that's all for today. You can shut her down. Tomorrow we have to work on the two jumps. Plan on a long day."

THIRTY-SIX

To bypass the jumps, the previous day they had run the cars with an inserted bridge section simulating the correct arcs. Today they removed the extra lengths of steel and their supports and faced the issue squarely. The most important things to test were the laser guidance system, and the spinners, and the TOA mechanism. The plan was to start with optimum conditions—dry track, no wind, normal temperatures, and a set car weight—and then move on to testing inside their operating parameters. But even though the acrobatics they were putting their vehicle through had never been tried before, they were not really flying blind. The tenth-scale layout had answered most of their velocity and trajectory calculations. What they were working on now was fine-tuning the jumps' backup systems to make them a hundred percent safe. These two systems were capable of moving the nose of the full-scale vehicle almost eight feet in a 360-degree circle, more than enough leeway to insure the mating of the train's funnel-shape catchers with the track's continuing rails. In the worst case scenario, as Garvey had calculated it, an unexpected sustained gust of wind of up to eighty miles per hour would deflect the nose of the vehicle 6.8 feet. Since the system was designed to correct deviations instantaneously and automatically as they were noted by the laser monitors, the deviations should never accumulate beyond a few inches at most.

Garvey watched intensely as the first vehicle was loaded on the red track with the simulated passenger weight, then released from the start position. It climbed slowly up the first hill, then glided away over the track that had been shimmed to perfection the day before. It approached the first jump less than a minute later and without hesitation, flew over the open space like a champion steeplechase horse dispensing with a routine hedge. Garvey glanced at the numbers on a computer and noted that it had been dead on course. He watched as it continued around the track and approached the second jump. Again it flew over the space effortlessly and landed on the Kevlar catch rails with the smallest swishing sound. Twenty seconds later it was back at the start position.

"Congratulations," Jason said with a broad grin on his face.

"Red track," Garvey said. "Let's try the blue one."

A second car was loaded in the start position of the blue track and sent up the start incline. A minute and a half later they had the car back with the same good results.

"This is ominous," Garvey said with a smile. "Only a minor problem on jump two."

"How about together?" Jason urged.

Garvey thought for a moment. "Why not?" he said finally. "We're on a roll."

The two cars were released simultaneously, which was the way the ride was designed, as a kind of race. Watching it in tenth-scale layout was not the same as watching it like this, on a scale one could imagine real people riding on. Once again the cars started along their separate tracks, but now they were keeping pace with each other, heading through their series of acrobatics toward the place in the layout where the tracks stopped and there was only air. They hit their jumps at the same moment and flew upward, one angled higher than the other. They passed each other with only eighteen inches of clearance between one car's wheels and the other's top. Neither Garvey or Jason said a word. They continued watching as the two cars continued onto the second half of their tracks, negotiating the inversions, fan turns, helix spins, and camel-back bumps. Again they hit the jumps perfectly timed and crossed over each other, landing without incident on the final section of track.

"It works," Jason said almost incredulously.

"Quarter scale," Garvey said soberly. "But damn if that wasn't pretty." He walked over to one of the computers to check some numbers. "Blue was deviated left point-thirteen percent on jump two again, but other than that, things looked good. Let's address that, then run a recheck."

Jason nodded, went to the blue track, and pointed to where a shim was needed. One of the crew came over and started hammering it in. After a few minutes they ran the test again and this time the numbers came up perfectly.

"You want to run the crosswind tests or the variable TOA weight tests next?" Jason asked.

Garvey thought for a moment. "Let's try the TOA."

They reset the cars, but this time they added more weight to the red car and reduced the weight to the blue car. They watched as the subtrack pistons cranked up or down in response. When the cars completed the next run as smoothly as they had the previous one, there were smiles all around.

"Son of a bitch, I can't believe it's going so well," Jason said.

"Sometimes life cooperates," Garvey said with a smile. "Enjoy the moment."

THIRTY-SEVEN

Four days later they were finished. They had put their models through every permutation of operating conditions, noted any problems, and adjusted their onboard and sub-track guidance programs to correct them. At no time had either car not completed a jump successfully. A few of the landings had been very rough but still within their safety margin. The work with the tenth-scale model had paid off handsomely. What they originally thought would be several weeks of testing had been accomplished in less than one. Everything was documented for submission to the state licensing board and a day was scheduled for the following week for a board engineer to come and observe a final round of the quarter-scale tests. Things were moving with surprising smoothness and they were slowly gaining on their original schedule for an opening on September 3, now less than two months away. Garvey was so pleased he decided to give Dominici the positive news.

The corporate headquarters of the Angelus Corporation was at Angel City in one of the soaring towers that gave the park its long-distance profile. Garvey waited on the twenty-fifth floor and looked out the window. From up here it was clear how much of an alien environment the amusement park was. Outside the park's lush landscaping and friendly wooden-edged walkways, a more hostile, dry, and windswept flatland was visible, broken only by the spiderlike roads that led up to the front gate. Around here, everyone was friendly to Angelus because of the revenues it brought to the county and state. It could do no wrong, which was one of the reasons that Garvey was so confident there would be no problems with the licensing. Just as long as it was safe, and he was well on the way to proving that. He shifted his gaze back to the receptionist, who was concentrating hard on a Danielle Steel novel. She put a hand to her earphone and looked up.

"You can go in now, Dr. Garvey."

"Is he in a good mood at least, Mildred?"

"Sounds pleasant," she said and went back to her book. Garvey headed for the corner office.

The Angelus Corp. CEO was sitting behind a beautiful blond fruitwood desk that had definite Biedermeier lines. The rest of the office was subdued in its elegance but equally expensive. There was not a thing in it that could be found at Wal-Mart . . . not even the lightbulbs.

"I heard Ralphie was acting up a little last week," Dominici said before Garvey even had a chance to close the door behind him.

"Excuse me?" Garvey ticked off in his head all of the people he knew at Angel City, and not one of them was called Ralphie.

"At school," Dominici continued with an awkward smile. "Ralphie's got a competitive streak in him just like me. I had no idea your daughter was in the same grade. Schooling is his mother's area. He's a cutup, that boy is. My older son was the same way. Sorry if there were any misunderstandings." Dominici looked at him with his smile still fixed. "The school had called but said everything was taken care of."

"No, no misunderstandings," Garvey said. "I think we straightened things out. It's a small world . . . I had no idea he was your son."

"Freemont? An exceedingly small world. But he's really a great kid at heart, little Ralphie. Some of the things he gets into . . ." He smiled and shook his head. "I suppose he could use a little more discipline." He leaned back in his comfortable, oversize chair and his lighthearted expression changed as quickly as the weather in south Texas. "So, how are the trials going?" It was more of a demand than a question.

"I guess you'll be happy to hear we're finished," Garvey answered. "Except for the observation. We have a shot at catching up with the schedule."

"That's great news," Dominici said. "You had me worried there for a while. Christ, we can't afford to be late on this. The stockholders would eat me alive. Not to mention the board of trustees."

"Well, I thought you'd like to know as soon as I had some positive results. We're playing things pretty close to the vest now."

"Damn right, Sam, we don't want things leaking out to the press prematurely. Those financial writers are vultures. Any scrap of information they blow up out of proportion and then stock values go crazy. Just keep things to your team and me."

A picture of Hotchkiss floated briefly through Garvey's thoughts.

"Yes, sir. I'd say about another week and the first sections of full-scale track will be coming in. Madondi is on a guaranteed July delivery schedule for the full-scale cars. Things are looking good."

"Best news I've had all day," Dominici said and stood up. "Keep up the pace. And if there's anything you need, anything, just let me know. The closer we get, the less I want some little obstacle standing in our way."

"I certainly will," Garvey said and turned to leave. "Oh, you could notify the landscape crew to go ahead with the next phase. There won't be any changes based on the trials."

"To tell you the truth, Sam, I've already done that," Dominici said. "I have great faith in you." Another smile flashed out but somehow it looked wooden.

"I'm honored," Garvey answered and walked out of the office.

THIRTY-EIGHT

The phone booth was in a corner of the Wrangler Snack Bar, seventy yards away from the screened-in outdoor test track. The Wrangler served barbecued ribs, fries, burgers, and other fast-food items with which amusement park goers expected to fill their stomachs. It was noisy, smelly, and crowded, which was exactly what Jason wanted. He stepped into the booth, closed the door, and turned his back. He dialed, and after a few moments a familiar voice came on the line. Jason spoke a little above a whisper.

"You didn't tell me everything."

"Everything you needed to know," the man answered.

"You didn't post anything on the Internet?"

There was silence for a long moment.

"Shit." Jason's voice rose. "Are you crazy?"

"Crazy enough to know you won't do anything. You're in too deep."

There was another silence as Jason tried to take it all in. "No, from now on you're on your own," he finally said. "This is getting out of hand. I had no fucking idea—"

"You had every fucking idea. What'd you think we were doing, playing jacks?"

"Screw that. I'm out."

"Not so fast," the other man hissed. "I've got recordings. Your voice on the phone . . . all your reports."

"Fuck your recordings," Jason said.

"And fuck the money?"

"That too. Just get yourself another boy to do your dirty work. I thought it would stop after the first one. I had no idea where it was going."

Jason slammed the phone down and held his head for a moment. Dumb, dumb, dumb! He put his hand on the wall of the phone booth to support himself. Maybe, just maybe, he was clear of it. Maybe it would all go away. The person waiting to use the phone pushed past him, but he didn't notice. He didn't notice the scores of harried parents balancing trays of food on their way to their screaming kids. All he saw was, in his mind's eye, a picture of twisted metal and bodies at the bottom of the Cyclone start hill and the Boblo loading platform and he felt sick. So sick that he sat down in one of the empty chairs and put his head in his hands. But it didn't go away. None of it did.

THIRTY-NINE

Hotchkiss was a bachelor and lived alone in a rented trailer over by Furness, five miles outside of Angel City. Garvey had been there only once, when Hotchkiss's car had been in the shop and he had asked for a lift. Garvey remembered a small trailer court with maybe a dozen units, and a grudging attempt by the management to provide some landscaping in the form of a gravel driveway and inexpensive yucca plants. A line of willow trees backed the little complex, showing that it was next to a small river. A sign out front indicated that there were still furnished units for rent by the month.

Garvey pulled up to the trailer he remembered and cut the engine. It was nine o'clock at night and dusk was just sliding away for the evening when he knocked on the door. This had to be done, he knew, had to be faced up to. This confrontation had been coming for a long time. Hotchkiss had been the weak link on the team, even though he was there only for the VE side, the electric visuals and decorative lighting. They'd inherited him from Angelus because he did all the decorative lighting for the new rides. He was totally in the pocket of Dominici and the corporation, was less trustworthy than a Greek bearing gifts, and had already leaked information on the Jumper. But now this was much more serious. He was one of a few people who knew Garvey had been in New York . . . Periclymenus also knew.

There was no answer. He knocked again, this time louder, and waited. A light was on in one of the side windows and the air conditioner was humming from around the back. Other than that, there were no signs of life from inside. A dog barked from one of the other trailers a dozen yards away, then quieted as Garvey waited. Still nothing. Garvey pushed lightly against the front door and was surprised when it yielded. Inside the trailer was dark. Garvey could just see the outlines of another door from the light that escaped around its edges. He hesitated for a moment, then took a step toward it. His foot came down on something soft, something that made a squishy sound, and he recoiled backward. His eyes were just getting accustomed to the light and as he looked down he saw something dark and bunched . . . a wet towel. He breathed in deeply and looked around. He was in the front room, kind of an everything room, a kitchen, dining area, plus a living space with a couch and TV toward the end. The room with the light must have been the bedroom. He stepped over the towel and slowly worked toward the closed door. It was now deathly still inside the little trailer. The noise of a cricket outside by the front door sounded to him like a firecracker.

He put his crutch on the door and pushed. Slowly the thin door swung inward and Garvey called out softly.

"Hotchkiss."

The dog started barking again, but Garvey's mind was focusing only on what he saw. The inside of the little bedroom was bare except for a bed and a night table. The bed clothes were rumpled, but on top was a twisted doll-like shape. The arms were at a strange angle and the legs were akimbo. The face on this strange apparition was truly garish, a cross between a Mardi Gras reveler and a dancehall prostitute. It took Garvey a few seconds to realize that he was looking at one of those soft, vinyl inflatable dolls, the kind advertised in the back of stroke magazines in porno bookshops. He was so shocked he never heard the person enter the trailer behind him.

"What the hell are you doing here?"

Garvey spun around and faced Hotchkiss. He was standing there with a small fishing rod in one hand and a jar of worms in the other. The expression on his face was a mixture of anger and embarrassment.

"I . . . I came to talk to you," Garvey stammered.

Hotchkiss flicked a light switch inside the main room and threw his rod down.

"You usually enter someone's house when no one's there, Garvey? Where I come from that's illegal."

Garvey turned away from the small bedroom and walked over to one of the chairs.

"You mind?" he asked. "It's important."

Hotchkiss shrugged. "I got nothing better to do now. The fish ain't biting." He walked to the refrigerator and put the jar of worms on a shelf inside. Then he pulled out a beer. He came and sat down next to Garvey and stretched out on the couch. With a foot he reached out and casually moved the wet towel to a side of the linoleum floor. "What's so important that you came all the way over here when you should be working on the quarter-scale tests."

"They're finished," Garvey said. "Didn't you know?"

Hotchkiss shook his head. "No one tells me anything. I'm just the VE guy, remember." He said it in a challenging way, throwing it back in Garvey's face the way he had been hit with it earlier.

Garvey let it pass. "Whatever disagreements we may have had in the past, Martin, this has nothing to do with that. This is different. It's beyond the Jumper."

"Beyond the Jumper?" Hotchkiss said with a grin. "I thought nothing was beyond the Jumper, Garvey. Not with you."

"This is." He sat down and leaned forward. "About three months ago I went to New York for personal reasons. I've been going over in my memory how many people I told and I've narrowed it down to three."

"So?" Hotchkiss took a swallow of beer and looked at

Garvey out of his narrow eyes. If he was nervous he didn't show it.

"Someone is using that information to frame me." Garvey watched Hotchkiss. "It wasn't one of the three people who knew because they're all people I'd vouch for. It wasn't someone looking through credit card records because I paid cash. And you can't go on a fishing expedition with the airlines companies. It had to be someone one of the three told inadvertently." Garvey leaned back into the chair. "You, for example."

Hotchkiss took another swallow and a little frown crossed his face. "I don't know what you're talking about," he said flatly. "I had no idea you went to New York except for the time with the Cyclone investigation."

"No, this was before that, end of March."

"Uh uh." Hotchkiss shook his head. "Your information is wrong."

Garvey got angry. "Listen, Martin, it won't be that easy. You just can't deny it. I'll call the police if I can't get you to tell the truth."

"You sound like a petulant little boy, Garvey, but the truth is I never knew."

"Jason said he told you."

"Your boy Jason is lying. And if he's one of the three I'm surprised you'd vouch for him. You ever wonder where he got the money to buy his new Miata? On what Angelus pays him?" Hotchkiss snorted. "Look around."

"If Jason said he told you, then he told you."

"Loyalty is so touching," Hotchkiss said and took a long swig of beer. "How late in March?"

"The eighteenth. I told Jason the day before I was going."

"Well, let's see." Hotchkiss stood up and walked over to a desk on which the television was resting. He opened a drawer and pulled out a little book the size of a paperback. As he flipped through the pages he slowly came back to the couch. "March eighteenth, huh. Yeah, like I thought." He looked up with a smile. "Did Jason say he phoned me with this information while I was visiting my sister in Canada? Up in Edmonton?" He turned the pages of the book toward Garvey and there in black was written through the week of March fifteenth to March twenty second: *Visit to Martha in Edmonton. United Airlines, confirmation WDZQ7408.* "You want to see my canceled ticket? My American Express receipts? Maybe you want to call my sister and confirm this with her?"

Garvey was stunned. "You weren't here, in Freemont."

Hotchkiss shook his head. "And Jason never told me. Before or after."

"No, he said it was before. That you came looking for me the day I was gone."

"Impossible." Hotchkiss upended the beer and tossed it in the direction of the sink. It hit an edge and rolled neatly into the cluttered basin. He turned with a smile toward Garvey. "Now what?"

Garvey was silent. He concentrated momentarily on a spot above the couch, away from Hotchkiss's mocking eyes. He felt confused, as if he'd just witnessed some natural law being broken, gravity upended. His head was spinning. Jason had lied to him? Garvey had to stand up, had to move away. He picked up his crutch and took a step toward the door."

"Not so smug now, Dr. Garvey."

Without bothering to reply, Garvey went out the front door and down onto the gravel in front of the trailer. Yes, he was angry, but some of it was for his own stupidity. Naïveté was only charming in the young. In someone his age it could be fatal. He limped through the gravel to his car, the sound of the still-barking dog behind him.

By the time he got home, Rosita had her coat on and she and Sarah were playing patiently by the front door. He looked at his watch and couldn't believe the time.

"I'm sorry, Rosita, I had to see someone."

"Eees okay. I tell my son I call heem. Sarah's waiting for bed story."

Sarah jumped into her father's arms. "Where have you been?" she asked in between big hugs. "I was waiting so long."

"Dinner?" he asked Rosita absently as she made her way toward the phone. "She eat anything?"

"Some refried beans and rice. Hot dog. Still in microwave, you want."

"Thanks." He put Sarah down. "How was school?"

"Good."

That was the best he could hope for. Only occasionally did he get elaboration, and then only for something transcendent, like the time the gerbil got out of her cage and fell into a toilet. "Show me what story you want," he said. "It's already past your bedtime."

Sarah went to her bookcase and pulled out a large book, one with an enormous elephant pictured on it.

"No poetry tonight?" he asked.

"No, I want Horton. He's so funny."

"Dedicated is what I would have said."

"What's that mean?" Sarah asked, open-eyed. "Deci-dated."

"D-e-d-i-c-a-t-e-d." He spelled it out. "I guess it means sticking to something. Not giving up."

"Uh hunh," she said and snuggled into his arms on the bed. "Read me about Horton."

So Garvey started out on the Dr. Seuss story about the elephant who sat on an egg and wouldn't give up until it hatched. When he had finished the story his daughter smiled up at him.

"Now I know what dedicated means."

"Good," Garvey said, getting up and pulling the blanket up to her chin.

"Like Jason."

Garvey stopped and stared down at her. "Like Jason," he repeated curiously. "How like Jason?"

"The time he was here. Remember, you had to go to New York."

"I remember. He read you all those Ogden Nash poems. I'm not sure I'd call that dedicated, honey."

"No, not that. We played a hide-and-seek game. He wouldn't give up until he found the cookie."

"Uh huh," Garvey said, sitting back down on the bed. "How long did it take?"

"Long time."

"And where did you hide it?"

"Well, he said I could hide it anywhere in the apartment. I put it in the hall closet."

"And where did he look?" Garvey was afraid of what was coming.

"Well." Sarah smiled again. "I really fooled him. He looked everywhere. In your bedroom, in your drawers, in your closet, under your bed." She thought about it a long time. "He looked in your room for a really long time. Wasn't that silly? But he was very ded-i-cated," she said it carefully, "and he finally found the cookie."

"Yes." Garvey frowned and tucked the blanket in. "I bet he did. Good night, honey, I'll see you in the morning." He bent down and kissed her.

"Good night, Daddy. Can Jason come again and baby-sit me? He was really fun."

"Maybe," Garvey said. "I'll be sure and ask him tomorrow when I see him." He got up, turned off the light, and closed the door slowly behind him. He thought to himself that there was a lot he had to ask Jason.

FORTY

Garvey looked impatiently at his watch again, as if that, by itself, would make the door open. It was well after ten o'clock, and whatever beef he had against his assistant, Jason had never been late before. If anything, he was usually there well before Garvey and had things set up for the day's work. A nervous thought gnawed at Garvey, overlaying a jumble of confused emotions. Jason was still a colleague, a friend, a young man whom he felt close to . . . and now this unexplained deviation. He tried concentrating on some of the landscape drawings, but within a couple of minutes he found himself once again looking at his watch. Finally he picked up the phone and dialed the young man's number.

But there was no answer, as there had been no answer a half hour earlier. This was becoming frightening, like waiting for a child after a curfew had passed. He found another number in the company phone directory and dialed that.

"Security, I wonder if you could help me," he began.

The death was called an accidental overdose. Jason had been dead for over five hours when he was found so there had been no attempt to administer naloxone to counter the effects of the heroin. One look around the apartment told the paramedics all they needed to know, that and the syringe still stuck in the victim's left arm. A subsequent blood analysis confirmed their call. Jason had probably died within a few minutes of shooting up. A sample of the heroin still left showed that it was unusually pure and probably the reason he died. Perhaps it was his inexperience that had also contributed to his death. He had not been a longtime user from the unmarked look of his arms.

All this was told to Garvey after he waited hours for the report outside the coroner's office later that day. But he knew differently, knew all along. He was certain Jason had been murdered. His assistant, whatever bad trouble he had gotten into, had never experimented with drugs. He would have known, would have seen it working day after day so close to him in the lab. And he was certain of another thing. Jason's death had occurred somehow because of him. This was not a random killing. Garvey didn't believe in coincidences. Someone had beaten him to Jason before he had a chance to question him. Someone in Freemont, Texas.

It scared Garvey. For himself, for his daughter, for the Jumper. Whatever else it was, Jason's death was another warning.

Garvey left the coroner's office, got in his car, and headed home. He would call Rachael, would insist that she come. At the very least she could help him explain to Sarah how come Jason would no longer be reading her poems about animals of the bovine ilk. And then, he thought, maybe they could figure out what the hell was going on.

When he got home, there was a message waiting for him. A Mr. Mooo had called from Colorado. Rosita pronounced it Meeester Mooo, but Garvey knew right away.

"Can you give me ten minutes," he asked Rosita. "I have to return some calls."

"No problem," she said. "I wait."

FORTY-ONE

"You ever meet Milly when you were here?" Moore asked after the preliminaries.

"That nice old lady with the diner?" Garvey said after a moment.

"Roadhouse," Moore corrected. "Yeah, that's the one. I'm there so often it's like a second home. Great cooking, friendly atmosphere . . ."

"Colorado's a great place, I know," Garvey said impatiently. "But Patrick, I don't have the time right now—"

"Hold on, Sam, I'm not giving you some travelogue. I'm working up to something."

"Listen, we've had a real bad day here. My assistant died."

"Jesus, sorry to hear that. I better get right to the point. It's Milly. She actually gave me the idea, talking about a trip she was planning to go on down to Juarez. You listening?"

"Go ahead." If Garvey didn't know Moore so well he would have postponed this conversation for another day, but his friend was not someone to call long distance just to chat.

"Mexico," Moore continued. "Who would have thought? I told you I was looking at this little entertainment company over in Nevada and found some funny backslapping going on. So I tried to get to the bottom of it and kind of reached a dead end. Small stuff, really. A hedge fund was laundering some of their cash, in turn supporting the price of the fund. I could report it, but why? Then Milly casually mentioned Mexico and I figured I'd see if they had something else going down there. What the hell."

"And?"

"Well, it's funny. This Virtuland company, turns out

they're floating high-interest bonds to some local banks down there. I called the Mexican bond rating company I know and they tracked the company down. There's not much, really, couple million. But borrowing from Mexico? Some people would call it creative financing. Usually it's the other way around."

"And you?" Garvey asked.

"Well, at fifteen percent, I'd call it foolhardy. I don't know all the details, just the size of the offering and rate. The funny thing is that they could have done much better here. I've seen their balance sheet, and it's solid enough to have found financing at around twelve percent, maximum. My guess is that the extra three percent went to buy something they could only get across the border."

"Like what?"

"Anonymity. A shield from the prying eyes of domestic analysts. At least for a year, and maybe more if they get creative and pay it off, then refinance."

Garvey was silent for a moment. "Patrick, I don't think I see the significance," he said finally. "Where does it lead?"

"Nowhere, really, not with Virtuland. They're a small cap stock, very thin. Whatever they're playing at with their balance sheet is small potatoes, like some kid cheating at marbles." Garvey could almost hear the smirk on the other end of the phone. "But then I asked another question to my friends at the bond rating service. I mean, I'm a curious kind of guy. I asked if there were any other U.S. entertainment companies that had floated bonds down there. But this time I set a floor of ten million . . . just to get a feel for how big this was. I'd never heard about it before. And guess what, I came up with a list of about twelve companies that have been doing it. Maybe for years. Very cozy with the Mexico City banks."

"Yes?"

"So guess who's the biggest borrower?" Moore waited a beat and then answered his own question. "Angelus Corporation . . . to the tune of forty million dollars."

Garvey whistled. "You're kidding?"

"Nope. I thought you'd like to know that. Your Jumper is flying on dollars *and* pesos. How do you like those enchiladas?"

"I don't think many people know that," Garvey offered. "I mean, at the stockholders meeting there was no mention of Mexican bonds. In fact, Dominici said there'd be no new borrowings."

"Strange, huh. I guess he's going all out to do whatever he can to get your project up and running."

"Looks that way," Garvey said slowly. "But still, seems a little irregular to me."

"Me too. That's why I called. Has nothing to do with the other thing, but interesting nonetheless."

"I suppose. Patrick, you're not going to tell anybody, are you?"

"Knowledge is power, buddy. I'm giving you a gift."

"Thanks."

"I figure you need all the help you can get. I mean after that Internet posting. I'm surprised you haven't had a visit yet from my two favorite FBI agents."

"The FBI doesn't want me, they want the person who murdered my assistant."

"Murdered?" Moore repeated slowly. "You didn't tell me."

"Like you said, knowledge is power," Garvey said. "In Jason's case, it appears too much was fatal."

"I'll keep that in mind," Moore said and rung off.

FORTY-TWO

Garvey replaced the phone and sat on his bed looking at it. He had resolved to call her, ask her to come down, but now he hesitated. He felt like a high-school sophomore calling on a first date. But what he was asking was over the edge. She had a job, had a life up in Washington. What could he be thinking? It was just the shock of Jason's death and the pressure of getting the Jumper ready on time . . . that he felt he needed someone to talk to, to be with, someone he could trust. It would pass, he thought. He got up and started to walk into the living room when the phone rang. He turned and picked it up.

"I've been reassigned," Rachael said angrily. "Can you believe the sons of bitches? Pouncy got to my boss. Because I went out to dinner with you in Ohio."

He felt a flood of relief come over him. "Rachael, I was just going to call you."

" 'Socializing with a suspect,' " she continued. " 'Very compromising.' What shit."

"How'd they find out?" Garvey asked.

"It's the FBI for God's sake. They have a lot of resources."

"Not enough, apparently, to figure out what the hell's really going on. So you're off the case?"

"I'm off the case. I was asked to turn over all my notes and field studies to an associate. They gave me some stupid six-month-old commuter plane mishap. No fatalities, just a near miss. In this agency it's what passes for being taken out to the woodshed."

"Sorry to hear that. Rachael, listen—"

"And you know who's coming your way. They're probably there right now. Delaney and Jacobson."

"I wonder if you could come down . . . ?" He blurted it right out, surprising even himself. "I need help on this. Jason was murdered today."

He heard Rachael catch her breath.

"Jason. Your assistant, the guy that gave me a lift to the airport?" she finally asked.

"Yes. Somehow he was involved in this. The one person I trusted the most down here. I don't know where to turn. I don't even know if these phones are tapped or not."

"Sam, can't you meet me somewhere?"

"There's Sarah. I can't leave her now. I'll have to tell her about Jason."

There was silence on the phone for a long moment. Rachael was considering. Finally she said, "Well, I have some vacation coming. I suppose I could put this commuter thing off. Tell them I was visiting a friend. Maybe I'll be lucky and they won't notice who the friend was."

"You could stay here," Garvey said. "Keep a low profile."

"Oh, they'll find out," she said. "But as long as I'm not official on anything . . ."

"I don't want you to get in trouble," Garvey said.

"I think I already am," she said with a little laugh. "In my own way. Pick me up at the airport?"

"Let me know the flight and I'll be there."

She flew in the next evening in one neat package; a small clothing suitcase, her laptop computer, a pair of jeans, some T-shirts, and a baseball cap. This one said MACANUDO CLUB.

"You smoke cigars?" Garvey asked after giving her a hug. He picked up her bag and thought to himself, Boy, that felt good.

"An old boyfriend did. This is the only thing he gave me that mattered."

"That good, huh?"

On the trip into his apartment, he told her about his misgivings. How Jason had snooped around his apartment and the lie he had told about Hotchkiss. Rachael listened in silence.

"You think this has anything to do with the accidents?" she finally asked.

"Everything to do with them," he said. "This posting about me on the Net leads right through Jason to Periclymenus."

"He's here?"

"Not necessarily. Jason had plenty of time to call someone after I told him about the posting. Plenty of time for that person to travel here to kill him. But . . . why Jason?"

"More important, why you?" Rachael asked. "Why should anyone want to frame you? You have any old enemies floating around?"

"You may not believe this," Garvey said, "but I'm pretty well liked in this industry. A model citizen in my community. Upstanding, considerate, brave. No enraged ex-lovers . . ."

"Don't brag."

Garvey looked at her sideways. "I really don't know, Rachael. I've been going over it in my mind since I called you. Why I've been singled out . . ."

"What about the Jumper?"

"What about it?"

"It's your big project. What if you're so compromised, or even distracted, it fails to open? Who benefits?"

"No one. Well . . ." he reconsidered. "Maybe some other amusement parks, our competition. But the nearest park is in Austin, over two-hundred miles away, and that's only about a quarter of our size. The Jumper is more likely to draw from the bigger parks, the Astroland in Houston, places like that. Except they also have their own new rides in development. It's a constant game, we bring on line something new, then they do. One year it's our turn to steal customers, then it's theirs. But no one uses murder for a competitive edge." He shook his head. "We'll have to look elsewhere."

"Just a thought," she said. "Is this where you live?"

Garvey had pulled into a driveway and cut the motor.

"It is. You remember Sarah?"

Rachael nodded.

"See her looking at us from the window? She's probably been waiting since I left to pick you up."

"How's she doing about Jason," Rachael asked.

Garvey looked sheepish. "I haven't told her yet. I was waiting for you."

"I see," Rachael said. "Real brave."

There is no good way to announce a death to a child. Garvey tried to be as gentle as he could, pulled out every metaphor he could think of, and still Sarah cried. The tears came softly in that special understated way children have of grieving when something truly hurts, unlike when a simple barked shin or cut finger elicits shrieks of pain. She cried because she felt a special trust had been broken, that he had unthinkingly violated a secret gift she had given him, her friendship. Then she remembered the details, his sweet smile and the games he played with her, and she felt even worse. This thing that grown-ups did—this disappearing thing—she hated it. Couldn't understand it, hadn't the faintest clue when and why they chose to do it. All she knew was that it hurt, and the only thing that made it feel any better was to hold on to someone very tight . . . preferably a daddy.

"I'm sorry, honey," Garvey said hugging her. "I know he was special."

"But why?" she asked, her face still wet with tears. Garvey looked helplessly at Rachael.

"I don't think anyone knows," she said, "but I do know this. All those people up in heaven . . . and not one single roller coaster in the whole place. I'll bet Jason is going to build one for them, and it's going to be the best one ever.

Maybe the ride will take all day, and a single loop the loop will go around the moon. Won't that be fun to build?"

She looked at Rachael and a smile began to form on her face. "And Mommy could ride it too. She always liked the rides in the parks."

"Yes, sure," Garvey said. "And Jason will tell her all about you, how big you are and what a wonderful hide-and-seek player you are."

"Uh huh," Sarah said, wiping her eyes. "But I'd still like to see him again."

"We all would," Rachael said. "But he's in your heart, you can see him there."

"I guess," Sarah said and wiggled down from Garvey's neck. She looked at Rachael sitting on the couch next to them. "Maybe you could play with me sometime."

"I'd love to," Rachael said. "How about tomorrow?"

Sarah frowned. "I've got to go to school. Will you still be here in the afternoon?"

"I'll be here for a week, Sarah, we'll have a lot of time to play."

"Great," she said. "And you can read me some silly poems."

"Some silly poems," Rachael repeated, nodding.

"Good." She said it with a certain relief. "Daddy, could you read me a bedtime story now? I think I'm ready to go to sleep."

"Sure, honey." He took her hand and walked with her toward her bedroom. "Which one?"

"Any," she said. "Except Horton."

FORTY-THREE

Garvey stayed with Sarah until her eyes fluttered shut and she slipped into a peaceful sleep. He turned on the night-light, closed the door carefully, and came into the living room. Rachael was on the couch waiting for him.

"She's the brave one," Rachael said. "Just to be young today. You can only hope that you'll get it right."

"Get what right?"

"Growing up."

"I suppose some of them are better at it than others," he said and came to sit down next to her.

"Usually the ones with good help." She looked at him and smiled. "You really are a good daddy, Sam. It's the side of you I like best."

"Well, I sure appreciate any help I can get. This Mr. Mom role can be confusing at times. Thanks for making it easier."

"Thank you," she said, "for letting me see what it's like. I've never had that opportunity."

"Your choice, I bet."

"No, I just never met the right person."

"Mr. Macanudo?"

"Definitely not." She laughed. "He was great for the short run, but not for extended play." She put a hand out and touched his shoulder. "Now you," she said, "have a different problem. I'm afraid your extended play is going to be spent at some penitentiary."

"Very funny."

"You think I'm kidding, Sam? Jacobson and Delaney are not softies. They'll chew you to pieces looking for stuff."

"They won't find anything. Just like they didn't with Moore."

"Moore had never left Colorado. And he wasn't being framed."

"Are you trying to scare me?" he said and reached out for her hand. "Or just to excite me?"

"Trying to wake you up, damnit."

"I didn't think I was asleep. At least not every part of me."

She laughed and gave his hand a squeeze. "And sometimes you can be very amusing." She hesitated. "But I'm not sure this is the right time."

"You'll let me know," he said and got up.

"I will."

"Right now I suppose it's time to throw on some spaghetti." He walked to the kitchen. "I've got puttanesca or marinara. You have a preference?"

"Yes," she said. "Butter and Parmesan."

After dinner they cleaned up the dishes and sat down to talk. There was nothing he could do about the FBI investigation, but he wasn't about to lie down on Jason's murder.

"I want to find out what happened," he said simply.

"How? The police haven't taken it seriously."

"All the better," Garvey said. "That means they probably just went through his apartment casually . . . looking for drugs and paraphernalia. I'm going to look for other stuff, the things that would lead to his killer."

"You have a key?"

"No, but neither did the killer."

"When?" she asked slowly.

"Tomorrow night. I was hoping you wouldn't mind baby-sitting."

She shook her head. "Are you kidding? I'm going with you."

"No you're not. I need someone for Sarah. Besides, just in case something goes wrong, it will mean your job . . . maybe your future. I can't ask for that."

"You're not asking, I'm telling. Besides, I'm a trained investigator. I search for things for a living." She held his steady gaze without moving. "Isn't there someone else for Sarah?"

"There's Rosita. I suppose I can see if she's free. But, Rachael, you're down here on vacation. Are you sure . . . ?"

She nodded. "You're not going in there alone, that's settled. Now," she looked around, "if I'm down here on vacation, show me the amenities."

"Well, the best I can do for accommodations is this couch."

She sighed and her bright blue eyes were quizzical.

"You don't have a bed?"

"Well, yes, I mean, only one," he said awkwardly.

"We only need one," she said. "Now help me unpack."

He held her closely in the bed, breathing in the warm scent of her body. It was late, past two o'clock, but he felt elated. They hadn't stopped touching each other since they had slipped between the covers three hours earlier. To Garvey, lovemaking was like a ride on a wonderful coaster, all spinning lights and sounds and jolts and rushes and amazing loops, then an eventual slowdown and run-out. With Rachael it had been like a dozen rides, one right after another, and no run-out until the end when, emotionally, he felt at rest. He couldn't remember a time like this. Maybe early on with Fran, but later, when her back spasms hit, the infrequent lovemaking was always joyless.

He propped his head in his hand and grinned at her.

"Was it my spaghetti sauce?"

"No," she said, sighing. "It was your crutch. I've never made love to a man with white hair and a crutch before."

"What crutch?" he said and both of them laughed. He

reached up again, kissed her gently, then put his head back down. "Sarah will be up early for school."

"You want me to sleep outside," Rachael asked. "Is this too shocking for her?"

"Too shocking for me," Garvey said. "But I think Sarah will be all right. Let's get some sleep. Tomorrow's going to be exciting."

"No, tonight was exciting; tomorrow is going to be dangerous."

FORTY-FOUR

Jacobson and Delaney were waiting for him outside his house the next morning. They were sitting in a rental car, cups of coffee in their hands, watching the front door. He was glad he had left Rachael sleeping late but there was Sarah to think about. He didn't want anything to scare her, anything like an official bracing by the front door on the way to school. He left her eating her Cheerios and walked out to them.

"Delaney and Jacobson, right?" he asked.

They weren't pleased. Delaney was about to ask how the hell he knew their names when Jacobson shook his head.

"Driving your kid to school?" he asked casually.

"How'd you know?" Garvey asked tightly.

"We know a lot about you, Dr. Garvey. We've been asking a lot of questions, but now it's your turn. I don't suppose though you'd want us to begin right here in front of her. We're considerate, Dr. Garvey. You play ball with us, and you'll be surprised how agreeable we can be."

"Sure," Garvey said angrily. "Like I have a choice."

"You don't," Delaney shot in. "So, how about you drive her to school, then you meet us outside. We'll follow you."

Garvey was disgusted, but he had known it was coming. The best thing now was to cooperate.

"Okay," he said looking at his watch. "Give me ten minutes." He turned and stalked into the house. It was a good thing Rachael was asleep. No telling what she would have said to them.

He was a long time in the backseat of their car. He answered all their questions, surprised at the details they had uncovered. Rachael had been right, they knew who he had phoned and when, what restaurants he had eaten at, where he had shopped, how much his rent bill was, and dozens of other seemingly inconsequential facts of his life. They wanted him now to put it all into context; why he had traveled somewhere, what he had purchased at the hardware store, why he had called Moore in Colorado. And up to a point he obliged them. The sooner he got this over with, he figured, the sooner they would get off his back. But then the questions began taking on a more challenging note and his patience started fraying.

"No, I did not go back to Cincinnati to see the accident at Kings Island."

"You'd just been there a few days before. Why'd you go back?" Delaney asked.

"I told you why I went originally, to get some cars rebuilt. You can check on that, ask Don Madison at Madondi."

"We have," Delaney shot back. "We're asking now about your trip back three days later. You go back maybe to retrieve a tree saw?"

"I went back to see a friend."

"A friend?" Jacobson asked. "Could that have been one Rachael White?"

"Why don't you ask her." Garvey said with annoyance. "Listen, I've got a job to do and I've been talking to you for over an hour. You want me to answer more questions you'll have to either arrest me on some federal warrant or else talk to my boss. The schedule I'm on doesn't have any room for casual FBI fishing expeditions."

"One last question," Jacobson said, "then you can go. "Where were you when your assistant was killed?"

Garvey didn't say anything for a moment. He tried to look blankly at the two men turned around in the front seat, the young, athletic Delaney with the shock of blond hair and the older, more cynical-looking Jacobson. "The police here thought it was an overdose," he finally managed.

"Yeah, it was meant to look that way," Delaney said, matter-of-factly. "So where were you?"

"Sleeping. No alibi." He looked blankly at them, daring them to do something.

"You have any ideas," Jacobson said after a moment.

"No," Garvey said. "None."

"He a dope head?" he continued. "I mean, you would have suspected something, no?"

Garvey put his hand on the door lever and pulled. The car door swung open and he put a leg out.

"Jason was a good worker," he said. "I can't say that he ever came in impaired. Besides, he was my friend."

"So, you didn't kill him then?" Delaney asked casually.

Garvey pulled himself the rest of the way out of the car and shut the door.

"We were both working on the same project. Now I have to work twice as hard to get it in on time. Does that make any sense?"

"There's not a lot that makes sense about this whole thing, Garvey," Jacobson said. "Least of all why Rachael White should be hanging out with you."

Garvey walked away at that, not willing to give them a look at his red, angry face. "You want me again, call my lawyers," he shot back over his shoulder. He limped quickly the rest of the way to his car and got in. When he pulled out of the parking lot and turned toward Angel City a minute later, their rental car was nowhere to be seen.

Had they gotten anything, he wondered? Or were they just trying to push his buttons, trying to get him to do something incriminating? He'd have to be careful, he told himself. Real careful.

FORTY-FIVE

Assume they're looking," Rachael told him later that night. "Assume they are out there somewhere, hiding, and when we break into Jason's, they'll have all the cause they'll need for an arrest."

"We'll have to fool them, then," Garvey said. "You think it can't be done?"

"You're a scientist, Sam, not a cat burglar."

"Yeah, well, wait till you see this." He pulled a package out of his briefcase and put it on the table in front of them. "I put it together from some things I picked up in the lab."

Rachael looked at it for a few seconds without saying anything. "What's it do?"

"Well, I figured the FBI has too big a budget and too much equipment to be old-fashioned. They'd simply put a little GPS transmitter in my car. It was outside all last night, they had plenty of time." He patted the machine. "This little device picks up the source of transmissions and tells me where the thing is so I don't have to rip my vehicle to shreds to find it. Then I take it out and we have a little fun with them."

"You're sure about this?" she asked nervously.

"Hey, you'll remember this night for years."

"I'm afraid of that," she said, touching the little device cautiously.

* * *

They started out two hours later. Sarah had been asleep for over an hour with Rosita contentedly watching a movie on the local Spanish-language channel when they left. Garvey took two flashlights and some thin track shims to use on Jason's door. Rachael brought the little black package that they had found taped under the windshield fluid reservoir and the map she had marked up to give to the taxi driver. Then they piled into Garvey's old station wagon and noisily backed out of the driveway.

When they turned the corner onto Davis Street a mile away they spotted the cab waiting for them, the motor idling just as they had instructed. There were no other cars in sight and the thick bushes along the street hid both vehicles. Quickly, Rachael jumped out and gave the driver the package and map and got back in with Garvey. The taxi immediately headed south on Davis while they made a U-turn and headed north.

"I told him to be back here in an hour and a half and to keep moving the way the map shows," she said. "It should keep him from being spotted. You think they were following us?"

"Well, even if they weren't, it's cheap insurance. Let's go," he said. "It's at least ten minutes to Jason's." He stepped down on the gas and the car rocketed forward.

They parked in the big employee resident lot and walked arm in arm toward Jason's building. The last thing they wanted to do was raise suspicion with some casual observer. They looked innocent enough as they walked slowly into one of the entrances and climbed to Jason's door. Garvey busied himself with the shim and in a minute they heard the latch click and the door swing in. After a quick look up and down the empty hall, they pushed inside and shut the door.

There was enough light coming in through the windows

143

for them to see the layout. He motioned and she closed the venetian blinds before he turned on his flashlight. Then he walked close to her and put his lips near her ear.

"Start in the living room," he whispered. "Look for anything unusual."

"Like what?" she whispered back.

He shrugged. "Papers, names, records, that kind of stuff."

She nodded and flipped on her light.

"I'm scared to death," she said slightly above a whisper. "I've never done this before."

"You never had sex with a man with a crutch before either," he shot back.

In a minute she was rummaging through the drawers of Jason's desk. Garvey headed for the bedroom.

The police had cleaned up some of the mess. The drugs and paraphernalia had been taken away for sampling and the bed had been stripped, but otherwise it looked pretty much the way Garvey figured Jason had left it. Old magazines were on the nightstand, his bureau held some pennies and paper clips and mints in a tray alongside an open wooden box of cheap jewelry. On top was mostly sterling rings, bracelets, single earrings. Garvey started in on the bureau drawers. There wasn't much, some T-shirts, collared shirts, underwear, cotton sweaters, shorts. The usual men's selection. Nothing hidden between or under any garment. Then Garvey removed the drawers and shone his light inside the empty bureau and then under the drawers. Still nothing. He got up and turned toward the closet.

"Nothing in the desk," Rachael said from the doorway, proud of herself. "Now what?"

"If something's here it won't be obvious," he said softly. "Look under things, behind . . ." She nodded and drifted back into the living room.

Jason's closet was fuller than he would have expected. Besides the light summer jackets and pants, one side was covered with a sheet. When he pulled it away he saw heavier clothing, woolens, knitted sweaters, coats. This was unusual. Garvey thought that Jason had always lived in Texas. He'd never mentioned living anywhere up north. Garvey looked in all the pockets but besides some loose change and pens, he found nothing. He looked under the small rug, under the mattress, and in the upholstery of an easy chair positioned under a wall lamp. When he was satisfied that the bedroom held no secrets, he looked at his watch. They had been at it for half an hour.

"Find anything?" he asked softly as he came into the living room. Rachael was in front of the bookcases flipping through some books.

"Not yet." She pointed to the desk. "What about his computer? It's a little laptop."

"We'll just take it. I'll look at it at the office. I can always say he brought it there. It's a perfect cover."

"He's got more books here."

"Okay." Garvey was about to leave her when they both heard the sound from outside. Someone was walking slowly toward the door. They held each other's eyes and waited. The footsteps grew louder on the cheap wood tiling of the hallway, stopped for a moment in front of Jason's door, then kept moving. Rachael's face looked tortured.

"This is what it must feel like to have a stroke," she breathed.

"Keep looking," he said. "I've still got the bathroom."

He walked quickly back into the bedroom. The bathroom was opposite the bed and was as spare as the builders at Angel City could have gotten away with and still provide basic body amenities. There was a toilet, a bath, a sink, a medicine cabinet, and a towel rack. Very basic. Garvey flashed his light around, but there were few places to hide anything. He opened the medicine cabinet and aimed his light, but again, there was not much to look at: some mouthwash, medicine containers, shave lotion, aspirin. Maybe, because of that, he decided to look at the medicine bottles closer. He picked each up, shone his light, and read the prescription. On the third, he felt a jolt go through him. A prescription for Vicodin ES by itself was not unusual. It was an effective painkiller and many people took it. This Garvey sadly knew because it had been the pill Fran had tried to ease her pain with, swallowing enough to double the toxicity limit in her blood. So the word *Vicodin* by itself conjured up painful memories. But what had him stunned, with the bottle still clutched in his hand, was the name of the doctor who had prescribed it for Jason, Dr. Paul Ivey, the same doctor Fran had used. Written right there, on the little label. With an address in Boston, here in a medicine cabinet in Texas. This was not just a cruel coincidence. A sense of dread, of something terribly wrong was seeping into his consciousness. How, he barely managed to think, could this possibly be? Ivey was a Boston doctor, Jason had never been to Boston.

"Come here," Rachael called softly from the bedroom door. "I found some pictures."

He was barely able to move out of the little bathroom and find her. He walked as though in shock. The little bottle was still in his hand although now he couldn't bear to look at it.

Jason had a notebook, one of those black artist journals, and in it were crammed some loose photos. Rachael had them out and spread over a little table that he had used as a dining table. There may have been three dozen photos, many of Jason with friends. The backgrounds were interesting. Most were taken in what looked like Texas, or at least the Southwest, but a few were winter scenes with people in heavy coats.

"Know any of these people?" she asked him.

He was afraid to look, not because any full idea had formed but because of the dread that had rooted from the moment he saw the word *Vicodin*. He looked reluctantly, and there, after a moment, he found her, in a group photo of people in front of Boston General Hospital. He recognized its facade; they had gone there often. There were six of them, he now remembered, all in the pain-management clinic. Jason was the second from the left in a dark turtleneck sweater, the same sweater Garvey had just seen under the sheet in his closet. Fran had been two people away, When had that been? He tried to think. Six weeks, nine weeks before that fateful night in April? Oh, Christ. He wanted to cry. He sat down heavily in a chair and put the bottle on the table next to the picture.

"Something evil," he said heavily.

She looked at him, anxious now. His face had gone the color of parchment. "Let's go," he continued.

"The computer . . ." she began.

He looked idly at it. "Yes," he said slowly.

"What is it?" she asked, then looked back down at the picture in front of him. "Who is it?"

He was silent for a long moment, then said, "Fran." He looked up at her with eyes so vacant, so punished, that he could have been inebriated. She put a hand out to him, touched his shoulder.

That seemed to rouse him. He nodded, pocketed the medicine bottle, labored up, and put the laptop computer under his arm.

"Let's go," he said again, this time with more resolve. "We have to get back for the taxi."

They were careful to leave everything the way they had found it. All the doors and drawers were closed, the blinds reopened, the books put back. Then they cautiously looked out into the corridor and quickly exited. In Garvey's pocket were the bottle and the picture.

"You'll tell me when we get back?" she said.

"I'll need some help," he told her. "We have to work this out together.

FORTY-SIX

"For a whole year there was only one thought in my head every day I woke up. What could I have done to help her?"

"There was nothing you could have done. It's . . ." Rachael was hesitant, ". . . a familiar story."

"I guess so. Except, rarely with this kind of ending."

It was late and they were at his kitchen table over two cups of steaming tea. They had gotten back without a problem; picked up the little black GPS tracker from the taxi driver, who had reported no incidents, and continued on to Garvey's place. Sarah was quietly sleeping.

Garvey continued. "I don't know how to feel. I think maybe he killed her. The coincidence is chilling."

"How could he? Where was she found?"

"This hurts so much," he said. Tears welled up in his eyes and he pushed back from the table. Rachael leaned across the table and hugged him, held him until the crying trailed off and he was left wiping his eyes on his sleeve. "I'm sorry," he offered.

"Tell me about it. Maybe it can help us now."

"She left the house around noon to go to the clinic. Often afterward she'd go to a Starbucks for a coffee; there was one right nearby. Lots of students there, reading books. Someone noticed around four P.M. that she was asleep, but she seemed to be in an awkward position. Two of her fingers were still looped around her coffee mug handle. When they tried to wake her up they realized she was nearly gone . . ." his voice trailed off.

"The police investigated?" Rachael asked.

"No. I told them the circumstances were not unexpected.

I think they interviewed the half dozen people who had been there."

"Had she been sitting with anybody?"

He shrugged. "No one seemed to notice. They did a blood chemistry and found what killed her. The pills were in her handbag. I thought . . . what else could I think . . . that she had given up on the clinic's method and was going to do it her way, the way she had always wanted . . . with bigger doses."

She got up from her chair and walked around the table.

"Okay, let's take it one step at a time, Sam, see if we can piece it together. She's at this pain clinic, trying with all her might to keep the drugs down, and she meets this guy. We don't know how Jason managed to get in there, he must have faked some untreatable back pain to Ivey because he also gets a prescription for Vicodin from him. Everyone's tight, friendly, all suffering a similar anguish. They take group pictures. And Jason, he's attractive, charming, unthreatening . . . of course she's going to have coffee with him after their meeting. Maybe often, and he easily worms his way into her confidence. Does he give her more of his pills to take so you won't notice and she downed too many on his encouragement, or does he just lace the coffee with a half dozen extra? It doesn't really matter. I think you're right, he had a hand in her death. The question is, why?"

Garvey looked up and shook his head. "This is all too painful."

"Why? Why did he go after her to begin with? Why did he wind up as your assistant? Why did he need her dead? Why was he in Boston when he told you he'd never been there? There is indeed, as you said, something evil going on here, Sam. And only you can possibly answer those things."

He nodded sadly. "There is an answer," he said. "And it's absurdly simple. Fran's death brought me to Texas, brought me to Angel City."

"That's it?"

"That's it. I had been approached for months, even before Fran's pain clinic, to come and work on the Jumper. Fran refused to go. She didn't want to take Sarah out of her nursery school. She didn't want to leave the city she loved. She didn't want to take herself and her pain to someplace unknown, and ultimately, she didn't want me to go to work for Angel City because when I told her about the project, she thought I'd fail. She was very protective of me, and I had just been through the debacle of the Demon Dipper. That was the last thing she wanted to see happen to me again."

"And you told the people recruiting you that that was the reason why you wouldn't go."

"I did. I should have said nothing, but instead I told them and sealed her fate. Getting rid of Fran would get rid of that opposition."

"And that became Jason's job." Rachael added.

"I was being set up, like a piece in a chess game," Garvey said disgustedly.

"And that's what we have to find out now. Why were you so important to someone to kill for? Not once, but twice. Now there's Jason's murder."

"More," Garvey said. "Many more. All of the deaths in the three accidents."

"Yes," she said, nodding. "I almost forgot."

"It was Dominici," Garvey said softly. "He was the one who wanted me so badly. He called me every week."

"Dominici? But that's crazy," she said. "The person behind this is trying to frame you. That would jeopardize the Jumper. Where's the logic?"

"Logic?" Garvey repeated. "I don't think I know what that means," he said. "Not after tonight."

FORTY-SEVEN

The next day, Saturday, Rachael kept her promise to Sarah and took her on a drive to a lake nearby where they could have a picnic and play a lot of hide-and-seek. Garvey was pleased that she was gone, away from the changed, somber mood into which he had fallen.

He brought Jason's laptop into the office, thinking he might get an early chance to try getting into the files, but there was too much to do. With Jason gone, and the full-scale Jumper green-lighted, he had to make scores of changes. He tweaked all of the joint butt-plate angles where they had placed shims on the quarter-scale model to allow for the increased space, then he called Madondi with the new numbers and faxed them a back-up set. Then, even though he had told Dominici to go ahead with the ground work, he double-checked with the landscape foreman that the extra few inches of track sweep wouldn't be a problem. Then he walked in on Hotchkiss and reviewed the decorative external lighting to make sure the changes from the shims could be dealt with. Finally, at around two P.M. he sat down in front of Jason's little computer and turned it on.

But when he tried to open anything he got the expected password-request screen. He looked at that for a moment, then something clicked. Jason's SAT score . . . like the password he had suggested for the Jumper files. It had to be below 1600 but not less than 1200. That was only four hundred attempts at the right number, which should only take him a couple of hours. He sat down with a cup of coffee and stared at the screen that requested the password entry.

He thought for a moment and punched in 1600. Give him credit, he told himself, he was a bright kid.

Forty minutes later when he entered fourteen sixty eight, the password request screen evaporated and in its place appeared a list of files. Some of them he recognized as games, some as word-processing and spreadsheet programs, and some as personal planners and schedulers. He had no idea what he was looking for, but he knew it would be somewhere in one of the programs.

So he proceeded slowly, looking even in the game files for hidden caches of information. By five o'clock his eyes were bleary from looking at all the dancing pixels and he took a break. Nothing even remotely incriminating had shown up. The phone was nearby and he dialed to check up on Rachael and Sarah.

"Jacobson and Delaney have been by," Rachael said when she picked up. "They didn't seem surprised to see me here so Pouncy must already know. I feel a little exposed, Sam."

"You knew they'd find out. He won't do anything. He's already had you taken off the case. What did they want?"

"They didn't say. You should have come to the lake with us," Rachael said. "We had a lovely day."

"I'm glad someone did. I'm getting nowhere," Garvey said. "I'll see you later, maybe an hour."

He hung up and looked back down at the computer. It's here somewhere, he thought, and dove back in.

After another half hour of going through dozens more files with extensions like .DTF, .WPS, and .DOC, he had still found nothing of interest. He was coming to the end of the list and knew that the odds were thin that the file he was after was one of the last ones. Unless Jason had deliberately placed it last. Garvey scrolled down to the file called XKANG.DTF and opened it. A list of numbers flashed down the screen. It was some type of rudimentary code. Garvey recognized after an initial two letters a six-place entry most likely for the date and then a forward slash and then a run of digits, possibly for a dollar amount. All of the entries were under the letters *AT* with the last one from no more than ten days before. Garvey scrolled down to the end of the file, hoping, but not really believing in good fairies, but there it was. A footer describing that AT stood for Alameda Trust of New Mexico. Apparently Jason never expected someone to ever get this deeply into his computer. There was a single account number, 578092-P, plus entries showing that for the past eighteen months Jason had socked away a total of over one hundred thousand dollars. And the source of all this money? Nowhere listed. But Garvey made some notes and shut off the computer. He sat back and thought for a moment. XKANG? Now who, or what, the hell was that? And why New Mexico? And how did he hope to get information on someone's private bank account? As he sat an idea came into his head, and he toyed with it for a long time. Then he stood up and walked over to one of his cabinets and found the personnel file on each of the people working for him. He saw Jason's right away, and after a moment's browsing he found what he was looking for. He made another note, then slowly closed the file and put it back. Albuquerque. His mom was listed as living there. He found a map in another cabinet drawer and opened it to New Mexico, and after no more than thirty seconds he spotted Alameda. He didn't even need to measure the distance; Alameda was a suburb of Albuquerque, no more than ten miles from downtown. The pieces were dropping into place. He came back to his desk and looked at the little note he had written. Then he took a moment to collect himself and slowly dialed the number.

The voice that answered was not that of Jason's mother. It was a gruff man's voice, a voice that had been scorched by bad liquor, too much smoke, and maybe a lot of loud cursing. It was the voice that filled countless late-night pool halls and dusty country stock-car tracks, and it asked, quite unambiguously what the hell he wanted.

"Mrs. Roper, please," Garvey said.

"You're a little late, buddy."

"How's that?" Garvey asked.

"Justine's dead. And I'm sure you ain't nobody she owed money to or else you wudda heard. She's gone maybe nine months."

"I'm sorry," Garvey said quickly. "I was looking for Jason Roper's mother. He never told me she died."

"Jason? That little son of a bitch wuddana cared. Those two never got on."

"Are you Mr. Roper?" Garvey asked hopefully.

The other man made a noise like he was choking on a bad cigar; a peculiar way, Garvey thought, of laughing.

"She fuckin' wudda liked that," he rasped. "No, I ain't Mr. Goddamn Roper. I musta asked her a dozen times but she didn't wan' no strings. Said they only grabbed at you. That was Justine. If you're lookin' for Roper, that cocksucker's dead too." There was a moment of silence on the phone, afterwhich the other man came back suspiciously. "Why you lookin' for Justine, anyway? Somethin' happen to the kid?"

"Listen, did he have any other relatives or friends in Albuquerque? Maybe someone over near Alameda?"

"I asked you somethin'," the other man came back.

"Yes, Jason's had an accident. I was looking for someone to contact."

"And who are you . . . a cop?"

"I am . . ." Garvey hesitated. "I was his boss."

"Dead, huh?" the other man said, reading into Garvey's message. "Never thought he wudda made it past thirty-five. That kid was bright, but there wasn't much he wouldn't do for a buck. I remember—"

"Alameda," Garvey prompted again.

"Yeah, there's Trish. His younger sister. Lives in Alameda.

I suppose that's the closest relative he's got. I think they were on speakin' terms."

More than that, Garvey thought. "You got an address or phone number for her? There's all his stuff here."

"His boss, huh? I wish I had a boss like you. All the ones I ever got wuddana given a shit if I died. Yeah, Trish, let me see, last I heard she lived on Pinyon Street, I think. She's in the phone book. Never married. You should be able to find her. Christ, Alameda's not a big place."

"Thanks," Garvey said and hung up the phone slowly. Six hours of driving time to Alameda. Maybe by tomorrow afternoon he could find out what the hell was going on. He pocketed the address and turned to leave the office. But, he thought, he couldn't take Rachael. He needed her for Sarah now. And to keep Delaney and Jacobson in town, watching. Someone else, someone who knew about banks and just how to apply enough pressure to get results. He sat back down and picked the phone up again.

FORTY-EIGHT

The airport in Albuquerque was buzzing with activity, but it wasn't hard to spot Moore as he stepped through the exit gate. It wasn't so much the large gray ten-beaver Stetson he was wearing as it was the dark blue John Weitz pinstriped suit that it shaded. He was the most elegant man on the plane, probably in the whole airport, and he came right over and gave Garvey a bear hug.

"Thanks for coming," Garvey said when he came up for air.

"A friend calls and I come," the taller man said. "Besides, it was only a little hop for me. I just took the afternoon off." His sixty-year-old eyes fairly twinkled. "And if it's about what I think it is, I can't wait to lend aid and assistance to the enemy . . . of the FBI, that is. They came to Ironwood and it took a coupla weeks to undo the damage they did me."

"Well, they're still on my case," Garvey said. "Come on, the car's nearby."

On the way to Alameda, Garvey filled Moore in on everything, including the part about Fran. This new revelation seemed to deflate the banker.

"It's too sad to contemplate," he said. "Fran was real special." He put his hand on Garvey's shoulder and shook his head. "How are you holding up, my friend?"

"I don't know, Patrick. I'll feel a lot better if we find out something this afternoon. Fran is gone . . . It's the people who are still alive I'm worrying about."

"Don't let the pinstripes fool you, Sam. I can get pretty nasty when it comes to tracking down money."

It didn't take them long to find Pinyon Street. It meandered leisurely around the northeast part of Alameda, never venturing more than a block away from the intertidal zone of desert-suburban overlap. This was the domain of tired-looking squat ranches with their landscape of disembodied engine blocks, homemade carports, and inverted truck-tire planters.

Garvey turned in at number 45, the address he had gotten from the phone directory. It was a small house like many of its neighbors except that there was nothing to indicate the presence of children. No bicycle, no basketball backboard, no errant skateboard littered the postage-stamp lawn. Just a large, semi-awake dog who eyed Garvey with a mixture of curiosity and hope. The two men edged past him, and Garvey rang the bell next to the aluminum storm door. Even though it was two P.M., an old Honda waited on the cement parking pad, and Willie Nelson was singing out of a tape deck inside. Someone was home.

It didn't take long for the door to open. If her dog's look

had been inquisitive, the woman who faced them now looked seriously suspicious. She looked both men up and down, and her eyes narrowed.

"Yes?" she asked.

She was mid-thirties, and her short haircut made her two hundred plus pounds more noticeable. Her clothes were neat, large, and made clever concessions to her body's profile.

"Are you Patricia Roper?" Garvey asked.

"Who are you?" Her eyes went from one to the other.

"This is Patrick Moore, on the Colorado State Advisory Board of Banking Regulations. My name is Samuel Garvey. Your brother, Jason Roper, was an employee of mine. May we come in?"

She looked behind her quickly. "I wasn't expecting anyone."

"We'll only be a minute," Garvey pressed. "It's important."

She shrugged, then turned and led them inside. The little house was spotless, and like her personal dress, everything seemed to serve its function well. The two men sat down in easy chairs facing a couch that had a distinct southwestern style. The coffee table between them was an old wagon wheel covered with thin glass.

She took the couch and looked at her watch.

"I have to go to the hospital in fifteen minutes," she began. "I hope it won't take longer . . ."

"You're sick?" Moore asked.

"No, my job. I'm a nurse's aide."

"It's about your brother, Ms. Roper," Garvey began. "He's had an accident. Several days ago." He watched her closely, but there was no response. "He was found in his apartment, apparently a victim of an overdose of narcotics."

She took a deep breath, but that was all. And continued to watch them carefully.

"And we have to ask you a few questions. As the next of kin."

"You're not the police?"

"No, ma'am," Garvey said.

"We weren't very close," she finally offered. "Last I saw him was maybe two years ago. I guess I should be sorry, but he wasn't, you know . . . exactly the best of brothers. He worked for you so you probably saw he wasn't that reliable."

"On the contrary," Garvey said tightly. "He was very good at what he did. He was very organized." Garvey let that sink in.

"The burial?" she asked.

"His body is in Freemont, waiting. That's one of the reasons we're here."

"There are others?" But she looked somewhat relieved.

"His personal effects. You can probably claim them," Garvey added.

Her look now went almost friendly.

"There much?"

"Enough," Garvey said. "Computer, television, furniture, clothing, that sort of stuff. Oh, and a bank account."

"I see." She relaxed into the cushions of the couch. "What do I have to do?" she asked.

"There's one problem," Moore interrupted. It was the first time he had spoken but she still had her friendly face on. "The bank account was illegal."

Her expression changed as quickly as if she had been handed a full bedpan. "Illegal . . . ?"

"Account number five-seven-eight-zero-nine-two-P at the Alameda Trust right here in town. An account of yours that at this moment contains one hundred twenty-three thousand, nine hundred eighty-seven dollars and twenty-three cents. Please do not deny you are aware of its existence. I have copies of deposit slips with an individual's handwriting. It would not be hard to subpoena samples of your own handwriting to match with them."

Patricia Roper was silent, not trusting herself to say a word.

"With all due respect, Ms. Roper, I think you knew your brother a lot better than you want us to think, and were in touch with him a lot more often." Moore sounded angry and his long frame leaned closer to her. "In criminal matters of this kind, phone records can easily be gotten."

"Criminal matters?" She looked now utterly deflated. "What criminal matters?"

"And as an owner of this account, Ms. Roper, I'm afraid you are also greatly in jeopardy." This came from Garvey, but his tone remained even. If Garvey and Moore were doing a good cop/bad cop, they had gotten their parts down perfectly.

"Perhaps you didn't know where your brother got the money you deposited for him," Moore continued. "Perhaps you did. But you certainly knew that the method of handling it was highly suspicious. That makes you look like a part of the whole scheme."

"I didn't do anything wrong. I just took it to the bank," she said, looking frightened now.

"The checks?" Garvey asked.

"Yes. They were made out to me and I just endorsed them in."

"Every month," Moore supplied. He took a paper from his pocket and held it up to her. "Like clockwork. And you didn't ask Jason what this was for? All these checks? That amount of money? You weren't curious?"

She shook her head vigorously. "No, I swear. I never asked. He told me it was a job he was doing and he couldn't get the payment direct. It was just a favor I did him."

"A favor that could get you in a lot of trouble," Garvey said. "All you've worked for, all this . . ." he waved his hand around the trim living room, "could be history."

"I wasn't part of anything." She said it loudly and certainly more in fear than in defiance.

"Federal banking regulations allow that illegal activity is not contained to the beneficiary. Anyone involved in the process could be implicated. So, what we need to find out here," Moore persisted, "is just where the money came from. Who was paying it. If there was a name on the checks," he prompted, "an address, some indication of what illegal activity your brother was involved in. That would be one way to convince the authorities you were not a part of anything."

"But there was nothing," she said. "I mean no indication of where it was all coming from. All the checks were without a maker's address. I think they were from a bank somewhere in Kansas. The postmark was from New York. The whole thing made me nervous if you really want to know—"

"We do really want to know, Patricia. It's very important. Your brother is the key to some very dangerous activities," Moore pressed.

". . . because he told me not to tell anyone," she continued. "And that he'd give me something."

"He's dead, Patricia," Garvey said. "He can't give you anything. The only person that can help you is yourself. Wasn't there anything you can remember? The signature even?"

She glanced slowly over at the two men. In the silence as they waited, they heard a little chiming clock that came from over the false mantelpiece.

"I did have my suspicions," she said finally. "Every damn time I went into the bank with a deposit. So I guess that's why I tried so hard to decipher the signature. It was mostly a scrawl at first, but then I finally saw it clear on one check a couple of months ago."

The name?" Garvey asked.

She nodded. " 'Frank Tartaglia,' if that's how you pronounce it. I hope that helps." She smoothed out her cotton shift as if to indicate that's all she had to give them.

Moore frowned. "Tartaglia?"

Garvey glanced at him. There was something in his friend's voice.

"That name . . . ," the banker said, "but damn if I can place it. I hear and see so many over a week." He cupped his palm over his forehead. "Frank Tartaglia," he repeated.

"Yes," she said. "Now I really have to go. I'm already gonna be late."

"Wait," Garvey said. "One more thing."

"Tartaglia," Moore said again, trying to coax his memory into an association.

"Something with an X," Garvey asked. "On the checks somewhere? XKang or something?"

Moore turned to him with a look of sudden surprise.

"What did you say?"

"XKang. It was the file on Jason's computer where all this was."

"No," Patricia Roper said.

"XKang," Moore said close to Garvey's ear. "XKang... out of Kang. D. Kang to be exact, a hedge fund. And Frank Tartaglia, now I remember, is one of the directors. That's where I saw the name. Except when I called for him, he wasn't in, Robert Massio was. But I know where they are, phone number and everything." When he leaned back his face had broken into a smile. "Thank you, Ms. Roper. You have been a great help."

"Yeah? So, now what do I do about the account and Jason's other stuff? The TV and computer," she asked.

"Not to mention the funeral," Garvey added. "Freemont, Texas." He said, standing. "Call the police there. They'll know what to do. Now tell your dog to behave, please. We're going."

FORTY-NINE

On the ride back to the airport, they tried to put it together. Jason had been getting money from D. Kang, a hedge fund that was also involved with laundering money for entertainment companies like Virtuland. So, what was he giving D. Kang? Virtuland had floated some high-interest bonds in Mexico, presumably for reasons of anonymity. Angelus Corporation floated similar bonds in Mexico. Jason worked for

Angelus, but his role was not financial. Still, he must have known something sensitive—but what? And what the hell was Jason's tie-in with the roller coaster accidents? A pall of confusion hung over everything.

It was obvious that D. Kang had to be the key. But apart from casual information gleaned from leaning on one of the front investors, neither Moore nor Garvey had any idea how to proceed. Moore got on the plane back to Colorado, trying to come up with a legal way to crack their books. But hedge funds were notoriously private, and short of a plumber's job, it looked hopeless to him. Garvey was not encouraged either. He drove all the way back to Freemont in a funk that made the long miles seem endless. He arrived in the middle of the night and, after checking on Sarah, crept into bed exhaustedly.

Rachael was there, huddled into a tight ball, hugging a pillow between her arms. She shifted with the new weight in the bed but didn't open her eyes. Garvey looked at her wonderingly, and even in his fatigue couldn't believe that she was still there. He put an arm around her and went to sleep quickly.

In the morning he awoke with an idea. It was a cheap, immature, unsophisticated little gamble that one would expect from a private detective with an eighty-square-foot office and filthy venetian blinds. But he acted on it anyway, and at 9:45, in his own office, he picked up the phone and dialed the main number.

"Mr. Dominici, please," he asked. In a minute he heard a woman's voice.

"Mildred, is that you? It's Dr. Garvey. I need to get a telephone number I think you have. A D. Kang company. Someplace in New York."

"Hold on," she said. After a minute she came back. "Sorry, Dr. Garvey, it's not on my Rolodex."

"How about Frank Tartaglia or Robert Massio?"

"I'm supposed to have these?" she asked.

"Mildred, come on, it's for the Jumper."

"Lord. Everything stops for the Jumper. Just a minute."

Garvey held the receiver tightly, waiting. She was back in no time.

"Nothing for Massio or Tartaglia either. Where'd you get this notion I'd have them?"

"You're sure?" Garvey pressed.

"Listen, I'm good at what I do, and one of the things I do is keep my phone records up to date."

"Sorry, Mildred, I must have had the wrong information," Garvey said deflatedly. "Could you give him a message for me, then. Tell him we're moving along rapidly on the final installation. The steel track is arriving today and I have a message here from Madondi that the cars should be in next week."

"I'll tell him when he gets back. He's out of town right now. In New York."

"Oh?" Garvey said sharply. "I didn't know. When did he leave?"

"Last night. He'll be back tonight," Mildred said. "Something came up suddenly."

"Do you know with whom he's meeting?"

"He didn't say, Dr. Garvey," Mildred said somewhat icily. Her patience was wearing thin, or the Danielle Steel novel was calling.

"Thanks anyway," Garvey said and hung up slowly. New York, he thought. A lot of people go to New York. It's a big place, right? He got Moore on the phone a minute later.

"What's the telephone number of that fund in New York?"

"Got an idea?" Moore asked.

"I don't know. It's a long shot."

"I've won a few like that," the Colorado banker said.

"Not this long."

163

FIFTY

Garvey had to time it right. He waited forty-five minutes, then dialed; ten-thirty in Texas meant twelve-thirty in New York.

"Hello, D. Kang. How can I help you," a woman's voice answered.

"I'm sorry to trouble you," Garvey began. "This is really stupid. I'm supposed to be having lunch today with Mr. Tartaglia and I've forgotten the restaurant where we're meeting. Has he left yet?"

"Geez, I'm sorry, he just left five minutes ago."

"You think you could find out where it is?"

"Geez, I don't know. I'm the only one here. Massio went with him."

"Do you think you could look at his appointment book?" Garvey asked pleadingly. "It's an important meeting. Christ, I'm hung if I miss it."

"Hey, hold on. If you were supposed to meet him maybe I could look." Garvey waited nervously and in three minutes she was back.

"He didn't have anything written down."

"Damn."

"But it's usually La Marmotte. That's where he likes to go with clients. Over on Fiftieth Street. You could try there."

"Thanks a lot," Garvey said and put the phone back down. Now for the creative part. He had to get a photographer outside the restaurant within forty minutes, some stranger who would trust that he was good for the money. He turned to his terminal and jumped on the Internet. In five minutes he had

164

scrolled through a Yellow Pages search engine and had written down ten names, all listed under photographers, wedding. He started dialing.

In another ten minutes of frantic cajoling and negotiating, he finally found Burt Tarshis, from a company called Brides and Slides. Burt allowed that even though he was somewhat slow that afternoon, someone who was available on a moment's notice with all the required photo equipment and who appreciated the fact that speed and discretion were of the essence, that person should be paid a handsome fee. Garvey made a final offer of one hundred and fifty dollars and Burt grudgingly took it. After getting Garvey's Visa number and the address where he was to send all the prints, he did have one question.

"So, I mean I don't need to know if it's your wife or not, but maybe you could tell me what she looks like? I could concentrate better."

"Everyone, absolutely everyone that leaves," Garvey said with force. "Concentrate on that." He hung up and sat silently for a moment, wondering if he had just thrown away a hundred and fifty dollars. Maybe they weren't even going to La Marmotte. The more he thought about it, the more he realized it was insane. So he turned away from his desk and opened the installation charts for the final track that was coming the next day. At least that was real.

FIFTY-ONE

The twelve tractor trailers were waiting with their motors idling long before Garvey arrived the next morning at eight A.M. Each was neatly stacked with twenty tons of precisely labeled steel track. Six trucks had the straight pieces and four had the curved sections. A final two held the supporting angles and connector rods, each machined to fit perfectly into its matching member. Madondi had always been obsessive when it came to providing every last nut and bolt to construct one of their coasters. They had been even more thorough with the Jumper. The blueprints ran to one hundred and forty pages, each one detailing no more than sixty feet, ten sections of running track. Each print showed elevation and plan views and the precise number of each part and which truck on which it could be found. It was a bravura performance by the men from Cincinnati. Following them, the erection crew from Madondi was scheduled to arrive the next day.

He had already scheduled the concrete trucks for two days later when the footing could begin. Two 180-foot tower cranes had been rented and were on site. Two crane operators for each crane had been booked in case of overtime requirements. Hotel rooms for all the installers had been reserved and a special air-conditioned mobile snack/coffee unit had been outfitted and moved over from the restaurant services building. And these were only the large items to be dealt with; Garvey was also point man on such basic concerns as how many Porta-John units were needed, and which names went on the yellow parking permits. Constructing the Jumper was only manageable if approached like a big-budget film and broken down into its component parts.

The entire job of the steel erection was supposed to take no more than two weeks, a surprisingly quick time considering how many pieces were to be welded or bolted together and how many concrete feet were to be poured.

Concurrent with the steel erection, the boarding station was to be constructed and the electrical controls installed. Final landscaping would come in at the end when all the construction equipment had moved out.

In all this frenzy, Garvey found he had no time to think of anything not Jumper related. This was the most critical phase of coaster construction. What went in ground stayed in ground, and no matter how good all those months of planning were, or how all the little tweaks on the quarter scale got all the alignments right, if something was not placed correctly now, it would throw everything off.

As the installation began, Garvey checked and rechecked the drawings and placements. He carried with him a two-foot steel angle gauge and would shamelessly check angles that had been checked a minimum of a dozen times before in factory and on the ground. He was everywhere, and after the first three days of work, he finally made it home one night before seven o'clock.

Rachael was there with Sarah, and next to the front door was her small suitcase and computer. Sarah had an expression on her face like she was about to lose her favorite puppy.

"It's time?" Garvey asked with surprise.

"You knew that," Rachael said. "The week was over three days ago. I have to start that commuter investigation."

"Can't she stay, Daddy?" Sarah asked pleadingly.

"I wish it were up to me." He looked carefully into Rachael's eyes. "I'm sorry I've been so busy. It's the worst time, and with no help . . ."

"I understand," she said. "My plane doesn't leave until nine tonight. I thought maybe we could go out for a farewell dinner."

"I would love that," he said. "Let me just call the Madondi engineers and let them know where I'll be. We're operating on a double shift to make it in time."

"They can't do without you for a couple of hours?" she said, teasing.

"I don't give them that option," he said. "Let me just wash up. Where do you want to go?"

"Someplace intimate," Rachael answered, "for just the three of us."

"How about Casa Beffi? It's so intimate it doesn't even have a kid's menu."

"Yuck," Sarah said. "Candles and tablecloths."

"Oh, this package came for you," Rachael added. "Looks like it's from New York."

"Bring it along," Garvey said casually from the bathroom. "I doubt it's anything. Just some photos of power lunchers."

On the surface, Casa Beffi was a shameless collection of every cliché of Italian dining. Checkered cloths were on the tables, murals of Venice and the Colosseum were on the walls, Mario Lanza sang from overhead speakers, and there wasn't a pasta shape forgotten on the menu. Still, most of the ingredients were fresh and the sauces had enough zip to make a meal there reasonably enjoyable. With Sarah there, the conversation tended to be restricted. They stayed away from the Jumper and the accidents and got through dinner talking mostly about when they were kids, making Sarah laugh to think that her dad had actually been one. An empty bottle of wine was still on the table, as well as three plates of half-eaten canoli, when Garvey finally brought out the envelope of photos and slit it open. He cleared a space in front of him on the table and brought out a fistful of black-and-white glossy four-by-six prints.

Rachael watched idly as he slowly ran through the images. The cameraman had been positioned across the street from the restaurant and every picture had roughly the same look. Except for a few shots where the subjects had turned their head at the moment the picture was taken, people's faces were in focus and easily identifiable.

They were mostly businessmen in suits and ties, and all seemed to be pleased either with themselves, the company, or the meal. Smiles abounded. The few women captured in the photos looked well-coiffed and fashionably elegant. It was obvious from the pictures that this was an expensive restaurant, one a world apart from Casa Beffi and its Chianti-bottle candleholders.

"Who are those people, Daddy?" Sarah asked.

"New Yorkers," he said simply.

"Can we go there again?"

But they were not all New Yorkers. He stopped flipping through the prints about halfway down when he came to one of three men. Two of them were strangers, but Dominici's face never showed more self-satisfaction. Rachael saw Garvey's reaction and leaned closer to look.

"It's him, Dominici," Garvey said softly. "I can't believe it."

"What's it mean?" Rachael asked.

"What's it mean?" Garvey leaned back. "It means the son of a bitch is dirty. I don't know why, or what he's doing, but I'll bet I know who the other two men are. They're managers of a sleazy fund that specializes in laundering gambling money, among other things. But more important, they were the ones paying money into Jason's secret little bank account."

"Dominici," Rachael said. "Your CEO? What was be doing with men like that? Murderers?" She was raising her voice.

"I don't know," Garvey said throwing up his hands. "Dominici has a history of unusual associations."

There was silence at the table for a few moments.

"So, what are you going to do about it?" she finally asked.

"Do?" He looked confused. "The truth is I don't have time to do anything now. I'm going crazy with the Jumper, which can't wait. We're in midconstruction, double shift. The company has millions riding on it."

Rachael said slowly. "You're working for the people who arrange—uh—homicides." She took a sideways glance at Sarah. "I think," she continued on slowly after a moment, "that this calls for some rethinking."

"Rethinking?"

"I mean," she said, "that besides being inappropriate for you, building the Jumper could be very—unhealthy."

"You can't be suggesting that we delay," he said, surprised.

She shook her head. "No, not delay. Abort."

"Abort," he repeated quizzically.

"At least temporarily, until you can figure out what Dominici is up to. The last thing you want is to be associated

169

with those men and their activities. And the only power you have now comes from stopping work on it."

"But, Rachael. It's too far along. It can't be stopped. Besides, it's . . ." He ran a hand through his white hair nervously. "Well, it's one hell of a ride. The best one I've ever done."

"And maybe your last," she said curtly.

"Daddy, what's Rachael saying?" Sarah suddenly said, looking up from the pictures.

"Nothing, honey. It's just about Daddy's new coaster," he said.

"Daddy's new coaster," Rachael repeated with an edge of sarcasm. "Seeing it built no matter what. Think about what your true motives are, Sam. You don't have to prove yourself, even after the Demon Dipper."

"You think that's what this is about," he looked hurt. "It's not."

She looked down at her watch. "Sam, I can't force you to make this decision. For one thing, my plane leaves in forty minutes and I've got to get to the airport."

"I'll drive you," he said. "Listen Rachael, I'm . . ."

"What?"

"Sorry. But this is just one of those times when there's no little black box giving the right answers."

"Not one we've found yet," she said, standing up.

FIFTY-TWO

He drove her to the airport and said good-bye in an awkward and troubled mood. Being in love did not mean never having to say you're sorry. He'd already crossed that bridge and it hadn't helped at all. Not with Rachael. She was, in her own right, as frosty and remote as he had ever seen, even more so than when he had made the mistake of asking if she approached her job like a game. Principled people had a special hierarchy, he thought, where love stood in line after perceived morality. He just knew that the idea of turning his back on the Jumper was as unacceptable as turning his back on his daughter. With such confused thoughts he watched Rachael's 737 climb into the night sky, then turned away and led Sarah back to the car.

"Did you and Rachael fight?" she asked.

Garvey looked at her and nodded. "I guess we did. Sometimes people do that even if they care a lot about each other."

"She's not going away for good?" she asked nervously.

"I hope not," Garvey said.

When they got home, he read her a quick Ogden Nash poem about a seagull wanting to be an eagull, then made himself a cup of coffee and sat down at the dining room table with his briefcase. With all the work on the installation of the Jumper, he hadn't had a chance to look over actual expenditures versus the budgeted numbers. Containing costs was an important consideration, but in the heat of every installation it was an issue that got compromised in many small ways. If there was a bottleneck in setting in the electric, more electricians were called in. If some of the threads on the pipe connectors were scored, new connectors were called for rather than taking the time to retap new threads. All these unexpected costs added up, and Garvey now wanted to make sure they were not getting out of hand. He sipped some of his coffee and spread several pages of financial reports on the table in front of him. Columns of numbers glared back at him. On the left were the budgeted items in black, on the right were the invoiced amounts and their dates. Red numbers showed where the invoices were greater than the budget. He made notes as he worked on a legal pad, culling out those items that he thought needed monitoring. After an hour, he had used up two sheets of paper and was starting in on a third. He leaned back, finished the cold coffee, and rubbed his eyes.

Number work, how he hated it. What he really wanted to be doing was either installing a section of the Jumper, or making love to Rachael. And if he were really truthful with himself in the quiet and emptiness of his little house, he knew now which he'd prefer. But she was now probably thousands of miles away with a heart so cold he doubted she'd even open an e-mail message from him. Damn, he thought. Why had he been so defensive?

He leaned forward again, picked up his pen, and half-heartedly looked back down at the numbers. But now, instead of seeing individual entries, he took in the whole page. Perhaps it was because he was thinking of Rachael, or perhaps it was because he was so exhausted he couldn't concentrate on any one of the entries, but this time what he saw made him start. He quickly pulled from his briefcase a recent set of his engineering prints, looked carefully at it, then turned back to the budget printout. He put his pen on the top of the date column, then slowly brought it down in a neat line. Then he did it on the next one, and the next. Then he looked at the previous five typed pages for the same thing. Only then did he lay his pen down.

Peculiar, he thought. More than peculiar, irresponsible. The last numbers in every date column were the same, which was to be expected since all the expenses had been incurred that year. What had caught his tired eyes was the fact that they were all only two digits long, not the four they should have been. Here it was, only a few months after the turn of the year and a millennium bug was still lurking in the Angelus Corporation's financial programs. His engineering files had been fixed already, as he confirmed from his prints, why not the financial ones? He made a mental note to ask about it in the morning, then reached over and turned off the light. It was past midnight, and he needed his sleep. Tomorrow they were erecting the steelwork for the two jumps and he wanted to be as alert as possible. Curious, though, he thought trudging off to bed. And very careless.

FIFTY-THREE

Garvey believed in the notion that evil flowed unevenly in fits and spurts. The following day was one of those times when everything came together in the worst possible way. Nothing fit, pieces were mislaid or lost, several key people were missing, and, finally, the sky opened up with six hours of rain that was akin to a Bangladeshi monsoon. It was a day when Garvey worked through frustration, anger, confusion, and finally exhaustion before calling it quits at nine P.M. Relatively little had been done; certainly nothing substantial on the jumps. It was almost as though some devilry had been dogging his footsteps, and yet there was not one single cause behind it. Two crane operators had been out the night before on a binge and were sleeping off a hangover. An important connector had simply fallen off a pallet and rolled unseen behind a tarp. A strut had been welded in the wrong place because its identification tag had been misread as M-809 instead of 608-W. That kind of day. Garvey only hoped it had cleared away further mishaps so that the rest of the week would run smoothly.

But like a baseball player in a mysterious slump, a whole week went by with the same problems. Garvey never felt he was ahead on the count. Maybe it had something to do with karma, with Rachael leaving in such a foul mood and him feeling guilty and defensive. Maybe evil worked by exploiting the least little weakness, like air pressure on an overinflated balloon. He would be the last to fall for any New Age explanation, and yet he couldn't explain the run of ill luck. He thought about her a lot in the brief time before sleep overtook his exhaustion at night, but in the morning the day's first problems crowded out his evening's remorse. Finally, by the end of that time, the jumps somehow got built, and some more of the remaining track structure put in place. Saturday was the first good day; nothing went wrong and Garvey breathed easier. If they didn't run into any more problems, he figured they had a fighting chance to get the Jumper finished and ready for safety tests and certification by September fifth. They wouldn't make Labor Day, but they might be able to open up for the public a week later. Even though the kids were back in school by then, the weather would gradually start to turn cooler and bring people out of their air-conditioned living rooms. Like groundhogs popping up to look for their shadows in February, Texans emerged to walk the earth again sometime in September. That was three weeks away. He put a third crew on, midnight to eight, and hoped that the increased pace wouldn't result in some horrible oversight.

But the oversight was his own. Even though he had made a mental note a week earlier, he had completely forgotten to follow up on the curious, neglected Y2K correction until things were finally running smoothly. Six days had passed.

In a quiet moment with a cup of coffee and a bagel, it finally dawned on him. The Angelus Corporation financial programs hadn't been date fixed. He got up abruptly from the little snack bar before the thought could flee again and headed for the computer department at the Corporation Center. He had fifteen minutes to spare, it was only one question, and he knew just whom to ask.

Dale Frazier was the kind of guy everyone made fun of in high school. He was always too precise, too thoughtful for the Kansas farm children with whom he rode the school bus. But his father was a scientist with the state agricultural extension service posted just outside Topeka and had started Dale in on computers before the kid was old enough to throw a baseball. By the time he had graduated from Carnegie Mellon he still couldn't hit a meatball from a JV second-stringer, but he could program a computer like no one else. Angelus hired him right out of school, promoting him over seven years until he wound up as head of computer operations.

Frazier was ubiquitous, as likely to be seen puttering around with the landscaping department's watering programs as he was with the purchasing department's monthly requisition schedules. He was always looking for new upgrades to old programs, new technology and equipment, and easier ways to accomplish basic reporting. Everyone around Angelus liked him because he was friendly, helpful, honest, and supremely competent. There wasn't one employee who hadn't experienced some form of computer hell, and when they did, Frazier was always the person to whom they turned.

Garvey found him in his little office behind four operating computer monitors. On the tables around him were literally a hundred software disks, each precisely labeled and color-coded.

"Morning, Dale," Garvey began. "Got a minute?" The other man motioned him in and pushed a seat at him.

"Give me a moment, will ya. I'm running a new attendance regression." His slender fingers punched some buttons, and Garvey watched as a flood of numbers tumbled down one of the screens. After a minute, the flood stopped with a screen of numbers frozen in place. Frazier leaned closer. The glow off the screen bathed his prematurely balding pate in a soft light.

"Did you know," he said, "that the families that come with three or more children have an average of fifty-nine percent boys?"

"I'm more interested," Garvey said, "in why the financial programs haven't been Y2K updated yet."

Frazier leaned back in his chair and slowly swiveled to face Garvey. "You and me both," he said. "But I just do what I'm told."

"Excuse me?"

"It came down from the top, from Dominici. He asked me how much time I needed to correct the financials and I said I thought I could do it in two months."

"And you're just waiting?" Garvey asked incredulously.

"Just waiting," Frazier said, nodding, "until the Jumper is on line. That's what he said, and he's the boss. He told me I'd lose my job if I started changing the program before then."

"Until the Jumper is done?" Garvey couldn't believe what he'd just heard. "What the hell does one have to do with the other?"

"I don't know, buddy, I just work here. The financials is the only program still left to go Y2K compliant."

"I want to know the relationship."

"I can't help you," Frazier said. "I don't think I was even supposed to let you know what I did just now except that you came in here asking. It's not that I volunteered it." He looked at Garvey hopefully.

"It won't get back," Garvey said to reassure him.

"Thanks." He shook his head and continued. "I mean, the financials are different from the other programs. Those were pretty simple to fix. The financials are all about numbers. You got to be careful . . ."

Garvey thought for a moment out loud. "I don't understand why he would deliberately delay at all. What happens when you fix the programs?"

Frazier shrugged. "You have to write a new program, an expanded program based on the model of the previous one. I mean, an exact model of the original one, which requires a real close reading. Then the new program has to have all the previous data entered, which is what really takes the time. Like spoon-feeding a kid his dinner."

"Someone has to look at all the previous data?"

"Of course. It's slow, tedious work. Don't you remember how long it took with your engineering computers?"

"I do," Garvey said. But he wasn't thinking about his own computers, he was thinking about an entire army of accountants going over the Angelus Corporation books and reentering figures into the new program. Fresh eyes going perhaps where only select eyes had gone before.

"When did Dominici tell you to delay the financials," he finally asked.

"Long time ago," Frazier answered. "It must have been close to a year ago. Let's see, yeah, just about the time you came aboard and the Jumper got green-lighted. I've been sitting on it ever since. I don't mind telling you I was a little nervous about it on New Year's Eve."

"And I'm the first person to ask about it?" Garvey said.

"Yup," Frazier said with a smile. "Everyone else thought I had it under control. And I don't like getting blamed for things that're not my fault. Now, at least someone else knows. I don't feel so exposed."

"You're not the only one that feels that way, Dale." Garvey stood up and slid the chair back. "Thanks."

"But what it had to do with the Jumper," Frazier said as Garvey started to leave, "I couldn't figure that out."

"Neither can I," Garvey said.

FIFTY-FOUR

Frank Danville here," the voice on the telephone said. "I have a note to call you this month on the progress of the Jumper."

"Who?" Garvey said. He had just gotten back to his desk when the phone rang.

"*Amusement Monthly* magazine. You remember, you told me

several months ago to call now for an update. Target date was September third, you said."

"Oh, yes, I remember. We're still trying for that," Garvey said. "Listen, I'm a little pressed now as you can understand."

"I can. But just one more question. Is there any truth to the report that the Angelus Corporation is way out on a limb on this project? That there are some Mexican loans outstanding to bankroll all you've gone over budget?"

"Sorry, no comment." Garvey slammed the phone down and cursed. Then he yanked it up again and dialed Rachael's number in Washington. In his heart he hoped she wasn't there, but she picked up right away.

"Danville just called me," he said. "How could you? That was information I told you in confidence."

"That's a nice way to start a conversation after you haven't called for a week," she said smoothly.

"I've been busy, in case you haven't noticed."

"I have, Sam, but you've been busy looking the wrong way. Besides, I did try to call you this morning, but you were out. I didn't know Danville would call you first." She hesitated. "I had to scare them," she said finally, "before they did something tragic."

"Them? Who?"

"The people Dominici is playing with. I understand what the game is now. Who Periclymenus is. What they're planning. I haven't been idle here, Sam. I'm not building the Jumper, but I am working overtime."

"Rachael, what are you talking about?"

"It's all about money," she answered. "You've been too close to it to see. Periclymenus is all about money. If the Jumper fails, guess what happens to the stock?"

"The stock? You mean Angelus Corporation's?"

"Yes. Hocked-to-the-max-in-Mexico Angelus Corporation. Everything-riding-on-the-Jumper Angelus Corporation. What do you think? It's now at forty. Where do you think it would sink if you never got the Jumper to work. Or worse yet, if you did and Periclymenus sabotaged it?" She took a breath. "You ever hear of selling short, Sam?"

He sank down in his seat. "Selling short?"

"Just an idle inquiry on my part, after working on the commuter crash, that is. I had some time so I called this friend over at the SEC. Not that it's not public information to begin with. Angelus Corporation traditionally had a neutral-to-positive long-short ratio. At least until a year ago, just about when the Jumper was given the go-ahead. Then dramatically the open interest changed and the ratio turned south. You want to know what it is now?" She didn't wait for his answer. "There's over six million shares open, that means short and uncovered. Here's the part that's not public. My friend tells me that some unnamed hedge fund has bet its ass the company is going to take a dive. And I think you and I both know which one it is. The stock plummets ten points and they're sixty million dollars richer. Twenty points and it's a hundred and twenty. You get the idea? And here's the beautiful part, the part that hit me last night like a ton of bricks. It's much easier orchestrating a disaster than it is orchestrating a smash success. All you need to do is set up an impossible goal, get a starry-eyed idealist to try and meet it, and wait. But just for insurance, just in case your best-laid plans backfire because your idealist is actually good enough to pull off the impossible even after all the monkey wrenches you've thrown his way, why then you hire a Periclymenus. Except you pull a few stunts first so his real target is camouflaged. Along the way you frame someone else to muddy the waters. Then, either way, as soon as the Jumper dies or crashes, your bet comes in big-time." She stopped and listened. "You still there, Sam?"

"I'm listening."

"I'm afraid that's why he needed you so much. Why Jason had to get you to Freemont at all costs. Why Fran. Because only the absolute best person in the country heading the team could have convinced his board the Jumper was feasible. Without you, they never would have agreed to such a risky gamble, or gotten the Mexican banks to throw in either. You and your reputation were the key to the whole scheme, one that was over a year in the making, maybe more. It's real clever, Sam, don't you like it?"

He was silent.

"Except there's one problem I can't figure out," she continued. "They also needed Dominici. He was pulling all the strings, hiring you, going for secret loans. I can't understand why any CEO would deliberately shoot himself in the foot like that, even for that kind of dough. Even if Periclymenus took the rap, Dominici would be out on his ear for exposing the company to such a risk. Doesn't make sense why he did it. So, I don't know, maybe the whole thing is wrong. It's a serious weak link."

"No," Garvey said slowly. "You're right. You're right because Dominici would have been out on his ear anyway as soon as they reprogrammed the financial programs for the Y2K fix."

"They haven't done that yet?" she asked incredulously.

"I was surprised too," he said. "So I followed up. That's where I was when you called. They would have found the years of skimming and laundering and all the other schemes that Moore uncovered when he looked at other associates of D. Kang. Dominici must have hidden it for years, hidden until all of a sudden the whole system had to be overhauled. And yes, he saw that coming years ago."

"It fits," she said simply.

"So now what? I don't think this bunch scares easily, Rachael."

"No, there's only one way now. You have to build the Jumper. You have to force their hand."

"A few days ago you wanted me to shut it down."

"A few days ago I didn't understand what this was about. Besides, it's what you wanted all along, to see your work of art soar. We force their hand and then we wait for Periclymenus."

"What if . . ." Garvey stopped and looked down at the set of blueprints on his desk. The intricate lines of steelwork

and electrical work made patterns that were truly like fili-
gree. "What if Periclymenus figures a way to bypass us."

"That won't happen," she said, "You're too careful."

"Thanks," he said. "You willing to back that up with an
opening-day ticket to ride the Jumper?"

"I'll come," she said. "But you know I hate heights."

FIFTY-FIVE

He didn't ask any questions or worry if he was stepping on
anyone's toes or going over budget. He simply called the
Angelus security office and told them that the Jumper site
was now off limits to the two full-time details of special
guards they had posted. Then he phoned Brinks, a company
that had no association with Angel City, and hired his own six
daily guards. He gave strict instructions that absolutely no
one without a new photo ID pass be allowed inside the barriers. Then he reprinted the new set of numbered passes and
delivered them in person to each member of the Madondi
team. That removed one of his concerns; trusting any Dominici
employee inside the barriers.

Then he purchased four black-and-white TV security
cameras and mounted them so that no area of the site was
uncovered. Their feeds went to four cassette recorders,
tapes from which were reviewed nightly, and to a bank of
monitors stationed in the Madondi work trailer, where several
eyes were watching. There was already a temporary eight-
foot plywood fence braced around the site, but he increased
its height with the addition of two feet of barbed wire.

All of these precautions did not go unnoticed. A day after
the wire went up he got a call from Charlie Szep, the head of
security. There was a rumor going around that Szep had

smiled sometime in the eighties, but no one could be found to confirm it. Surly, suspicious, protective of his turf, Szep did not take to the new security measures easily. He challenged Garvey's authority to make the arrangements without his approval, challenged the expense, and finally complained about the effect it would have on his men's morale. Garvey held firm, threatening to stop work if his precautions were not adhered to. It escalated over two days and finally came down to a shouting match held at seven P.M. one evening in front of the snack trailer. Szep was the taller man, but Garvey held the trump cards. They were less than three weeks away from the scheduled licensing tests and Szep ultimately didn't want the responsibility of having to explain why all work had stopped. The wire stayed up, the camera tapes were reviewed only by Madondi, and after a few days things quieted down.

Garvey considered the site now as secure as he could get it, but that did not keep him from putting in two extra hours daily going over every square inch of structure to insure that there had been no tampering. He found he was getting only four hours of sleep a night, and as his consumption of black coffee went up, his patience with slow and inefficient work went down. It got to the point where one morning Sarah burst into tears when he barked at her for being late getting dressed for school. He never shouted at his daughter, and her tears reminded him of how close to the edge he was getting.

But the Jumper was moving along swiftly. At the end of a week and a half, all the steel was in and all the electrical hookups made. Still to come were the hydraulics, the lifting motor and cable, and the safety control systems. The structure of the faux lake the cars dove through had been built. The rest of the landscaping, at least for the first year, was slated to be pretty basic. The sod, wood chips, and small trees were scheduled to be laid in after the certification tests. The passenger loading and unloading station was already built, and a special Madondi art crew was working on interior decoration.

In the last several days, other than the fracas from Szep,

everything had gone smoothly. Yet Garvey could not get over his growing feeling of nervousness. It was a big project, and there were a lot of possibilities for mischief. He finally listed on paper all the critical areas where sabotage would be most effective. The list was long enough to make him shudder.

While this was going on, the Angelus corporate publicity department was in feverish high gear. Besides churning out radio and television spots throughout Texas about the new ride, they had invaded local supermarkets, toy stores, auto parts distributors, and home furnishings discounters with flyers about the Jumper. There wasn't a person within one hundred miles who didn't know that by mid-September, something frighteningly wonderful would be unwrapped at Angel City.

Then there was the contest. Americans all over love contests, but in the South they are elevated to some higher, religious status. It is not unusual to find, in rural sections of Dixie, people whose sole daily occupation is to scour newspapers and periodicals for new contests to enter. Publishers Clearinghouse is only the top of the pyramid for many of these addicts. They are on a ceaseless hunt for the scores of local pizza parlor or car dealership giveaways, for which they merely have to fill out an entry form. So it was not a big stretch for the publicity department to come up with the notion of the Jump of Courage contest.

It was solely for children under sixteen, who were asked to write in a story about their most frightening moment ever. The writer of the winning letter would be given not only bragging rights to the first-ever Jumper ride, but also two free all-year passes for all of Angel City's rides. Before the ride, the contest winner would have his or her picture taken with Mario Dominici, the chairman of the board of the huge Angelus Corporation, and Dr. Samuel Garvey, the noted builder of the ride. Already, with several weeks to go, the publicity department had received over five thousand entries. It had been determined that the winner would be announced September eighth. Now, Garvey was reminded by the overworked letter readers, all they needed was a ride for the winner to go on. More pressure, he thought. Just what he needed.

FIFTY-SIX

The last two weeks were a blinding rush to the certification tests. Postponed twice, they were finally fixed for September seventh, the day before the contest winner was to be announced. That meant that by the fifth, the Jumper had to be ready for Garvey to run his own final tests. The worst thing that could happen would be to uncover some embarrassing flaw in front of one of the state inspectors. As tired as he had been the weeks before, the final week showed Garvey just how little sleep a person could get and still manage to stand upright. He took catnaps when he could, sometimes even sleeping for a few hours in his office. He somehow managed to convince Rosita to come live in for the final weeks so that Sarah would not be alone. He hated himself for abandoning his daughter, but there was another truth, and it lay somewhere private at the juncture of pride and honor and commitment. The fact was, like a long-distance runner on the last half mile, he was in the zone, slotted, and immutably focused. This was no longer just a job, it was Samuel Garvey and thirty years of expertise, concentrated in a single shining effort. He could not stop the process, nor did he want to.

He got some help. Madondi sent over an extra engineer when they saw what he was putting himself through. It was just enough to get him over the hump and somehow, miraculously, September fifth dawned on a completed Jumper. Everything was in place for their in-house tests.

Garvey shut down the site to outsiders. Like a film set with a high-budget star doing a nude scene, no one was allowed to be a witness who was not absolutely necessary. That meant only Garvey, two Madondi engineers, and the foreman of the construction crew. It was a perfectly airless day, humid and in the nineties and the track was dry. The cars were positioned for their first full-scale debut.

The cars had always been something of a hybrid conception on Garvey's part. Like traditional cars, they were not enclosed, giving the rider a sense of speed and exposure as the air whipped by their bodies. But they were not articulated or jointed and flew as one solid unit, thirty feet long. On the outside, they looked something like a silver missile with ailerons and phallic thrusters, but their front funnel-shaped catchers gave them an alien appearance.

The cars hadn't yet been cleaned for the test. They still had their protective plastic wrap coverings, their yellow china marker instructional notes, and paper taped over the contoured vinyl seats. But that was only cosmetic. Their meticulously tuned moving parts were ready to go. Garvey sat in the glassed-in small control room twenty feet down the loading platform. In front of him was an electric panel with several buttons and levers surrounding two computer screens. Along one side of the panel were gauges indicating temperature, wind speed, car weight, and time. Above his head were additional television monitors for observing every inch of the ride.

The three other men waited expectantly behind him.

"Everything's checked?" he asked without looking at them. "Simulated passenger weight in range?"

"Twice," the chief Madondi engineer answered. "Weight's at three thousand."

"Well, then, here goes," he said and put a hand up on the main switch.

He took several deep breaths, then finally pushed the start switch. There was a loud click from the releasing air brakes. Then the two cars, side by side, glided out of the start house

185

and rose on their individual pipe tracks. Garvey sat back in his chair to watch. It was eighty-seven seconds to the first jump, and in that time it seemed as if no one in the control room moved. They didn't need to watch the monitors because both jumps were in full view of the booth. The timer counted up to eighty-seven and then all of a sudden, both cars were airborne, one skimming over the other by only a few feet. Ten tons of steel hurtled through the air with enough combined momentum to crush a house. Then, like two aerialists, the cars were caught by the welcoming rails on the other side of the void.

"Goddamn," someone said.

The cars continued around the ride, dipping under the fake pond, pounding around fan turns and over camelbacks, doing their figure eights, out and back, until it was time again to go weightless. The second time they did it as flawlessly as the first. The Kevlar coatings on the rails and catchers muted the sound of the impacted steel. What came to them was a sort of *thwack*, a noise that Garvey had actually dreamed about but had never heard. A half minute later the cars were back in the loading house as if nothing had happened.

In the tiny booth, no one spoke. At least another fifteen seconds went by before the man behind Garvey said evenly, "I guess it works."

"I'd say it was fuckin' brilliant," the foreman said.

"Thank God," Garvey added with relief.

FIFTY-SEVEN

The promotion department had gone crazy with the Jump of Courage contest. After whittling down their eight thousand entries to ten finalists, they then attacked the media. For two weeks, all the supermarket discount coupon sheets had a banner header announcing the drawing. There wasn't a half hour stretch of airtime on local radio when an innocent listener wasn't hit with the news. They were informed that Sam Witherspoon, the current NCAA record holder in the broad jump, would be picking the winner, and that each of the runners-up would be given a fifty-dollar gift certificate to Angel City, an official WBA hickory-handled jump rope, and a True Value top-of-the-line twelve-volt jumper cable. An additional half hour of children's programming time Saturday morning on the CBS-TV affiliate WFRT had been taken by Angelus Corp. to read Mark Twain's *The Celebrated Jumping Frog of Calvaleras County*, interspersed, of course, with reminders of the drawing. The promo department had left few stones unturned, and those it had, presumably, would be flipped for the actual opening day festivities.

As it was, the drawing was something of a circus. It was held in the loading platform building in front of the two shiny cars. Several news crews were there, having determined that it was the hottest story of the day. Every old NFL player and retired big league baseball player who could be pried off his ranch or favorite barstool was hustled into attendance along with a local roadhouse comic named Jimmie Flanders, who had been chosen as emcee.

But the ten kids looked like they were loving it. Any college admissions diversity committee would have been proud to field such a collection of eager, expectant faces. There were four whites, three blacks, two Hispanics, and one Asian. Five boys and five girls.

The parents were there too, proud of their gifted children who had managed to beat out several thousand other hopefuls for the two free Angel City passes. Fortunately, no one had told them that the glazed-over judges' final selection had been made solely on the basis of legibility and brevity. But there was not a single negative note to the whole affair. Klieg lights lit up the venue as if it were Oscar night. Cameras rolled, shutters clicked, and Jimmie Flanders kept things lighthearted.

"What's the last thing you usually hear before a redneck dies?" he asked the crowd. " 'Hey, y'all, watch this.' " He looked around the room with a big grin. "I guess that went over your head, huh? Shoulda realized this was a younger audience. Well, okay then, kids. You know there are three kinds of people in the world, don't ya? Those that can count and those who can't." The laughter that came back was mostly polite and from the parents. The kids were too busy looking at and touching the sleek metal cars.

"Well, anyhow, I guess it's time. Welcome to our little drawing, everybody. I'm sure no one missed seeing Lance Garber over there, the nineteen-seventy-six National Football League's leading punt returner, or Joe Caravagas, third-base coach for the Rangers in nineteen-eighty-four." He waved at two men who looked like they could be drivers for the city pound. "Then, of course, there's Sam Witherspoon, who will be picking today's lucky winner. Sam currently has the NCAA broad jump record, and he comes, believe it or not, from the University of Texas. Hiya, Sam, what do you eat in the morning for breakfast, refried beans? Ha ha. Now, let me introduce Roger Stokes, the head of promotions here at Angel City, who has a few words to say to you."

Flanders stepped away from the microphone, and Stokes took over. He was a man of about forty with curly hair, engaging eyes, and a friendly smile. He looked as if he could be trusted, up to a point.

"Let me just begin by saying that Mr. Dominici was supposed to be here today, but he was called out of town suddenly. I'm kind of his replacement, but he will be back in time for the gala opening. Now, I want to assure everyone that the Jumper is on schedule and will take off from this very spot on September fourteenth. Just yesterday we got our clearance from the state regulators after they held an exhaustive safety review on every phase of the Jumper's operation. Certification will follow in a day or two, so it is a go, and I can tell you we're very proud that we've managed to bring this wonderful new ride to the community when we said we would." A smattering of applause filled the room, but now everyone was looking at the fishbowl, which was on a small table in front of Stokes. Ten little pieces of paper were inside, each with the name of one of the children waiting with sweating hands. On a side table behind Stokes lay nine envelopes, nine jump ropes, and nine jumper cables. Clearly, being a runner-up today was not going to make anyone real popular at school.

Stokes rambled on, mostly to the television cameras. "And let me add, that if you think today is special, wait until the fourteenth. Mr. Dominici, CEO of Angelus Corporation, will be here to cut the opening ribbon, Dr. Garvey, the builder of the ride, will throw the switch, and there will be no less than a dozen celebrities who have been invited to attend this historic event. So please, even if you don't win our contest today, I urge you all to come back and see for yourselves why this new ride has been billed as the most unique and memorable roller coaster ride in the country."

"Draw the name," someone yelled from the small crowd, and Stokes nodded.

"Yes, it's time. Sam, would you do the honors."

Witherspoon stepped up, a tall, sleek athlete in a Hawaiian shirt. He dipped his arm into the bowl and grabbed a piece of paper.

"So many, many good essays," Stokes said, "but here it is . . ." He unfolded the paper Witherspoon gave him. "The winner, Jane Atwood."

A little squeal went up from the back, and a black teenager, no more than fourteen, wearing blue jeans and a T-shirt, threw up her hands.

"Me," she said and came rushing forward. "I'm Jane Atwood."

There was another smattering of applause, but now it was truly halfhearted. The losers and their parents had gone on to new concerns, such as how to get out as soon as they could with the off-grade loot and not look boorish.

"Congratulations, Jane," Stokes said, pushing Wither-spoon to one side as he handed her a letter and two laminated passes. "I am sure you will enjoy our amusement park and tell all your friends what the first ride aboard the Jumper really felt like." He put an arm around her short frame and faced the cameras. Like a true marketing professional, he was milking the moment for all it was worth. But there wasn't much left. In ten minutes everything was over and the lights were turned off. The losing children shuffled by the Jumper cars with their giveaways under their arms and slipped back into the amusement park. Only Jane remained behind with her mother. They looked confused, as though there should be more. It had all ended so quickly.

Garvey, who had been watching from a corner, came over and introduced himself.

"I only want to know one thing," Mrs. Atwood said. "Is it safe? She pestered me till I was crazy. I really didn't want to say she could. These things scare me so."

"She'll be all right," Garvey said.

"Your word?" The equally small-framed woman asked softly. "You built the thing?"

"I did. And you have my word. I'd put my own daughter on it."

FIFTY-EIGHT

That night, for the first time in two weeks, Garvey made it home for dinner. Rosita had prepared a Mexican meat loaf, ground pork with lots of salsa mixed in. Unbelievably, Sarah was enjoying it.

"You never liked any of the spicy foods I made," Garvey said.

"Your spicy is not as good as Rosita's." Sarah smiled at him. "But you make good desserts."

"Thanks."

"How's the Jumper?" she asked innocently, and Garvey had to smile. His daughter had a way of saying just the right thing.

"Coming along really good," he answered. "You want to ride on it? I think I could bend the rules one time even though you're too young."

She thought about that for a long moment. "No, it kind of scares me. I can wait," she said.

"Okay," he said and leaned over to kiss her. "You know, I really missed having dinner with you."

"Me too," she said.

Rosita came in with the tortillas and he was about to take one when the phone rang. He shrugged, gave Sarah a little pat on the head, then went into the living room to take the call.

Rachael sounded urgent.

"Sam, I just got a call from my friend over at the SEC."

"Rachael, we did it. The Jumper works. We got our approvals."

"That's great, Sam. But listen to this. Yesterday a big block of short sales came in on Angelus. From one fund. My friend couldn't tell me which one. But I think we already know."

"They're still selling short?"

"Another twenty million. You think they know something we don't?"

Garvey was silent for a moment. "But everything is okay. Every nut and bolt in the whole layout has been checked and double-checked. Security is so tight they won't even let me in without my pass. I don't understand, Rachael. How are they going to do anything?"

"Maybe it's not the Jumper itself. Maybe it's the people who run it."

Garvey thought about that for a moment. "I don't think so. We've been training six operators on simulators to work the shifts. Then there are the engineers at Madondi. There's plenty of redundancy built in. There's no one single individual that is key to everything."

"Except you," she said.

"My job will be over on Saturday," he said simply. "By the way, you're coming?"

"Of course. I'll be there Friday night."

"Wonderful," he said. "I can't wait."

"Sam," she said, hesitating. "Be careful. No one throws twenty million away. You don't want this ride to be a killer."

"If it's anything, it must be with the mechanics. I'll double-check it again tomorrow. Thanks, Rachael, see you."

"Friday," she said, and rung off.

Garvey replaced the phone and stood there for a long time, thinking. The mechanics? What could he do with the mechanics that he hadn't already done. Nothing. He looked over at his daughter closely and a new idea began to form.

Maybe he hadn't covered all his bases.

"Listen, Sarah, you remember when you and the class went to the rodeo two months ago. It was on a Saturday, right?"

"I can't remember, Daddy. It was a lot of fun."

"Yeah, I think it was a Saturday. Not everyone came, but a lot of the parents loved having an extra afternoon free. You think they'd like to do that again?"

"Sure daddy, another rodeo?"

"Even better," he answered. "An amusement park."

"Oh, Daddy, could we?" she squealed.

"I'm going to try," he said. "With some free passes. Let's see what Mrs. Johnson and Mrs. Walker say.

"Yay!" she said, jumping into his arms. "You're the best."

But he didn't feel the best. He felt manipulative and evil. He only hoped it would work.

A day later he got his answer. The phone rang at his desk as he was going over some last-minute landscaping sketches.

"Yes," he said curtly.

"Dr. Garvey. This is Mrs. Johnson." There was silence on the phone for a moment as Garvey pried his eyes away from the drawings. "Sarah's teacher at school."

"Yes, Mrs. Johnson. You got the note . . . ?"

"Yes, and I want to say that it was very kind of you."

"Well, I've been thinking I must have come on a little strong the last time I visited the school. Kids sometimes are just . . . kids. I wanted to try and soften things a little, I mean with you and Mrs. Walker and the class."

"Exactly. They are sometimes little devils, but that is the nature of children, isn't it? It was so nice of you to offer the free passes to your amusement park and the opening of the Jumper. Of course, all the children know about it from all the ads around. I mean, everyone knows. At first I was a little doubtful, being a Saturday and all, but then Mrs. Walker and I talked about it and since we'd already done a Saturday field trip and since the children would be getting in for free and go right up front, why we thought it might be okay."

Garvey smiled. "How wonderful," he said. "I'll send the passes over early next week."

"With the understanding, of course, that we must have at least five parents to go with us. Fifteen children are too much to handle, especially where there are such crowds. Do you think you could arrange that? I mean calling up the parents to make sure we have adequate coverage. We are so busy here with the children's activities there's little time for phoning."

"I'll take care of it," Garvey said without hesitating. God knew when he'd get a chance for that in his busy schedule.

"Wonderful. I'm really looking forward to it and I am sure the children will be too. It was very generous of you."

He somehow managed to call enough of the other parents in Sarah's class that night to round up volunteers. But the only call he really cared about was the one to Luisa Dominici.

"You know, it's funny," she said after Garvey introduced himself, "Mario didn't want Ralphie to go to the opening. He said it would be way too crowded."

193

"How interesting," Garvey said. "But I am going to reserve a special place for the class."

"Ralphie put up such a fuss," she continued, "but Mario can be pretty stubborn when he wants. I guess you know that. But now, I don't know, if the whole class is going . . ."

"Everyone I spoke to so far is planning on it. He'll be with all his friends. How can you keep him away on such a special day . . . especially for him. He'll be so proud telling everyone that it's his daddy that runs everything. Otherwise, when he gets to school on Monday, everyone will kid him that he didn't come to his own party."

There was a heavy silence on the phone for a moment. "Maybe I could send him as part of the class project. I wouldn't even have to tell Mario."

"Good idea. Would you be coming? We already have enough parents. You wouldn't need to."

"Well, I was signed up for the golf tournament that day. I could send his sitter."

"No need. We'll count on Ralphie then."

"Okay, Dr. Garvey. Oh, and about last month. I am so sorry about his behavior. I don't know where he gets that from."

"I'm sure I don't know, Mrs. Dominici," Garvey said. "But it's already forgotten."

"Good," she said. "And thanks for arranging this."

"My pleasure," he said.

FIFTY-NINE

The schedule he kept this last week was cruel. He came home after Sarah was asleep, left before she woke up, and still worried that he was taking too much time away from the site. Garvey was taking no chances at this critical phase, except with his own safety. He refused to consider himself a target and ran his show and his life without once looking over his shoulder. It was understandable, then, that in his fatigued state, he never spotted the car that followed him Wednesday night. It was a Chevrolet, one of those seventies clunkers that should have been sent years earlier to South America to live a second life as a threadbare taxi. The driver had a linebacker's large upper body and big hands. On Thursday night, the man was again waiting for Garvey when he emerged from his office into the after-midnight, cooler air. The Chevrolet was parked at the edge of the parking lot, and as Garvey drove past toward the exit, the large man turned on his motor. He waited a minute, then pulled out. Unlike the night before, he left his headlights off.

Garvey drove out of Angel City and turned left, toward McKeeson Boulevard and the way home. There was nothing on the streets except an occasional person in a car or truck working their way home also. McKeeson was the kind of road that catered to automobiles, with its selections of gas stations, used car lots, muffler repair franchises, fast-food stops, and then long intervals of scrub grass and an occasional residential trailer. It was one of the roads that made Freemont, Texas, look like anywhere U.S.A., and at one-thirty at night it was dead quiet. The McDonald's was open, but Garvey passed that doing sixty and was two miles beyond when the Chevrolet pulled up alongside to pass.

Garvey was surprised by the noise. He had been thinking about which of the three operating crews to use on opening day and hadn't noticed the ghostly approach of the other car. Its lights were still off, so there was no reflection from its dashboard for Garvey to see the face of the driver. But then he didn't have much time to look. As the other car pulled even with him it suddenly swerved into his side. At first Garvey was merely shocked at the stupidity or drunkenness of the other driver. A wide-open road, only two cars, and he had to sideswipe him! He fought off his own car's mini-fishtail and put on his brakes to let the other car past. Then, all of a sudden, he realized—this was no accident or drunk driver, it was deliberate. Because now, the other car was slowing too and staying on his left side. Garvey gripped the steering wheel tighter. Once again the Chevrolet slid into him, but this time Garvey reacted with a little counterswerve of his own and the two cars bounced off each other and continued straight.

For no rational reason except that it just sprung out of his mouth, Garvey yelled out of his open window at the driver.

"What the hell do you think you're doing!" Then he honked his horn, but the effect of both of these things was lost in the next powerful sideswipe. Garvey saw himself being bulled over to the right side of his lane. He tried speeding up and this barely got him away, but only for a few seconds. A hundred yards down the road the other car was back, pushing at his side and forcing him over. The Chevrolet was bigger and heavier than his light Honda wagon, and it was all Garvey could do to keep his car on the road. But he could tell it would be a losing battle. He looked over again, trying to make out the face of the driver, but all he saw was a fleshy, flat-nosed profile behind the wheel. But he also saw something else that told him he couldn't just stop his car to keep from getting run off the road. Leaning against the backrest of the passenger seat was an automatic assault rifle.

His only chance was to keep going. But about five hundred yards ahead was the beginning of a stretch of road that had some thick cottonwood trees on its edge. In a flash he saw exactly what had been designed. He'd be forced off the road into one of the trees doing over fifty miles an hour and die in a fiery car crash. Maybe the other man had a bottle of liquor he would throw into the car before escaping to make it seem like Garvey had been drinking. Simple and effective, it was as mundane and exquisite a murder as anyone could plan for. Rachael had been right. Someone had figured, stop Garvey, stop the Jumper.

He wrenched his hands to the left with all his strength, but it was like trying to hold back a ferry boat. The metal of the two cars shrieked at each other and he heard his sideview mirror shatter, and still he was being pushed over to the right. At the pace and angle he was sliding, he would probably hit the second tree in line, if not that, then surely the third. If he kept going he had maybe four seconds to live, if he stopped, no more than a minute. He looked in the rearview mirror, hoping that he'd see another car, but both in back and in front McKeeson Boulevard was totally empty.

The other driver, for some reason, decided to turn on his headlights, maybe to aim his murderous push better, and in the second that he only had one hand on the wheel, Garvey managed to straighten out his car. And in that second, he also thought he saw the faintest possibility. But immediately he felt his car again inexorably forced over and now it looked for sure that he would run head-on into the third tree. He had to time it perfectly, to thread his car between the two trees and hope that what lay on the other side was not just as deadly. That meant angling through a gap of about twenty feet with a car that was close to five feet wide and eleven feet long doing over fifty miles an hour. There was also a curb to consider, but he had no idea what effect that would have on his trajectory. He watched as the trees came nearer, still struggling to hold his car to the left against his attacker. He waited, maintaining the same angle of drift until the last possible second. His wheels were a few inches from the curb and when it looked as though he would surely hit the tree ahead of him, he yanked the wheel hard to the right. He heard the explosion of his tire deflating as it hit the curb, and felt his car jump into the air. It flew to a height of over six feet for over thirty yards and miraculously cleared the two trees with no more than the width of a suitcase on either side. But the car was yawing over on its side as it landed, and Garvey wrestled with the wheel to keep it upright. For forty yards it plowed through the scrub brush balanced on two wheels then finally flopped onto its other two wheels. Garvey saw in his headlights a level field with mesquite and sage bushes. His car continued to mow over several of the sages before he was able to get it fully under control. He stood on the brakes and brought it to a stop, then turned to look for the other car.

He had heard something, but it hadn't registered in his struggle to keep his own car from flipping over. The sound had been that of classic collision, but not deep and final. What Garvey saw was the other car behind him on the shoulder of the road, smoke rising from its radiator and the fan making a noise to set a mechanic's teeth on edge. Apparently his assailant had been caught off-guard by Garvey's quick zag and had not straightened up in time to avoid hitting the tree. But he hadn't hit full on. The side of his car was smeared as if by a giant putty knife, but it was still able to move. The driver was trying to pull it back on the road to get closer to where Garvey was. It made a series of other complaining noises, but miraculously, it clawed forward.

Garvey didn't wait. He threw his car into low gear and headed back to the road. He knew his tire was flat, but maybe he could outrun the other car in its wounded condition. He had noticed some lights up ahead. The noise his own car made as he pulled onto the macadam was not comforting. The steel rim screeched and spun slickly, sending sparks up under the frame of his car. What remained of the tire slammed repeatedly against the wheel well and undercarriage and sounded like an animal being pounded to death. The car itself shimmied and sidled all over the road, but it was moving forward at about twenty miles an hour. When he looked in the rearview mirror, Garvey noticed that the other car was now about one hundred yards behind, but slowly losing ground. How long could he keep this up, punishing his car until it would either throw a rod, break an axle, or have a brake seize and spin off the road completely?

As he went over a little rise in McKeeson Boulevard, a minute later he saw the lights on the right and he remembered. He must have stopped here dozens of times before. It was a self-service car wash, apparently an all-night one because the front door was still open. It was a drive-through where you put in your money, guided your car into a track, and let the cogs pull you along. Garvey looked down the road past the car wash, but there was only more open road as far as he could see.

By now his car was making a new noise, and he felt it in his foot. The gas pedal was losing effectiveness. Every now and then the engine coughed and misfired and the car bucked. Apparently the flailing tire had ruptured or split the gas line and it was no longer delivering a steady flow of gasoline. He couldn't take his chances going on. The last thing he wanted was to come to a stop in the middle of an empty road and have his assailant come upon him. He did the only thing he could: He glided down the hill and turned into the brightly lit car wash. He looked behind him and saw his assailant's car just limp up over the crest of the hill.

There was no one else around, and only the one desolate cinder block building in the middle of the forlorn scrub brush. He had one slim chance, and he quickly fished in his pocket for the two dollars in coins he needed to start the car wash machine.

When the other man got close enough, he saw the tail-lights of Garvey's car going into the machine. Then everything was obscured by the whirring water jets and rotating brushes. A smile played over his face, like that of a hunter who knows he has his quarry trapped but wants to enjoy the moment. He pulled his damaged car around in back to block Garvey's exit, then calmly got out. In his hand was the evil-looking automatic rifle, pointed right at the place where Garvey's car would emerge from the car wash. The assassin took a few steps more to place him four feet away from where the driver's side window would pass, and waited. In this business, or any business for that matter, this was called a cheap shot. The driver didn't care. He had a job to do.

Garvey waited until he was in the middle of the wash cycle when the flying spray was like the inside of a steam shower and he couldn't see a foot outside the window. Then he quietly opened his door eight inches. Immediately he was inundated with hot water and the slightly caustic smell of detergent. But he painfully slid out onto his knees, reached back in and removed his metal crutch, then just as quietly closed the door. There was about half an inch of standing water under the car, but he rolled over and managed to lie flat between the wheels as the Honda slowly proceeded over him. He was drenched and the detergent stung his eyes, but he didn't dare move yet. The car finally passed over him and he painfully shimmied to a crouch behind it. The final scour cycle was just beginning, and from front and back, two curtains of flat, noodlelike pieces of heavy wet fabric started massaging every part of his car and his body. He spread a pathway through it and limped out the front entrance of the car wash.

But he didn't flee into the fields surrounding the building, or back onto the road. He knew this had to be ended right here, right now, because in the unlikely event that he could escape, he had the terrible fear that they'd go straight for Sarah.

He peered around the edge of the cinder block building and saw the front half of the other car blocking the exit sixty feet away. As he expected, the man was not in it. Garvey figured exactly where he would be to finish his job. He carefully limped up the length of the building, trying not to let the squashing in his shoes give away his position. He used the metal crutch halfway, then lifted it to his shoulder as he approached the edge of the building in front of him. Walking without it was excruciating.

Garvey's car emerged from the car wash as clean and shiny as the day it was purchased. As the water was still sheeting off the front window, the killer leaned a few inches forward and pulled the trigger. A burst of bullets sprayed the front windshield and exploded it into a thousand shards of safety glass. The bullets tore into the fabric of the driver's seat and punched out great gobs of mushroomed fabric from the rear side. The man emptied the entire clip in five seconds before he realized there was no one there. He stood there for another stupefied two seconds. On the chance his victim had slid onto the floor of the backseat, then he reached into his pocket for another clip. He turned as there was a squishing sound behind him, and was just in time to see the metal tube of Garvey's crutch arcing into his face. Garvey had used his best baseball swing and caught the man right over the bridge of the nose. He brought the crutch back and swung again, and this time the metal thudded into the man's temple as he slowly pitched forward onto his knees. The rifle clattered to the cement floor just a split second ahead of its owner. He lay in an awkward position, as though he had tumbled from a great height. He was crumpled directly in the path of Garvey's car as it lumbered out of the final few feet of track.

Garvey knew he hadn't killed the man, just stunned him. The first thing he thought was basic survival . . . retrieving the weapon. He grabbed for the metal stock of the rifle and pulled it toward him. But as he pointed it at his assailant on the ground, the car's wash chain gave the Honda a final good-bye push. It was a slightly longer shove than the others, long enough to roll the steel rim of Garvey's tireless wheel over the man's neck. He never had a chance. Garvey turned away from the gruesome sight and staggered to the edge of the building. He took a minute to get hold of himself and then turned toward the public phone booth on the building's wall.

SIXTY

By the time the state police let him go it was pushing two-thirty. A nice young trooper drove him the five miles home and waited while he trudged through his front door. Garvey simply took off his shoes and dropped onto his bed, fully clothed. In five minutes he was asleep.

In the morning he made some black coffee and toast and

sat there all alone, wondering what the hell to do. In twenty-four hours the Jumper would fly with live people on board, not simulated weights and computer dummies. And even though it had been certified, it was up to him to decide if it was safe. The cautious thing would be to postpone everything, but try as he might, he couldn't bring himself to make that decision.

But things went smoother than he expected. By eight that evening, Garvey had put the finishing touches to his next day's operations sheet. He had selected his crew, laid out the time schedule for the opening events, arranged for increased security, and generally made sure that all the little details had been addressed. There were still some lights and landscaping that needed to be installed, but essentially, by Friday night, the Jumper was ready to go. With the Madondi engineers, Garvey had once again pored over all the mechanisms, including the lifting motor and all the brake parts, the hydraulic adjusters and laser directional system, and found everything working perfectly. He sent a crew over the track again and was reassured by them that every inch of steel was tight. He even made them sound with tiny peen hammers to see if there was anything inside the steel pipes like a bomb on a timer. He could think of nothing further to do, and so he went to the airport to pick up Rachael.

When she saw him waiting for her at the gate, her face lit up. Worrying was a professional requirement for Rachael, but she wasn't used to it entering into her private life. She hugged him tightly, almost as if should she let go he would blow away.

"You were worried, perhaps, that I might not show up?" he said. He wasn't ready to tell her about the car wash. "Actually life has been pretty boring. Just work, work, work."

She smiled and the two of them walked to his car. "How's Sarah?"

"She's going to be better when she sees you."

He drove her home in the rental car and explained everything that had been planned for the next day. The crowds were estimated to be over five thousand people, most of whom would come not to ride the Jumper but merely see it in operation. Then he asked her the big favor.

"Could you play mommy for the morning? I can't tell you how important it is. Sarah's class is coming, and I need you to go with her and also . . ." he hesitated, "make sure they all get to the reviewing stand on time. There's a special row of seats."

"Of course," she said. "I know how proud Sarah will be. We'll make sure to get there on time. We couldn't be late for that. The whole class, you think?"

"Well, actually ten kids. The other five couldn't make it. There will be the teacher and other parents. It's going to be quite a day tomorrow," he told her. "So, what have you been up to?"

"After that lead-in," she said, laughing, "that's one hard act to follow. But let's try this out. I spoke to Pouncy this morning." Her smiling eyes turned serious. "Dominici is going down. I told him about the short sales and D. Kang and he put Jacobson and Delaney on the leads. They can do things you can't."

The color drained from Garvey's face. "They won't pick him up before tomorrow?" he asked.

"No. They'll wait until they get what they need. It's the right fish this time, but they want to sink the hook in good."

SIXTY-ONE

Garvey arrived at Angel City the next morning at eight o'clock. He had wanted to arrive by seven, but Rachael kept him in bed for an hour on some unfinished business. The night before he had had two conflicting priorities: to make love to her and to catch up on some sleep. His body, warring with itself, took the default setting and shut down before Rachael had emerged from the bathroom.

But Garvey found out that six A.M. is a delightful time to make love. Children are asleep, the only noises from outside come from the movement of wind and animals, and the low eastern sun paints walls fully with a fresh coat of roseate light. Morning love is sleepy love, that totally relaxed, dewy with hours of blanketed body-warmth love. Garvey wished he could stay in bed all day with her.

When he arrived at the park he couldn't believe the commotion. Earlier that morning, the camera crews of the three regional television stations had set up outside the Jumper where they thought they could get their best pictures. For that they had gotten permission from Szep. The head of security had also admitted two magazine crews, who were both waiting to interview Garvey. But the big surprise was the more than five hundred people waiting to get into the park. They would have to wait two hours for the opening, but they didn't seem to mind.

There was activity everywhere. But before Garvey dove into what he knew would be a last-minute whirlwind, he took a moment to look at his silent creation. At this hour with the low sun it looked like a ribbon of light forming a giant, silver, three-dimensional monogram twisting around itself to form letters that were hiding in the curves. It was supremely beautiful to him, rivaling even the sensuous curves of Rachael's body. He knew every inch in that silver form, every angle and twist, and for these few moments alone with it, like a lover, he was reluctant to share it. He stood there gazing at it, framed by a cloudless sky, and when he had had his fill, he lowered his head and walked toward the control room.

He passed by the raised platform area just in front of the loading station that had been built especially for the day's festivities. It was a space for about forty people, including a row of seats for Sarah's class, roped in bunting and framed by klieg lights with a lectern and microphone set up. Above it the art department had manufactured a colorful sign that merely said THE JUMPER, SEPTEMBER 14th, 2000. The platform was empty now, save for an electrician who was doing a final hookup to the loudspeakers that ringed the plaza in front of the loading station.

He had laid on a final test of everything for seven that morning and the engineers had carried it out, even though he had been absent. He looked at the report and saw, to his relief, that everything had worked flawlessly. Three perfect test runs. He checked again on the back-up generators, making sure that they were poised to kick in if something happened to the electric supply. He checked the air pressure gauges on the brake mechanisms, both primary and secondary, and then he rechecked each safety operational switch. He went over again the in-case-of-emergency procedure with the three operations crew members. Then, after forty minutes, there was nothing else he could check. The magazine people were waiting, and he graciously gave them twenty minutes. Then Garvey stood for photographs in the control room as he explained what everything did, and by nine-fifteen he was ready to go outside and see how things were shaping up with the crowds.

The gates were opened at Angel City at exactly ten A.M. and the pent-up flood of customers poured in. The festivities were scheduled for eleven, but people wanted to be early in line to guarantee themselves a ride on the Jumper. By ten-fifteen, the line was a hundred yards long, snaking back and forth through the neon ropes in the plaza. The front of the line passed to one side of the platform where Garvey now stood, waiting for the other officials, reporters, publicity flaks, and, of course, Mario Dominici. There was a definite air of excitement in the crowd as they gazed at the soaring structure above them. But what seemed to rivet their attention were the two gaps in the track, to which they kept pointing and shaking their heads.

At ten-thirty the lights were thrown on and the TV camera crews tested their equipment. A shout went up from the crowd in the plaza hoping that things would now start to move. But they'd have to wait a little longer. The mayor of little Freemont hadn't even showed up.

Rachael was pacing back and forth in front of the elementary school building, alternately looking at her watch and at the driveway. Nine kids had already arrived and five of their mothers and fathers were chatting and fidgeting with their cameras. Garvey had been specific . . . she shouldn't leave without them all, and if it hadn't been for Ralph Dominici, they'd be at the park already. Mrs. Johnson had suggested that they leave because of the crowds and that Ralph could catch up, but Rachael had insisted on another ten minutes.

Eight minutes later, the Jaguar came roaring into the driveway and Luisa, dressed in her golf culottes and Ellesse polo shirt, deposited Ralph on the grass next to Rachael.

"Sorry," she said casually, "I must have overslept. Have fun," she added and roared off. It took no time for Ralph to find his two closest friends. Then everyone climbed aboard the yellow school van and that too accelerated out of the school entrance.

"I just hope we're not too late," Mrs. Johnson said.

"Me too," Rachael said. "But I've been there before. I know some shortcuts."

By eleven o'clock, everything was ready. Mario Dominici stood in front of the microphone, staring out at the hundreds of people waiting in front of him. The platform was bathed in artificial light, illuminating the two dozen people standing there in an eerie daytime luminescence. There were a lot of people who were not in line for the ride but who had come to watch the ceremonies: workers on the construction crew, employees of Angel City, spouses and friends, locals, and even some people who had drifted over from some of the other rides to see what the fuss was about.

Dominici tapped the mike in front of him and stepped forward. He was dressed for the occasion in a light beige suit with a subdued paisley tie. He looked solid and in control.

"Good morning," he began, his voice resonating throughout the plaza. "I am Mario Dominici, the CEO of Angelus Corporation, and it is a pleasure to welcome you all here on this momentous day, both for Angel City and for the history of roller coasters . . ."

Garvey was behind him and to the left, scanning the crowd in front of the platform. Where the hell were they? The row of seats behind him was empty. At this point, with all the pushing and shoving he wasn't even sure they could make it through.

". . . I would like to thank all the officials of Freemont over the past few years for welcoming our company to their town," Dominici was saying. "I believe it has been a good association for the both of us . . ."

Garvey recognized a few faces down below: Dale Frazier, the computer guru; Martin Hotchkiss; even Frank Danville, the reporter from *AM* magazine. But still no Rachael. Come on, he thought anxiously looking at his watch. Don't blow this.

Dominici was finishing up his brief introduction. "And so now I'd like to turn the proceedings over to our own Roger Stokes, head of promotions." As he turned away from the mike, his eyes locked on Garvey, and for the briefest moment Garvey thought he saw a flash of anger. But it was gone in an instant as the CEO went and stood next to a few other suited men on the platform and smiled out at the crowd. Garvey let his glance brush over them, wondering who from the corporate offices had come. No one registered until his eyes lit upon the man standing next to Dominici.

He had seen him only once before, and then only in the picture that Burt Tarshis from Brides and Slides had taken in New York. It was one of the guys from D. Kang.

Rachael, with the parents and ten children in tow, reached the employee gate and flashed the passes. The guard, one of Szep's, was slow to look them over, but finally he handed them back and motioned them through.

"It's a madhouse," he said. "You won't get a ride on that thing today."

She led the children and the adults strung out in a row behind her toward the Jumper. The closer they got, the thicker the crowds became, until she was greeted by a solid wall of humanity. She could hear everything perfectly and see the lights, but she wasn't even in the plaza yet. She looked for an opening in the wall, a hard act for one, an impossibility for all of them. This wouldn't do, she thought, this definitely wouldn't do. She'd have to find another way. They backed out and angled toward the kiddie park. Fewer people got in their way and they could move faster, but the path was taking them away from the Jumper.

"Hurry up, children," she shouted. "This way!"

Stokes was loving every minute of this. It was what every promoter lived for . . . facing a phalanx of television cameras, reporters, and thousands of people, with the CEO and head executives of his corporation at his back. His voice had taken on a level of energy and rhythm usually reserved for evangelists and infomercial pitchmen. He thanked, praised, and promoted. It was his job to work the crowd and the media at this singular opportunity, and he was doing it with great skill. He got laughs, he got applause, but toward the end, he could tell the crowd was getting a little restless. They had been waiting a long while for the Jumper to begin its life and the line to move forward. He knew that timing was everything, so he held his hands up and hushed the crowd.

"And now one last introduction," he said. "Dr. Samuel Garvey, the man who built the Jumper." He stood aside and motioned for Garvey to come forward. The people had one last good round of applause left, and they gave it to him freely. He had known this was coming, but he wasn't ready, not quite yet. But the applause continued, drawing him forward, and before he could stop himself, he was at the lectern looking out at them.

Where the hell were they in this sea of faces in front of him?

"Thank you for coming," he began simply. "This has been for me a labor of love and it is wonderful to see that so many others can now share in my dream. I feel something like a father sending my child off to the first day of school. I'm sure many of you know that feeling."

There was a smattering of laughter and in the pause, Garvey continued to search the faces. Still nothing.

"And like a good parent, I want to make sure everything goes smoothly on her first day, for us and for you. However, while we've taken every precaution, we haven't held back on trying to give you the most exciting roller coaster experience in the world. And for you here today, and especially for those people on the first official run, it will be a once in a lifetime experience. Now," he said reluctantly, "let me introduce to you the lucky people who will be in those first cars. If they would come up, please . . ."

Rachael and the kindergarten outing worked their way in a large semicircle until they came to the back of one of the maintenance trailers next to the Aquaflume ride. From there they snaked their way under the supports for the Telemark Tramway and around the Bungee Bouncer ticket booth, and came out fifty feet from the side edge of the platform Garvey was standing on. But here the crowds got thicker and there were no further shortcuts. Sarah was pulling back, but Rachael gritted her teeth, wedged her hand in front of her, and rumbled, "Please, these children have reserved seats."

"And finally, the winner of our Jump of Courage contest, Miss Jane Atwood." Garvey reached down and helped the young black girl up the platform to stand behind him. "She will be joining the mayor, the director of State Recreation, the president of WKYV, and the other business community leaders who have been so helpful in sponsoring and supporting Angel City." As Jane Atwood went to stand with the other eight people waiting on the platform, Garvey searched the crowd one last time. After a moment he gave up and continued.

"After they are strapped into their seats, I will give the signal for the operator to start the ride with this red button." He pointed to the top of the lectern. "Then we can all just watch the excitement of the Jumper's first trip. After that the Jumper will open for business." He turned behind him, gave the passengers a last look, then motioned for them to go into the building. When the last of them had disappeared, Garvey turned and faced Dominici behind him. He was watching for a reaction, any reaction, but all he got back was a stony, unblinking stare. Garvey put his hand on the button and started to turn back toward the crowd when he heard something on the left. In the cacophony of noises, someone had shouted his name. He looked out and tried to place the location, but there were so many faces. And then finally he had her, struggling to move forward with her charges. She was about twenty feet back from the edge.

Garvey leaned forward and put his mouth near the microphone.

"There is one last thing," he said and the intimacy of his voice surprised even him. "A lot of you may be frightened by the notion of these trains flying through empty space, and so

210

we thought we'd reassure you that they are absolutely safe. Mr. Mario Dominici, the chairman of Angelus Corporation, has agreed to allow his little son, Ralph, to be on the first run. And here he is now . . . having a hard time coming forward. If you'll just make a way, please." Garvey hurriedly went off the platform and into the crowd and just managed to grab the little boy's hand. He had heard the announcement, and the look of joy spreading over his little face told Garvey he'd have no trouble getting him on board. He pulled him up to the platform, with Rachael and the other children and parents following. Then quickly, as Dominici started to come forward, Garvey led Ralph toward the door into the loading station. When he was through, he turned quickly to block the way. Dominici stood, red-faced, in front of him.

"What the fuck are you doing?" he hissed. "I never said anything about Ralphie."

"You didn't?" Garvey said. "My mistake."

"Take him off."

"Why?" Garvey said, watching carefully. "Everything's safe."

"Take him off," he insisted again, this time his voice rising.

"I can't, we've just told these several thousand people you've given your word."

An expression came over Dominici's face that was part pain, part helplessness, and pure hatred. He stood there, silently, every part of his body unmoving except his right hand, clenching and unclenching. Garvey slowly walked over to the button. But before he could get there, Roger Stokes was at the lectern and pointing at the other children on the platform.

"And isn't that your daughter, Dr. Garvey? Wouldn't she like to join her friend and ride too?" The director of promotion knew a golden gimmick when he saw one, and he was going to milk it big. He could see the headlines now: CEO AND BUILDER'S CHILDREN ARE AMONG THE FIRST TO PROVE THE JUMPER SAFE. But Sarah was shaking her head and there was a look of fear in her eyes.

"I don't think she's big enough . . ." Garvey began to say, but this time it was Stokes's turn to bring a child onto the ride.

"No, Daddy," Sarah whispered but the crowd wanted everything to begin and a rhythm of clapping began. "Put her onboard already," it seemed to say.

"Daddy!!"

Rachael bent low and whispered something in her ear. Sarah looked at her for a moment in doubt, then nodded slowly. She didn't look fully convinced, but Rachael put her arms around the little girl and picked her up.

"Okay," Rachael said to Stokes and Garvey. "She'll go if I go." She gave Garvey a long, meaningful look, then turned and walked, carrying his daughter into the start building. The front people in line had seeped forward when they thought Ralphie was the last to board, and now they had to try and clear aside to let them pass.

The crowd continued their rhythmic clapping. They knew it was time. But Garvey couldn't bring himself to continue, not now, not with his daughter and Rachael in the cars. He took the three steps over to Dominici, trying one last time.

"Tell me," he said softly, "or else we'll both have dead children to weep for."

"I can't," he said after a long moment. "It's too late."

"Then I'll stop everything. Call it mechanical malfunction."

"Yes," Dominici said simply. His head was bowed. "Stop it, and get my son off."

"Before I get him off, I want to know what it is, so I can fix it."

Dominici raised his eyes and looked at him with resignation. "It was a little virus, in the weight-sensing computer. It kicks in at exactly eleven A.M. today. Then all the readings go crazy and the angles all change. The cars will fly several feet short. Jason did it."

Garvey looked at him with contempt. "And before your son got on you were ready to let it happen? All for money?"

"Everyone wanted one last big score . . . before the game was over."

"Too bad," Garvey answered. "It's over now."

He turned back to the lectern to make his announcement that the ride was canceled when he saw a flurry of movement. He caught a glimpse of an arm reaching out, and before he could do a thing, Tartaglia's hand came down solidly on the red button. Garvey stood, riveted, halfway between the lectern and the door to the start house, and heard with horror the noise of the air brakes releasing on the two cars. The first ride on the Jumper had begun.

Garvey knew all the numbers. He knew it would take six seconds for the cars to fall to the lift cable, another twenty-four seconds for the cars to be hoisted to the top of the first big hill, then eighty-seven seconds to the first jump and another eighty-seven seconds to the final jump, and a final thirty-six seconds of roll-out and braking. A total of four minutes for the entire ride. He also knew that once the cars went over the first hill there was no way to stop them. But he had thirty-six seconds to push the emergency stop on the lift cable, which was only inside the door of the control room a few yards away. He didn't hesitate to look back at Tartaglia or Dominici, he simply rushed in the direction of the start house door.

But scores of people from the head of the line were now clotting the entrance to get in. They must have been ten deep and pressing forward. Garvey, with his bum leg, pushed, shouted, pried, and yanked bodies as best he could. But by the time he reached the front door nearly twenty seconds had passed. He limped through and down the platform to the control room glass door. It was locked, as it should have been, but when the crew chief saw him, he hurriedly released the electric bolt. Garvey lunged through and hit the switch on the wall, then looked at the bank of monitors. The lift cable made a clicking sound then stopped with a clean *thunk*. But as he watched, Garvey saw the two cars just float

213

over the apex of the lift hill and start down. He had been a few seconds too late. Gravity now held the two cars in its inexorable grip, the same force that would bring them crashing to the ground when they jumped too short.

And there were only eighty-seven seconds to do something.

Sarah snuggled under Rachael's arm as the lap bar came convincingly down, pinning them to the seats. Everyone else around them had a look of anticipation on their faces only slightly clouded by doubt. But they were making great sport of their adventure, calling to each other, telling nervous jokes. Sarah's face held only terror. Rachael pulled her closer as the sigh of the air brakes releasing filled the car and it descended toward the lift cable.

Garvey had left the ratchet dogs unmuffled on purpose. He had wanted the traditional slow clanking sound of the lift cable to add to the anticipation of the first hill, and as Rachael and Sarah started up, the rhythmic beat of the metal pawls punctuated their rise. Rachael was looking out at the other car, keeping pace only fifteen feet away, looking at the other people looking back at her, when she spotted out of the corner of her eye someone rush into the start house forty feet below them. Was it Garvey? She couldn't tell, but the very fact of the commotion below gripped her with fear. Something was wrong, but the cars continued to rise, and then, ever so slowly, they flattened out, topped out, and began to fall.

The first drop was eighty-five feet angled at fifty-two degrees and from the top it looked like the edge of a table. Then right at the base was a bow tie inversion element; a vertical figure eight. This was Garvey's way of waking everyone up and showing them what industrial-strength coastering was all about. Sarah held on for dear life and screamed as loud as her little lungs could manage, but the noise was lost in the yells from the other passengers. The track straightened out and ran true near the ground for a few score yards but it only served to lull the riders into a false sense of security. Before anyone could say, "That was nothing," the track went into a series of reversing flat, snakelike turns that created alternating lateral G forces. Lap bars dug into flesh, creating a sensation of being squeezed in two. Then a slamming corkscrew into a rising hill, a sudden drop that gave over two seconds of air time, and back up amidst the clatter of flying pocket change to the start of the lake plunge. All that and they hadn't come close to the jump yet. Rachael could only grip Sarah tighter and close her eyes.

Garvey pushed his way back outside, easier now because the people were all following the progress of the cars, and searched frantically for one face in particular in the crowd below the platform. There were so many colors, so much movement, impossible really, but everyone was looking up, and in a few seconds he had spotted Dale Frazier. He lunged down into the crowd, grabbed his arm, and started pulling him toward the start house.

"What the . . . ?" the computer expert said in surprise.

"Just come, I'll explain inside." Garvey nearly dragged him the entire dozen feet into the start house, closed the door behind them, then led him the rest of the way into the control room.

"There's a virus in the weight computer that sets the final track angles before the jumps. It went active at eleven," Garvey said breathlessly. "The cars will crash. Can we do anything?" He glanced at the elapsed time clock. Thirty-five seconds gone.

Frazier asked, "Where?" and Garvey pointed to a computer under one of the monitors.

"You have a reset in the program?"

"Yes, but that's no good," Garvey shouted. "It will reset to the same incorrect calculations."

"No, no," Frazier said. "We fool the computer. The virus went active at eleven today, right? We'll simply change the computer date. Make it a day earlier. Then reset."

"Christ, will that work?"

Frazier shook his head. "I don't know. Depends on how the reset was programmed. Will it use the old weight readings or wait for new ones?"

"Do it," Garvey said, looking again at the clock. Sixty-five seconds gone.

Frazier's fingers flew over the keyboard and mouse. He had to get back to the control panel, then to settings, then to the date function. Then he had to change the date. It took him a full fifteen seconds.

"Where's the reset?" he said frantically.

"Here, here." Garvey grabbed the mouse from him and clicked out of the control panel and into the program for the weight adjustment.

"Come on, come on," he coaxed. It seemed like an eternity to reboot the program but it was only five seconds when the screen finally filled with the familiar layout. He jerked the mouse up and to the left but he'd moved it too quickly. The cursor was nowhere to be found.

"Where's the fucking arrow?" he cried. His eyes raced over the screen from top to bottom until Frazier finally pointed at the bottom left corner. Garvey lifted it steadily until it was over the reset button and clicked. He immediately looked up at the clock and realized with a paralyzing dread he had again been a second or two late.

The timing had been so exquisite that both cars hit the last section of their tracks before the jumps at the same time. The angle hadn't changed since being set the moment the cars left the station. The first of their four sets of wheels released its grip on the pipes and whistled through the open air. Then the second set released, following the first in its fatally flat trajectory. But as it cleared, the hydraulic lifter came miraculously to life and rammed upward, lifting the second half of the rigid car with it. The third set of wheels flew off, then the fourth, and in a second, a thousand flash cameras from below exploded and lit up the sky. They caught the two cars as they sailed, like swan divers, one over the other in the most graceful of parabolic arcs. But unlike divers that plummet toward the sea, they were caught effortlessly in midair by their welcoming tracks, and with little more than a muted thud by way of thanks, they continued sprightly on their way. A shout of approval went up from the crowd and the crew in the control room but Garvey's voice was not among them. His throat was so dry he dared not swallow. All he could do was watch the monitor as the two cars continued their circuit. More fan turns, a helix corkscrew, two barrel rolls . . . everything flawlessly. It was only when they made the second jump as smoothly as they had the first that he realized it was finally all over. And then he felt like he wanted to cry.

SIXTY-TWO

He got up and walked to the exit ramp and waited for them to appear. All the dignitaries filed by first. If rubber legs and an observable air of imbalance were marks of a successful ride, then the Jumper was a smash. Few of the first riders walked down the ramp without at least a finger or two on the handrail. But all of them had smiles pasted on their slightly ashen faces. Garvey knew he had a winner. Then he saw

217

Sarah coming toward him, her arms outspread. He bent lower to scoop her up in a bear hug.

"Oh, Daddy, Daddy," she cried out. "It was so wonderful! I want to do it again."

"You do?" He looked at Rachael, who just rolled her eyes.

"I was a little scared at first," Sarah continued, "but then when it jumped it felt like I was flying. It was so beautiful and quiet. I felt like I was up in heaven with mommy." She gave him a big kiss on the cheek. "I wasn't scared after that at all. And the second was better than the first."

"I'm glad you liked the ride," Garvey said. "I was afraid it would be too much for you." He glanced again at Rachael. "And you?"

"Quite frankly, I'd prefer spending the afternoon in the inside of an industrial clothes dryer. But then again, I'm close to forty." She slipped her arm around the two of them and they turned to walk out.

"Seriously, it's a great ride, Sam. You should be proud."

"I have one more thing to do," he said. "Then we can go home."

"You look like you should go home right now," she answered.

"I have to find Frank Danville. I know he's here, in the crowd somewhere. I promised him a scoop, and I think it's time to deliver. In another month, Dominici won't have a job or hope of ever getting one. And when the feds get to him his life will be one courtroom and jail cell after another."

"He was Periclymenus?"

"He was. But he should have heeded another ancient. It was Epictetus who said, 'Chastise your passions, that they may not chastise you.' His passion was the sin of greed," Garvey said. "The deadliest of all." He opened the door and they emerged into the sunlit crowd clamoring to get on the Jumper. It was a killer ride all right, thank God for that.